The Glenwood Treasure

The Glenwood Treasure

~ a novel ~

Kim Moritsugu

SIMON & PIERRE FICTION
A MEMBER OF THE DUNDURN GROUP
TORONTO · OXFORD

Editor: Barry Jowett
Copy-editor: Andrea Pruss
Design: Jennifer Scott
Printer: Transcontinental

National Library of Canada Cataloguing in Publication

Moritsugu, Kim, 1954-
    The Glenwood treasure / Kim Moritsugu.

ISBN 1-55002-457-4

I. Title.

PS8576.O72G54 2003   C813'.54   C2003-903113-6   PR9199.3.M644G54 2003

1   2   3   4   5   07   06   05   04   03

THE CANADA COUNCIL | LE CONSEIL DES ARTS
FOR THE ARTS | DU CANADA
SINCE 1957 | DEPUIS 1957

Canadä

ONTARIO ARTS COUNCIL
CONSEIL DES ARTS DE L'ONTARIO

We acknowledge the support of the **Canada Council for the Arts** and the **Ontario Arts Council** for our publishing program. We also acknowledge the financial support of the **Government of Canada** through the **Book Publishing Industry Development Program** and **The Association for the Export of Canadian Books**, and the **Government of Ontario** through the **Ontario Book Publishers Tax Credit** program, and the **Ontario Media Development Corporation's Ontario Book Initiative**.

Care has been taken to trace the ownership of copyright material used in this book. The author and the publisher welcome any information enabling them to rectify any references or credit in subsequent editions.

J. Kirk Howard, President

Printed and bound in Canada.
Printed on recycled paper.
www.dundurn.com

Dundurn Press
8 Market Street
Suite 200
Toronto, Ontario, Canada
M5E 1M6

Dundurn Press
73 Lime Walk
Headington, Oxford,
England
OX3 7AD

Dundurn Press
2250 Military Road
Tonawanda NY
U.S.A. 14150

The Glenwood Treasure

From Rose Park: An Architectural Guide:

"Glenwood," 51 Highpoint Road (1854)

Named after the extensive wooded grounds which once surrounded it, this house is notable both for its ornately decorated exterior and because from 1915–1964 it was lived in by local builder and wealthy eccentric Jeremiah Brown.

In 1964, Brown pulled a hoax from beyond the grave when his executors found a handwritten note in his papers stating he had hidden $500,000 in cash somewhere on the Glenwood property, to be found by "a man with a dog who sees light in the valley."

After a thorough search yielded no treasure, the estate was sold, and the grounds were divided into smaller building lots. What remained of the wooded area was deeded to the city, which now maintains the ravine system as parkland.

The interior of the house was largely modernized in the 1980s, but the carefully restored exterior is an enchanting blend of the High Victorian and Italianate styles — it boasts a fine crested lookout tower, cut-out curvilinear bargeboard trim, a tri-colour roof tile pattern, original stained glass door transoms, and intricate patterns of yellow and red brick.

The cash may never have been hidden, but one look at this jewel-box of a house will convince the astute observer that there is still treasure at Glenwood.

~ Chapter 1 ~

I first heard about the Glenwood treasure from my father, who liked to deliver lengthy lectures about family lore, on what seemed like a weekly basis, in the cocktail hour before dinner. I was five years old when he started telling me the story of my Morrison ancestors, young enough not to question why I had to endure these history lessons, old enough to figure out that the Glenwood treasure part of Dad's recitation was the good part.

Picture me at five, sitting in the drawing room amid heavy draperies, stiff upholstered furniture, Persian rugs, mahogany side tables. My dark, shiny hair is held back from my face with a ribbon. The skirt of my smocked dress is fanned out behind me on the wing chair seat. My hands are folded in my lap, and my feet, clad in lacy-topped ankle socks and polished Mary Janes, are still. Under my mother's watchful and approving eye, I listen to Dad drone on, and when he takes a breath, I say, "Tell us about the Glenwood treasure, Daddy."

My brother Noel sits next to me in another wing chair. He is seven to my five, blond to my brunette, and prone to pinching me and leaving presents in my bed of slimy earthworms or stunned bees, but at this stage of the game that will be our relationship, we still collaborate on the occasional parent-manipulation manoeuvre. "Yes, please, Daddy," Noel says, his eyes big and round — he already knows how to assume a false mask of innocence — "tell us about the treasure."

Dad obliges, and treats us to his version of the story, which has less to do with the hidden money than with Dad's father, my grandfather, Robert Thomas Morrison, the executor of Jeremiah Brown's estate. According to R.T., Jeremiah Brown went a little strange at his end, had started to become so after his three sons died (two in the war, one in a car crash) and declined further when his wife passed away soon after the death of the youngest son. Call it strangeness or senile dementia, but R.T. was convinced Brown fabricated the treasure story, and never buried a cent.

Noel and I listened politely to Dad's lecture, to the official family line, but we didn't believe the hoax theory for a second. We both knew that there really was treasure hidden at Glenwood, and when my father's back was turned, we looked for it. We took our toy spades and shovels over to Highpoint Road and dug around on the Glenwood lawn, close to the street or under the trees, when the owners weren't watching. We didn't find anything, but we continued to believe in the treasure, each in our own way, for years to come. Which was remarkable, considering how few beliefs Noel and I ever had in common.

~

In May of my twenty-ninth year I planned a retreat from California, from the unbroken sunshine and my broken marriage, to home. The thought of living among Rose Park's deciduous trees, in a temperate climate, was a balm to my wounded expectations. When I closed my eyes, I conjured up images of dappled sunshine, of cool breezes causing leaves to dance on their branches, of crabapple trees in bloom, of waves of moral support float-ed toward me by friends and loved ones. That is, as usual, I was somewhat deluded.

I called my mother and asked if I could take up temporary residence in the coach house at the end of her driveway. "Just for the summer," I said. "I've signed a lease on an apartment in my old building to start September 1."

She went speechless for a second, and from across the con-tinent, I heard the clacking sound of pearls used as worry beads.

I said, "I'll pay you rent."

"Rent? Don't be silly. Rent's the least of my worries. But coming home is such a drastic step. Is there no hope you'll get back together with Gerald?"

Outside the kitchenette window of my sublet, I could see shiny, puffy-leaved foliage and springy tropical grass in my patch of garden, a tiny brown lizard on the windowsill. "No hope. Zero. What's the most of your worries?"

"None. I have none. Of course you can move in." The tempo and pitch of her voice had brisked up. From her kitchen, in Rose Park, she would gaze on a wide expanse of thin-blad-ed, northern hemisphere grass, on matte-finish foliage. "I'll tell your father. He'll be delighted. When will you be here? I'll have the place cleaned and aired out."

I thanked her, told her not to fuss, said I would arrive in early June, right after the Fairfield Day School's last day of term.

She said, "What should I tell people when they ask why you're coming back?"

"Who?"

"Friends, neighbours, people at the golf club." My mother's coterie.

"Tell them the truth: that Gerald and I have split up, and I'll be back teaching at my old school and living in my old building in September."

"What reason should I give for the split?"

"I'd go with incompatibility." A good one-size-fits-all reason.

"And if anyone asks what you'll do for the summer?"

"Say — I don't know. Say I'll use the summer to regroup." And to shake off the post-separation lethargy that had made the task of moving home seem like a Herculean labour.

"To regroup," she said, slowly, as if writing the word down. "Might you take a course? Or go on a trip? You're not going to just mope around all summer, are you?"

I reminded myself she meant well, that living in close proximity to the parents would be short-term, that they travelled a lot. "How about this? How about if, between moping sessions, I walk the dog for you? Once a day at least. More when you go away."

"You mean it? That would be a help. I'll tell Dad."

She talked on, I made appropriate responses, and I filled my mind with a greeting-card-perfect image of my parents' house, nestled under the majestic maple trees that form a canopy across their street.

~

Rose Park is known for its trees. If you look at an aerial photograph of Toronto, you can easily spot, to the northeast of the grey sea of concrete and steel and glass that makes up most of downtown, the green island that is Rose Park. Or rather, the large, flattish hilltop on which Rose Park stands, separated from the surrounding area by the ravines that border it on four sides.

In the mid-nineteenth century, when the city was a small grid of neatly laid out streets clustered around the harbour and named after kings, queens, and English market towns, Rose Park was a wooded area ten miles away where rich people built country houses. By the turn of the twentieth century, once-isolated estates had acquired closer neighbours in newly constructed manors.

Soon, roads were laid that linked Rose Park to its environs, and bridges were constructed across the ravines. With access came development, the building of more houses, many grand enough to confirm the neighbourhood's reputation as an exclusive, moneyed enclave. Emphasis on old establishment money, of my father's kind.

Dad is a third-generation lawyer. He grew up, as did generations of Morrisons before him, in the large house where he now lives with my mother, a like-minded import from Connecticut. More than a handful of my father's childhood friends still live nearby — fair-skinned, blue-eyed men who attended the same private schools as Dad, summered in the same lake district up north, belong to the same private clubs, support the same political party. But Dad and his ilk aren't the sole inhabitants of the neighbourhood. For every stretch of ravine-lot mansions with multiple car garages (and coach houses), there are a few blocks of modest, 1920s-era four-bedroom boxes. A short retail strip features railroad flats above the few stores. And here and there, on Rose Park's outer, lesser streets, are small, one-storey, never-renovated houses built as workers' cottages, some the size of a one-bedroom apartment.

Rose Park is not as homogeneous as it may seem, is what I'm trying to say, except when it comes to trees. The trees are everywhere.

~

My parents' dog Tup (short for Tuppence) jumped up and wagged his tail on my arrival home, pretended he remembered me and couldn't wait to begin our daily walks. I patted him in appreciation for this trick, said, "Good boy!," and turned to my mother. We hugged and air-kissed, and neither of us commented on the other's appearance. She bit her tongue about the wan, unhealthy look I was affecting, and I didn't comment that the widening white streak in her professionally coloured auburn hair had increased her resemblance to Cruella de Vil.

The house smelled the same as always — cool and leathery, with a base note of dog. It looked the same, too, notwithstanding the new living room drapes my mother pointed out, drapes that appeared to me identical to the heavy, formal, valance-topped set that had always hung there. I admired them anyway, followed Mom to the kitchen, and, over coffee and banana bread, listened to an update on the block's real estate transactions, followed by a report on the latest made-in-social-heaven marriages undertaken by the adult children of her friends. To match the job promotions they had recently received in their A-list professions.

A full twenty minutes of this chit-chat passed before Mom thought to mention the welcome back dinner party she'd organized for me, two days hence, when I wouldn't yet have adjusted to the changes in time, climate, and culture zones.

"How kind of you," I said. "But I'm not sure I'm ready to socialize."

"Better to show your face sooner than later. Let the world see that you're not down and defeated."

I faked a perky smile. "You advocate up and victorious as the surface mood to aim for, do you?"

"Don't act depressed and you won't feel depressed — that's my advice. How long since you and Gerald separated? Six months?"

"Eight."

"Definitely time to move on. That's why you came back, isn't it? To start over?"

Perhaps, though not so publicly. "Who did you invite?"

"Our usuals." She rhymed off the names of some of their couple friends, a few neighbours, an aunt and uncle who lived four blocks north, my married cousin and her husband from three blocks east. No one who had ever been close to me. "It'll be a festive start to your summer," she said, and stood up. End of discussion. "Shall we go over to the coach house now?"

The flat had been a tack room when the garage below it housed carriages, was converted to a spartan one-person dwelling sometime in the thirties, and had served as a home to various household staff for years after. When Noel and I were kids, a succession of live-in nannies stayed there. In our tween years, it functioned as a playroom, a kind of tree house, and Noel used it as a bachelor pad between terms at university.

The place had been uninhabited in the eight or so years since, so I wondered, when Mom unlocked the door, if I might find any signs of Noel's debauchery inside — a wrinkled condom wrapper kicked under the bed, maybe, or an empty amyl nitrate vial jammed in behind the fridge, a porn magazine rolled up under the bathroom sink. But no. The three small rooms were pristine, had been thoroughly cleaned by Mom's cleaning woman. The only visible evidence of Noel's former tenancy was a small cigarette burn on the arm of the tartan-plaid couch.

Mom opened the double-sash windows in the sitting room. "You might find it a little too cozy in here," she said. "But you can always come stay with us in the big house if you're not comfortable."

The old pine kitchen cupboards and the aged hardwood floors were of a worn golden hue, but everything else seemed to be white — white walls, white bedroom furniture, white bathroom fixtures (including a large clawfoot tub with a shower rigged up over top.) The fireplace mantel and surround were also white, and empty of decoration except for an earthenware vase filled with two stalks of white freesia that my mother must have arranged there. I saw her hand too in the placement of a worn leather armchair, perfect for reading, next to a window that gave out onto a beguiling view of sunlight, shadow, and leaves, and near a bookcase filled with the old books I'd stored with my parents when I'd moved to California. The overall impression was of a retreat, like a monk's cell in its simplicity. All that was missing was the hair shirt, but I already had the figurative one I'd been wearing for months.

My mother followed my eyes around, said, "It's rather austere-looking, isn't it? I'll run out and buy some throw cushions tomorrow to add some colour. In citrus shades, perhaps."

"No, don't. I mean, everything's perfect as is. Thank you. For letting me stay, for fixing up the place, for everything." This time, my smile was genuine.

~

Where was I, what day was it, and was I still depressed? These were the questions I was in the habit of asking myself each day before I opened my eyes. And on my first morning back in Rose Park, when I awoke in the chenille-covered double bed in the coach house, I thought the veil of sadness I'd worn for months might have thinned a little. Or maybe I should have pulled down the shades the night before — the sunshine flooding in through the windows was blinding.

I spent the day doing errands of the moving-in kind — I set up bank accounts, arranged phone, cable, and internet hook-ups, foraged among the boxes of my belongings in the parents' basement for various essential household items I needed, went out and bought a serious bicycle that I intended to use as my major means of transportation. At five o'clock, I walked three blocks to the local grocery store, an upscale emporium referred to by the locals as the Market. It sold flowers, fancy produce, all kinds of meat, sushi, baked goods, prepared food, fifty-dollar bottles of balsamic vinegar, and groceries, including the ingredients I sought for my dinner — pita, goat cheese, cream cheese, and chives. Since the breakup with Gerald, I'd often subsisted on a pathetic but satisfying single person's meal made by combining the cheeses and chopped chives, and spreading the mixture on toasted pita triangles. My version of comfort food.

I walked home from the store the long way, passed through a park called Cawley Gardens, sat down on a bench there, let the breeze blow my hair and my mind around, and rested my eyes on a house across the road, the house known as Glenwood.

If you didn't know the story about Jeremiah Brown and the treasure, you'd still notice Glenwood, because it's so pretty and colourful and ornamented, so different from its plainer neighbours — houses made of grey stucco or dull red brick, their only decorative detail sets of wooden shutters and the occasional concrete lintel. But, to me, who knew the story well, Glenwood was more than an architectural pin-up. I couldn't look at the house without thinking about Jeremiah Brown and its treasure, or about its current owners, the Greers, whom I'd met some twelve years before, when my mother had organized a welcome-to-Rose-Park brunch in their honour.

As soon as Mom heard that a heart surgeon and his author/illustrator wife had moved into the fiefdom, she contrived an introduction, invited the newcomers over to meet the neighbours who mattered. And vice versa. "They have a daughter your age," she said, after her initial reconnaissance. "Her name is Hannah. Maybe she'll be a new friend for you!"

I didn't bother to reply. I just gave Mom the look every teenage girl favours her mother with sooner or later — the I-can't-believe-how-much-there-is-to-me-that-you-don't-understand look. She carried on with her brunch plans regardless. She hired the two blunt-speaking, heavy-smoking, grey-haired ladies in maid's uniforms that she employed on these occasions to serve, she issued invitations on her monogrammed stationery, and she arranged for her caterer to supply quiches and salads and brown bread and the requisite side of smoked salmon garnished with capers, sliced onions, and lemon wedges. Mom's version of comfort food.

On party day, I hid out with a book in the glassed-in, fern-filled back room on the main floor that my parents liked to refer to as the conservatory. Soon after the party began, Mom swept into my hideout, trailed by the three Greers, and said, in her over-loud, over-animated social voice, "Blithe, what are you doing in here all alone? Come meet everyone."

I stood up and said hello. Mrs. Greer had a kind face, of a sparky and keen-eyed variety, as befitted a children's literature author. Her husband, Dr. Greer, was a polite presence beside her who would meet me ten or twelve more times before deciding that my identity was worth committing to memory.

"And this," Mom said, "is Hannah."

We shook hands, Hannah and me — her grip firm, mine more fish-like — and Mom said, "Blithe's going into grade twelve at Northside High this September, too!"

Neither of us judged this announcement worthy of a rejoinder. We were too busy assessing each other's appearance while pretending not to. Hannah was attractive, with naturally curly hair cut short, finely drawn features, and a slim build. She wore shapeless, dun-coloured clothes that seemed to be making a left-wing political statement, possibly related to South American revolutionaries — a folkloric bandanna was tied around her wrist, a hand-beaded belt held up the narrow waist of her pants. I could only imagine what she would make of me, in my more First World attire — a white shirt and khaki skirt.

Before our mutual regard could become awkward, Noel made his entrance and was introduced all around. He showed off his smarmy private school manners with Mr. and Mrs. Greer and favoured Hannah with a roguish grin. "How do you do?" he said. "I'm the more interesting sibling."

Hannah registered his WASPy, Dad-like looks — the close-set blue eyes, blond hair, princely forelock — glanced back at me, and probably wondered if I was adopted. Or the help. Noel winked at her, said, "I know what you're thinking. Sometimes I wonder how Blithe and I could be related, too."

"Oh, Noel," Mom said. She gave him an affectionate slap on the arm and said, to the room, "He's such a tease."

If the Greers drew any conclusions about our family dynamic from this exchange, they hid them well. All Hannah said was, "Blithe, would you mind showing me around the house? It looks so interesting and old."

Mom said, "I'm sure Blithe would be happy to give you a tour, wouldn't you, dear?" I agreed, and Mom headed Mr. and Mrs. Greer off to the backyard, where the bar, Dad, and more guests awaited them.

As soon as they'd gone, Noel moved in on Hannah. "Wouldn't you rather I showed you the garden?" he said. "I could cadge us some champagne on the way."

I waited to see if this come-on would work — sadly, Noel's lines usually did — and scored a small victory in our ongoing sibling war when Hannah said, "Maybe later, thanks. Where should we start, Blithe?"

I shooed Noel away and led Hannah into a book-lined room known as the library. Its main feature, other than old books, was a gloomy ancestral portrait over the fireplace. "That's Hugh Lawrence Morrison," I said. "He had this house built in 1847."

She looked around, at the picture, the leaded windows, the fireplace, the dark furniture, back at me. "Why are you called Blithe?"

"My parents are big Noel Coward fans. They named my brother Noel, and me Blithe. After the spirit."

"Poor you," she said, but she looked more amused than sympathetic.

"It could have been worse. They could have named me Cowardice." This was an old joke of mine that I trotted out whenever I could, despite the tepid reception it invariably received.

She smiled a brief, lukewarm smile, and said, "So was the guy in the portrait pretty rich?"

"'Comfortable' is the term the family's always used."

"Uh-huh."

Pause.

I said, "You're not actually interested in the house, are you?"

"Not really, no — I wanted to get away from my parents. My mother's been driving me insane with family togetherness since we moved here. I can't wait till school starts so I can leave the house without having to explain where in hell I'm going."

Uh-huh back to her. I sat down on one of the saggy leather chairs, gestured for her to sit, tried to think what innocuous but sociable remark my mother would make in this situation. "How're you liking Rose Park so far?"

"It's too quiet for my taste. The only people I've met are senior citizens and bratty kids. On our street, anyway."

"What street is that?" I hadn't listened when my mother had told me.

"Highpoint."

"Anywhere near number fifty-one?"

"What do you mean? We're in number fifty-one. In the house with a name: Glenwood."

I sat up. "You're living at Glenwood? I didn't know it had been up for sale. What happened to the previous owners?"

"They moved to France. Did you know them?"

"No. I only knew about Jeremiah Brown."

"Who?"

"You live there and you don't know about Jeremiah Brown?"

A flash of annoyance. "Obviously not."

So I told her about Jeremiah and the treasure and the man with a dog who sees light in the valley. "A book was written about the treasure years ago. It should be in this room somewhere." I stood up and started to search the bookshelves for it.

She put up her feet — clad in rugged, foreign-looking leather sandals that emphasized the slenderness of her ankles — on a cracked leather ottoman. "Tell me," she said, "what's Northside High like?"

I didn't turn around. "It's the usual collection of cliques. The athletes and the music students rule the place." Then there was me.

"Is there a darkroom in the school?"

"I don't know. Why? Are you into photography?"

"Do cats kill mice?"

Interesting analogy. Too interesting to comment on in any polite way. "You could probably start up a photography club at school if you wanted," I said. "Last year, Noel founded a rugby team there."

"But he graduated, right? Didn't my mother say he's going away to some Ivy League university?"

Where was that book? "Yeah, to Harvard, for economics and political science. Followed by a master's degree at Oxford, he's hoping. He has big plans for a foreign service career."

"Oh, does he." Not a question. "Is he as untrustworthy as he looks?"

He was worse than untrustworthy. But I'd been brought up to feign family loyalty, at least to strangers. "What do you mean? Did he look untrustworthy to you?"

"Never mind."

"Here it is. *Jeremiah Brown's Treasure.* Would you like to see it?"

She moved to a chair that faced the garden, sat down, opened the book, and read the title page. Through the window, Noel smiled at her, mimed drinking from a wine glass, and beckoned her to him. She turned two more pages before she said, "Do you think I could borrow this book? To show my mother?"

My smile was as thin as her long neck. "Sure."

"How about we go outside now, get some fresh air?"

"The indoor air suits me fine. You go ahead."

She got up out of the chair. Her movements were graceful, even in the baggy clothes. "See you later," she said. "Maybe you can show me the ropes at school."

I had a feeling she'd be able to handle the ropes fine without me, but to be polite, I told her I could be found, most lunchtimes, under a tree on the school lawn.

"Under a tree," she'd said, "gotcha."

Gotcha.

I shook myself free of memory, peeled my legs off the park bench, walked across the street, and rang Glenwood's doorbell. Maybe Mrs. Greer was home. I hadn't seen her for years, but I'd followed her literary career, owned all her books, had stocked my classrooms with the popular children's adventure novels she wrote.

She opened the door. Her hair was greyer than it appeared in her author photo, and her skin more lined. Her eyes were as warm as I remembered, though the friendly but inquiring expression on her face contained no speck of recognition. Probably because of the aged appearance of *my* hair and skin.

"Hi, Mrs. Greer," I said. "It's Blithe Morrison, Hannah's friend from high school. I was passing by and thought I'd say hello, see if you still lived here."

Her smile warmed up to match her eyes. "Blithe, of course! How are you? What are you up to these days? Are you living in town? Won't you come in?"

I declined entry, lingered on her porch, gave her the short answer on my life status — the divorced and back from

California to teach in September answer. "I'm glad to see you're holding the fort here. How's the writing going?"

"Busy. Actually, more than busy. I'm behind on a deadline and Larry and I are going on vacation soon and I'd be tearing my hair out if I weren't worried about losing it. How about you? What will you do for the summer?"

"Not much. Take it easy, read, relax."

For no reason I could see, these remarks elicited from her a furrowed brow, a speculative eye, and the comment, "You don't say."

"Good to see you. Say hello to Hannah when you —"

"Wait. I've just had a brainwave. A crazy one, but what the hell. Would you be interested in working for me part-time? I need a research assistant for a few weeks, and you'd be perfect for the job."

"Me? Why?"

Her eyes narrowed in concentration, apparently on an interior monologue. "Because the research that needs doing is on Rose Park, and who knows this neighbourhood better than you?"

"Lots of people. My father, for one."

"Maybe, but I'll bet your father isn't available to do some reading and site-visiting right now. And I've always thought you were the brightest light in your family anyway. What do you say? How about yes? Yes would be good."

The brightest light? "I, well, thank you, I mean, I'm flattered, but this is so sudden." And so difficult for my soggy, tear-logged mind to process. "I haven't thought beyond next week."

"When you do, think of me. Better yet, give me your phone number and I'll badger you till you agree. I'd love to hire someone reliable and smart instead of a callow university student."

I gave her my new phone number, said thanks and goodbye, took a flummoxed few steps away, and remembered why I'd knocked to begin with. "Oh, Mrs. Greer, have there been any developments with the treasure recently?"

She had on the friendly-puzzled expression again, like when she'd opened the door. "With what?"

"The Glenwood treasure. No one's found it in the last couple of years?"

Her laugh was chuckly, lively. "No, no one's found it. You're one of the few people who even remembers it was rumoured to exist."

"Other than you? I would have thought being mistress of Glenwood required you to be keeper of the treasure flame."

"You see?" she said, though I didn't, yet. "You *are* the perfect person for the job."

~

Ten minutes after the scheduled start time for my welcome back dinner, my mother called. "The guests are starting to arrive, dear."

"I'll be right over. Just combing my hair."

"You're not nervous, are you? Nothing to be nervous about. Chin up."

Cocktail chatter was underway when, chin aimed at the ceiling, I walked into a room occupied by about fifteen people, some of whom I knew. As soon as she saw me, Mom stood up from the sofa arm on which she perched with gin and tonic in hand, said, "Here she is!" and sent me a multi-part message with her facial expression and body language that included directives to smile wider and fix my posture. I attempted both corrective actions, and suffered the arm she placed around my shoulders.

"To Blithe, everyone," Mom said. "And to regrouping."

Dad said, "Hear, hear," and swilled back his own gin.

My father brought me a drink, my aunt asked me about earthquakes and California weather, other conversations picked up where they'd left off, and I was soon cornered by my cousin

Kerry, who saw in me a new audience for a recital of the many achievements of her four children, ages seven to fourteen. She spoke at length of private schools, academic prizes, ski teams, squash tournament wins, and horseback riding ribbons, and described a summer to come in which her kids would race sailboats and competitively wakeboard at the family cottage. Throughout the one-sided conversation, she showed no interest in my life, past, present, or future, a level of self-absorption that for once I welcomed. I nodded, said "Really?" at regular intervals, and let my mind wander back to my porchfront conversation with Mrs. Greer of the day before. Let myself bask for a moment in the glow generated by her random words of praise.

Kerry wrapped up her monologue with a question. "How's your gorgeous brother these days? Is he still in Geneva?"

I hadn't seen or spoken to Noel since his fly-in for my wedding, also known as the beginning of my marriage's end. "He's posted in London, now, I believe," I said, but Kerry's attention had shifted. "Look," she said. "Jane Whitney and her husband just came in. Do you know them?"

A fortyish couple was being greeted by my mother across the room. "No. Who are they?"

"James is a lawyer at your dad's firm. Jane is a curator of something or other at the museum. I've known her since we were kids, but they just moved onto this block a few months ago. Their daughter is in my Heather's class at Rose Park Elementary." She lifted her hand to her mouth, spoke from behind it. "I always feel awkward when I see Jane, because her daughter's a bit of a strange bird. To be perfectly frank, Heather and her friends can't stand her."

I looked down at the floor, diverted the glare meant for Kerry towards the faded patterns on the rug. Kerry was enough older than me, and enough uninterested, not to remember that I had inhabited my own strange bird phase during my elementary school career. "I guess someone always has to be excluded so the rest can feel superior," I said, and the taste of childhood hurt was so strong on my tongue I wondered if Kerry could smell it on my breath.

But Kerry yakked on as if she were named Blithe. "This Alexandra is a bright girl, no question, but she just doesn't fit in. She just doesn't get it. You know?"

I knew all too well, and was saved from making further barbed comment on the subject by the ringing of the silver bell that my mother used to announce the serving of dinner. The guests drained their cocktails and began to make slow progress towards the dining room, directed by Mom, who assumed a rear guard position from which she used both arms to make forward pushing motions. With a hitherto unnoticed third arm, she hailed me to come within muttering distance.

"You see my friend Marge there?" She indicated with a head gesture a well-groomed, Hermès-scarf-wearing woman of her generation, who was leading the charge.

"Is she the golfer or the bridge player?"

"The golfer. And she has a recently divorced son. His name is Phil. He's thirty-six, a lawyer, attractive. He has two small children, but he only sees them every other weekend. Should I pass on your number?"

"Are you kidding? No. Please. I do not want to be set up."

"Why not go out with him? One time. For fun. Take your mind off things."

"Mom, I said no."

She pursed her lips. "I was just trying to help. If you want to spend the summer sulking, go ahead."

The setting, my irritation with Kerry, my mother's tone, my insecure state — they all combined to make me rise to her bait. "I won't have time to sulk. I've lined up a summer job."

Mom's lips relaxed. "Why, that's wonderful, dear. What kind of job?"

Researching for Mrs. Greer, apparently.

~ Chapter 2 ~

M rs. Greer acted thrilled when I called to say I was interested in the research job, and after consultation of her fully loaded appointment calendar and my completely empty one, we settled on the following Friday morning to meet and discuss the details of the project, at a midtown haunt called Bagel Haven. "I go there every morning," she said. "I'm of the firm belief that breakfast should be consumed outside the home. Just because I don't work in a proper office doesn't mean I shouldn't share the rituals of those who do. Don't you agree?"

Did I? I wasn't sure. So on the Friday, I rode my bicycle to Bagel Haven, arrived early, and sat down at one of the small tables to observe the rituals in question. To see if, before Molly arrived, I could acquire a semi-informed opinion on the subject. On any subject other than my rapidly-becoming-boring state of woe.

In the five days since our phone conversation, I'd enjoyed the coach house's quiet, at least when the hammering and wrecking crews renovating a house two doors down took their lunch break, and between the debris-blowing and lawn-mowing sessions conducted by various gardening teams vying for the title of best simulator of jet takeoff noise. I'd also indulged in some spells of meditative solitude in the flat between visits from my mother, who dropped by daily with essentials like an extra pillow and blanket, fresh flowers, or rolls of toilet paper. (I'd have to start tipping her soon, and/or make up a Do Not Disturb sign for my doorknob.) But there were only so many hours I could sit in a chair with an open book in my lap, staring out the window at tradesmen's trucks jockeying for road space with sunglassed women in SUVs, and contemplating my inadequacy as a human, before I began to yearn for a change of scene and preoccupation.

So it was with interest that I watched the morning bustle at Bagel Haven. A grey-haired, jolly man with a British accent manned the till, a quick-handed woman in her thirties toasted and buttered, and a young guy in jeans, T-shirt, apron, and baseball cap periodically emerged from a back kitchen to unload hot bagels from a trolley into the display baskets at the front of the store.

A steady flow of people in office clothes took food to go, but those who ate in were a more mixed crowd. A man of about seventy, with a jaunty white visor on his head, chatted up the staff by name, ordered "the usual," dropped a dollar in the tip jar when his coffee and bagel together cost less than two, and sat down to read his newspaper. Seated in a corner with an infant in a baby seat was an exhausted-looking woman of about my age, clad in sweats, who closed her eyes in ecstasy when she took her first sip of latte. At five minutes to nine, in sauntered three city maintenance workers, dressed in orange coveralls and construction boots. All three ate bagels toasted with butter, and they sat at the table in the window to eat them, where they talked loud and laughed between bites. As if they liked their lives, the coffee break part, anyway. My eavesdropping on their conversation was interrupted by the arrival of Mrs. Greer, who, when I addressed her as such, said I must call her Molly, urged me to try a focaccia bagel, and introduced me to the jolly shop manager, name of Arthur.

"Welcome to Bagel Haven," he said. "What are you having today? A focaccia bagel and fresh-squeezed orange juice? That's a wise choice, to mix the bitter and the sweet. The choice of someone who's experienced both in life, I wager."

I smiled uncertainly, hoped my unhappiness wasn't so obvious that this stranger had seen it in an instant, paid for my order, followed Molly to a table, and said, "Does everyone get their breakfast order analyzed for its symbolic meaning, or was I just lucky today?"

She set down her tray. "Arthur considers himself something of a philosopher, but he's a good guy." In a more concerned tone, she said, "Was your divorce very hard? *Are* you bitter?"

To my dismay, tears welled up behind my eyes. I swallowed, said, "No, not too," and ran off to the condiment station, ostensibly in search of napkins but really so that I could blink the tears away, admonish myself to exhibit better self-control, and return to the table with a composed face and a change of topic. "What news do you have of Hannah? Is she still taking pictures for that wire service?"

She was. Somewhere in Africa that week, Molly thought. Israel the month before. "Wherever there's trouble."

"Hannah and I have lost touch," I said. "I invited her to my wedding, but she couldn't make it."

"She never can. I hardly remember the last time she was home." Molly's face went sad for a second, moved through hurt, and settled on proud. Similar to my mother's progression when speaking about Noel and his glamorous, globetrotting life. Time for another topic change.

"So I'd love to hear about the research you want me to do," I said.

"Yes, of course." Molly cleared her face of Hannah-related emotions, pulled a pen and pad from her purse, and told me that for years, she'd wanted to write an illustrated history of Rose Park for children, in a picture book format, with a puzzle on each page. "*The Rose Park Puzzle Book*, I'd call it." She grinned. "Catchy title, eh?" On the pad, she sketched an outline of an open book. "Every double-page spread would feature a different Rose Park landmark." She drew a house shape inside the book frame, added a few gables and a chimney and a wide front porch. "And alongside each illustration would be text that gives a history of the site and provides a clue or marker to a hidden feature in the picture."

I imagined her sketch come to life in full watercolour splendour, with every detail of the house realized, a path painted in, trees all around, rose bushes in bloom. I could almost hear a leaf-blower roaring. I said, "I like the concept, but are there enough picturesque landmarks with interesting stories in Rose Park to make a book?"

"When you take into account that each site will take up four pages — two to introduce the puzzle and two to reveal the answer — the nine sites I've picked should fill a picture book just fine. The problem is that I haven't had a chance to study them and find a feature at each that's hidden in plain sight. That's where you come in."

Next to us, the orange coverall guys stood up, scraped their chairs on the floor, tossed their garbage into the bin with basketball-type shots, made sports announcer commentary to match, and walked out. In the ensuing quiet, I said, "Could you give me an example of what a hidden in plain sight feature might be?"

She flipped the page over on the pad, started to draw on a clean sheet. "One landmark I want to use is the Field Street footbridge that spans the east ravine. Do you know it?"

"Vaguely." I wasn't a keen ravine-goer, never had been.

In a few quick motions, she had delineated a wooden bridge arched over a tree-lined chasm. "It could be something small." Her pen hovered over the drawing. "Maybe a workman carved his initials in the bridge supports years ago." Squiggles appeared on her drawing to indicate initials. "Or it could be something bigger. Like that on a clear day, you can see the harbour from a certain spot on the bridge." More squiggles suggested a far-off lake.

I closed my mouth, which had hung open while she'd drawn and talked, while I'd moved outside myself into a world of her creation. I won't claim a sparkle lit up my eyes, but a spot of colour might have come into my cheeks. "This sounds like it could be fun," I said. If I could remember what fun felt like.

"But do you think you can find me the nine hidden features in two weeks? I promised my editor I'd have a complete manuscript to her, including illustrations, by September, and I don't want to miss the deadline and give her an excuse to cancel the project, seeing as she only agreed to it in a weak moment when the first book of my twin detective series did so well. Though considering I'm behind on the new twin book, and Larry and I are leaving on Monday for a holiday in Nova Scotia, I'll still have to work like a madwoman when I return to finish everything on time."

"Two weeks should be fine." The guy in the baseball cap pushed a trolley full of bagels by us, and I caught an appetizing whiff of roasted rosemary and yeast. "I might even have time to come in here every day and keep your seat warm."

We discussed money next. I said I'd do the work for free, and she offered to pay me a high-sounding figure she said was a standard researcher's hourly wage. When we'd both said, "No, I insist," four or five times, I accepted her offer and we made a date to meet later that afternoon at her house for a hand-over of the puzzle book file. We parted outside Bagel Haven, she for a hair appointment at a nearby salon, I for the return bike ride home to bid my parents goodbye — they were going to England for one of my father's legal conferences.

Dad was standing on the porch, surrounded by luggage, when I wheeled into the driveway on my bike. "You all set?" I said.

He peered in my direction, appeared to recognize me. "Just about. The airport limousine should arrive any minute. Your mother's inside, on the phone."

From across the street and down a bit came the sound of childish voices, accompanied by kid commotion in front of a large white house halfway down the block.

"Blithe, you're here!" Mom emerged in her travel outfit of coiffed hair, gold jewellery, pantsuit, and pumps. "And we're off. I hope you won't be lonely with us gone."

Lonely? More like grateful my brooding sessions would be uninterrupted. "I'll be fine. Have a good trip."

"Shall I give your love to Noel?"

I was about to say no, I didn't think so, but she wouldn't have heard, was waving a cheery hello to a fortyish blond woman coming down the sidewalk toward us. The woman's small son preceded her on a tricycle. Twenty paces back, on foot, walked an older girl with long frizzy hair, reading a book.

"Who's that?" Dad whispered.

Mom whispered back. "Jane Whitney, your partner's wife. From down the street." It was the woman Kerry had spoken about at Mom's party, the museum curator with the unpopular daughter. She came within speaking distance, stopped, made cordial small talk to my parents about their imminent departure, and introduced us to her children. Joshua, the boy, yelled hi, then careened up and down the sidewalk on his tricycle making "vroom" sounds. The girl, Alexandra, stayed back, sat on a low stone wall in front of the house next door, kept reading, and raised a limp hand in a minimal greeting when asked to say hello.

"No school today?" Mom said.

"Josh only goes to half-day kindergarten," Jane said. "And I sometimes take a morning off with him." No explanation given for the daughter's presence on the street at ten o'clock on a Friday. Jane looked back at Alexandra and a ripple of something —worry? sadness?— crossed her features. Would she say more? No. Only, "Joshua, stay on the sidewalk. A car's coming." And to my parents, "Is that your limo?" In the flurry of baggage loading and bon voyaging that followed, Jane and her children made their escape.

Halfway into the car, Mom said to me, "Don't leave Tup alone too much. He'll start chewing the furniture if he feels neglected."

"I'll bring him over to my place as soon as you drive away."

She handed out a few more reminders about the gardener and garbage collection, Dad ahemed, and they left. I waved until they were out of sight, wheeled my bike up the driveway to the coach house, and caught a glimpse, through a gap in the cedar hedge, of the straight back of Jane's daughter, still walking fifteen paces behind her mother, still intent, to the exclusion of the world around her, on her book.

~

On the first day of school in my grade twelve year, *I* was reading a book, under a tree, at lunchtime, when Hannah showed up, plunked herself down on the grass, and stuck with me for the next two years. Why, I never quite understood.

My first guess was that she might be using me to get to Noel, but he was away at Harvard and rarely came home, and the few times I mentioned his name, she showed no interest, asked no questions. She asked a lot about Northside High, though. Which teachers were the biggest pushovers, she wanted to know, which the easiest to fool? Who gave the least homework? What school rules had to be followed and which could be bent? How could she find out about the darkroom? Did I have any idea why the student council social director, the very blonde Kathleen Caswell, was giving her hostile looks? And what was the story on Peter Matheson, who drove the green BMW convertible? He'd asked Hannah out already.

I didn't run with the likes of Kathleen Caswell or Peter Matheson, but I'd observed my peers in action long enough to know that Kathleen probably perceived Hannah as a threat. In the way that a new, pretty girl who doesn't shave her armpits and carries an important-looking camera slung around her neck can be to someone who started highlighting her hair at age fourteen. I told Hannah this, and that Peter Matheson was a stud looking to notch his jockstrap with someone new. I also passed on the information tidbit that Mr. Randolph, the physics teacher, had tried for years to get a Camera Club going, without success.

Is there anything as gratifying as having one's advice not just listened to, but heeded? In week two of school, Hannah obtained the key to the darkroom from Mr. Randolph and was told she could use it anytime, and order supplies for it from his departmental budget. By Halloween, she'd dated and dumped Peter Matheson — "He was such a boring lover," she said, as if I'd know what that meant — but not before driving his Beemer all over town. And she made no effort to seek more popular friends of the Kathleen Caswell variety, seeming to prefer my quirky company instead.

I decided Hannah must value me as a guide, a docent. Except that instead of interpreting Impressionist painters at an art gallery, I was leading Hannah through high school, summarizing the ethos of each social set with pith and insight. I didn't mind that image, of me as sage. It made a nice contrast to my regular role as the not as attractive or as smart sister to Mr. Golden Boy.

Besides, friendship with Hannah meant access to Glenwood.

~

Glenwood was number five on Molly's list of puzzle book sites. After a former schoolhouse, a former golf clubhouse, a former stable — all converted since to residential use — and a former manor house still surrounded by its original stone wall. "What do you think?" Molly said. "Is it too weird if I include my own house in the book?"

We were sitting in her kitchen, where I had tried and failed to pick up any hint of ghostly vibe or psychic spark from the long-departed Jeremiah Brown about the treasure, despite a concerted mental effort on my arrival in the house that involved much grimacing and had caused Molly to ask if I was feeling sick.

"Too weird? Not at all. You must include Glenwood. Glenwood is the best thing about Rose Park, the, the — " I remembered I was talking to a writer, considered and rejected referring to the house as a jewel on the crown, icing on the cake, or the top of the pops, settled for, "— the eye of the storm!"

Molly arched an eyebrow at me. "You're exuberant today."

She must have meant to say nonsensical, or maybe idiotic, but had mistakenly chosen the wrong word, an age-related habit I had noticed in my mother since my return home. I knew from experience that these slips of the tongue were better left uncorrected, so I said, "What's this? My parents' house is on the list? Why?"

"Because it's the oldest in Rose Park that's been continuously occupied by the same family."

And was about as boring to look at as such a description would imply. "Finding a feature to highlight there will be a challenge."

"I should mention that the feature you choose must be enduring; a flower that only blooms in June won't do." She twisted her mouth into a contemplative moue for a second before speaking further. "And it should be visible to the discerning eye, not to the careless glance, if you know what I mean."

"If a discerning eye's what you're after, too bad Hannah's not available to do the job."

"Actually, Hannah did some work on the project, briefly, years ago." Molly pulled an envelope of five-by-seven, black-and-white photographs from the file and passed it to me. "She took these pictures."

I opened the envelope and removed the first print, a photo of Cawley Gardens, the park across the road from Glenwood, once the site of a grand mansion. Hannah's picture of the park had been taken during what looked like a fierce summer storm — tree branches were bent over in the wind, and rain poured down in sheets.

"This is rather gloomy," I said.

"You know Hannah and her mood shots."

The next photo was of a wooded area. "What's this? Part of the ravine?"

"That's the site of a small lodge that was on Glenwood's property when that section of the ravine belonged to this house."

I hadn't known about any such lodge. And given my father's passion for local history, I should have.

Molly said, "There's a copy in the file of an old city plan that marks the lodge site. Hannah went down to the archives and found it for me."

I wrote, "Lodge? ask Dad," on my notepad, and flipped to the next photo, a shadowy, mysterious one of Glenwood. Hannah had shot the picture without any cars nearby, and at such an angle that you couldn't see the neighbouring houses, or anything modern like a telephone pole or hydro line. "Great picture," I said. "Very atmospheric." And much more haunted in feel than the cheery kitchen where we sat.

The next photo was of the footbridge that spanned the ravine up at Field Street, the bridge Molly had sketched at Bagel Haven. The "kissing bridge" the local kids used to call it. Noel had been there many a time in his day. Hannah, too, I was sure. "The bridge isn't very old, is it?"

"Not that edition, no, but there's been a bridge of some form in that location since the area was settled. There's a picture of an old iron version of the bridge in one of the books on the reading list I'm giving you."

There was no end to what I didn't know. "When did Hannah take these pictures?"

"When she was at art college. She was assigned a project on some technique or other — the use of natural light, maybe. So she made a couple of my sites the subjects of her photos; to kill two birds with one stone."

Or like a cat kills mice. I took the envelope, closed the file. "Tell you what: I'll go home, absorb all this, and call before you leave for Nova Scotia if I have any questions. Have you arranged for anyone to keep an eye on the house while you're away?"

"No, but we have an alarm system."

"You're not worried another Rose Park Burglar might come along?"

"Another? Who was the first?"

The Rose Park Burglar had haunted me the year I was fifteen, when a rash of break and enters was the talk of the neighbourhood. Most of the robberies took place when the homeowners were out, for the evening or away, but a few jobs were pulled while the victims slept, including one on my parents' own block, at the home of an elderly widow. No harm had befallen her — she didn't realize she'd been robbed until noon the next day — but the thought of a crime-bent stranger prowling the streets, our street, had spooked me badly.

The first night I heard the news of the burglar's spree, I lay in bed, unable to sleep, my anxiety the only defence I could muster against our house being next. I was tormented by the idea of waking up to the feel of a gloved hand across my mouth, or a pillow pressed down on my face. I called to mind, in a murky, green-tinged palette, with surround-sound, every graphic scene of violence or horror I'd been subjected to at movie theatres during trailers for scary movies I would never see.

Long after my parents had fallen asleep, I lay and listened too closely to the night sounds. The muffled moaning I heard was our dog Angus, Tup's predecessor. He slept on the second-floor landing and was known to have an occasional nightmare, despite a moronically sunny daytime personality. The rhythmic bangs that resounded in my room's radiator were furnace-related, I knew, and I also recognized the sound of car doors closing outside — one, then the other — that signalled the return of our gadabout neighbours, an empty nester couple more social than my parents.

With my paranoia-enhanced, superhero-level hearing, I could isolate, from the low hum of outdoor noises that leaked inside my locked windows, the jingle of the dog collar on the greyhound down the street who was walked each night at eleven-thirty. I knew not to panic when raccoons hissed and shrieked in the alley during their territorial wars over our garbage bins. But any other exterior sound had me up and at the window, straining for a glimpse of a black-clad burglar scaling our walls or trying to jimmy our windows. Any unaccounted-for indoor sound sent me racing to my side of the locked bedroom door, to press my ear against it and wish I had a spyhole to look through, or X-ray vision to go with the hearing.

Three nights of this routine, and I was a wreck.

On the evening of the fourth night, I pleaded with my parents, at the dinner table, to let me sleep on the chaise longue in their bedroom. Desperate for relief from my runaway imagination, I made a case for the chaise expressed with a fervour unseen since September of my grade three year, when I'd come home from my first day at Brookbank Hall, a private girls' school, sobbed for hours, and offered to perform Cinderella-esque chores for the rest of my childhood if my parents would transfer me back to Rose Park Elementary.

I'd been so compliant in the years since they'd withdrawn me from Brookbank that Mom and Dad were taken aback by my burglar-related outburst. Noel wasn't. At seventeen, he had painlessly passed through puberty and was enjoying an adolescence free from doubt or acne. He said, "You're being irrational, Blithe. We have nothing to fear. According to the newspapers, the thief is mainly after high-end audio equipment. Has it escaped your notice that we don't have any?"

"How's the burglar supposed to know that?"

Mom said, "You don't realize how impregnable the house is, dear. There are bars on the basement windows, Dad checks the other window locks every night before bed, and there's Angus to be our watchdog."

I snorted. "Angus is no help. He'd roll over and play dead for a breadcrumb."

Noel stabbed an asparagus spear with his fork. "Blithe has a point there."

Dad considered me the way he would a client in his office. That is, he gave me his full attention, for once. "I sense that the application of reason in this situation will not allay Blithe's fears."

Noel said, "So you admit she's crazy?"

Dad executed a facial move Noel and I had called the Angry Eyebrow when we were younger and on speaking terms. "That's enough, Noel. I'm not condoning Blithe's hysteric tendencies by any means, but I would like to finish my dinner before the meat is cold. Can we reach a compromise?"

Mom tossed her napkin on the table. "A fifteen-year-old should not be sharing a bedroom with her parents, no matter how fearful she is."

Dad said, "My proposal is that Noel and I move the chaise into Mom's dressing room and Blithe sleeps there. Behind a closed door, but close by. All in favour?"

I might have interrupted to ask them to stop referring to me in the third person, but the promise of a normal night's sleep kept me quiet.

Mom said, "I suppose I could tolerate that arrangement, as long as it's temporary."

Noel helped himself to another lamb chop from the chafing dish. "I still say Blithe's fears are baseless, but if I'm needed to move furniture around, we'll have to do it right after dinner. I'm going out tonight."

"On a school night?" Mom said.

He flashed her a phony smile. "I have study group," he said. In case anyone needed a reminder that he was the superior child.

Now, to Molly, I said, "The Rose Park Burglar committed a slew of robberies around here years ago. Before your time, I guess. But I'm just thinking I could drop over and pick up fly- ers from your porch if you like, move the mail out of your foyer, make it less obvious no one's home."

"I couldn't ask you to do that."

We played the no, I insist game again, and I won this time — we arranged that I would come by every few days, deal with the mail, water the houseplants, and nod in passing at various workmen Molly had lined up to perform exterior maintenance work during her absence. So when I walked out of Glenwood, I had with me the blue file folder, a spare key to the house, and, thank Molly, things to do.

~ Chapter 3 ~

The day after my parents' departure for London — my first day alone in Rose Park — I stayed home, luxuriated in the solitude. I ate a salad of bocconcini and tomato and basil for lunch, I read over Molly's puzzle book file, I walked Tup. At dinnertime, I rode my bike to an English-style fish and chip shop situated a twenty-minute bike ride away and pretended the calories I burned biking there and back might be equal to more than a minuscule portion of the calories consumed.

I spent the evening rereading the family copy of *Jeremiah Brown's Treasure* and didn't look up from the book and into space more than twice. I might have enjoyed a lie-in the next morning, but Tup whined and laid his nose on my arm and drooled on me at eight-thirty. So I got up, showered, dressed, had some coffee, filled a small backpack with supplies, and set out with him for a brisk walk to midtown.

When I'd tied Tup to a bicycle rack on the sidewalk in front of the library, I went inside and found the main space to be full of small children running amok, most of them in front of the door to the community room. A stencilled sign announced that a Red Riding Hood puppet show would be performed at 10:00 a.m., in fifteen minutes.

I stepped around the children and the strollers, past the harried-looking parents and nannies, asked a library staff person for help, and was directed to the "Of Local Interest" shelf. I was after two books from Molly's reading list: a recent publication called *Rose Park: An Architectural Guide,* and an old book entitled *Rambles in Rose Park,* by one Mary Elizabeth Bishop, published in 1910, which Molly had told me contained some interesting illustrations.

I'd thought my father's private collection of Rose Park-abilia constituted everything there was to know about the area, but after I'd pulled the architectural guide — a recent trade paperback, subsidized by the local historical society and heavy on black-and-white photographs — off the shelf, I located the Bishop book, a memoir of sorts, bound in an anonymous but hardy library cover that protected the yellowed pages within. I opened it at random, read a paragraph or two in the old-fashioned typeface, tsked at the author's breathy prose style, flipped through to the illustrations, and confirmed Molly's assessment — the frontispiece was a detailed etching of a now-demolished house named Norcastle that had once stood a few blocks south of my parents' street.

I took both books to the checkout counter, handed them to the clerk, and was standing, waiting for them, when I was tackled hard, in the shins, by a hurtling child. I cried out at the momentary splash of pain — there'd be a nice bruise the next day — bent down to help the boy up, and recognized him as Jane Whitney's son Joshua.

Jane ran over. "Joshua! Say you're sorry." To me, she said, "I'm sorry. So sorry." She hoisted a squirming Joshua onto her hip. "He's all hyped up for this puppet show."

I did not rub my leg or wince. I said, "It's quite all right," and took my books and due date slip from the library staff person. "I seem to have picked a busy time to drop in."

Jane set Joshua back on the ground. "Go see Alexandra," she said, and tilted her head to read the spines of my books. "Is that *Rambles in Rose Park?*"

"You know it?"

"I donated it to the library. Look at the bookplate."

Affixed to the inside front cover was a gold-rimmed label that announced Jane's gift. I said, "Was the author a relative of yours?"

"No, we don't go that far back in this neighbourhood. But the Bishop family built my parents' house, the house where I grew up. There were five copies of that book in the attic when my parents moved in. Self-published, and it shows. Why are you reading it?"

I gave her a short explanation about my research assistant work for Molly.

She said, "Well, don't believe everything Mary Elizabeth says. She wasn't the most careful chronicler of her time."

Joshua returned to Jane's side, picked at her jeans, and pouted. "Mommy, Alexandra told me to go away."

"Why don't you go find a book to read?" she said. "One with nice pictures." He wandered off again and she said, under her breath, "Alexandra's here under duress." She gestured to a chair nearby, half-hidden by a column, where Alexandra sat reading, oblivious to the preschoolers all around. Louder, Jane said, "Say hello to Blithe, honey."

Alexandra mumbled an uninterested hello and returned to her book, which some head-tilting of my own helped me recognize as *A Wrinkle in Time,* one of my old favourites.

Jane pulled me aside. The cloud of worry that had surrounded her in front of my parents' house was back. "You'll have gathered Alexandra's not big on social interaction," she said. I had gathered Alexandra used reading as a way to avoid social interaction, a coping strategy with which I had both personal and professional experience. Jane went on, so low I had trouble hearing her, "There was an incident this week at school — some in-group out-group nonsense among the girls in her class. It's been hard on her. "

I twinged with sympathy, and from behind us, Alexandra's voice said, loudly, "What's all that barking?"

The library's picture windows provided a lovely view of Tup straining on his leash and shouting his head off. "Oh no," I said, "that's my dog," and I ran off. Somewhere in my wake, I heard Alexandra say, "She has a dog?"

Outside, I yelled at Tup to be quiet, untied him from the bike rack, and saw why he'd barked: a pack of six dogs of varying sizes lay on the sidewalk. Unlike Tup, these dogs were peaceful and panting, and seemed well under the control of a young man in jeans and a T-shirt who sat on the library bench. He held the dogs' different-coloured leashes in one hand, and in the other, a paperback book — a mystery novel, it looked like. A baseball cap was pulled down over his eyes. He pointed to Tup, who had begun to sniff around the dog cluster. "Your dog?"

"I'm sorry if he was disturbed by your entourage there. He doesn't get out in public much."

He looked up at me from under the cap brim. His eyes were light blue, or rather, blue streaked with white. He said, "My entourage?"

"I meant all the dogs."

"I know what you meant. Is that black lab yours?"

"Yes."

"What's his name?"

"Tup."

"Yeah. I used to walk him."

I'm sure I looked as surprised to hear this news as I felt. "You did?"

"He was on my weekday run for the last couple of years." He gestured to the dogs at his feet. "With some of these guys. Are you the daughter that came home, then?"

I stammered yes and he introduced himself as Patrick Hennessy, a name that stirred in me vague recollections of a large family from a small house on Hillside Road in Rose Park. A large family that included several boys, though the one I could dimly remember had been older than me, and not named Patrick.

Alexandra's voice spoke up, tugged on my thoughts. "Can I meet the dogs?" She was standing on the library steps, very still, and making direct eye contact with me for the first time. Jane stood beside her, holding Joshua by the hand. "Alexandra loves dogs," she said.

"I can introduce you to Tup." I tugged on Tup's leash, got his nose away from another dog's behind, and showed Alexandra how to have him smell her hand, let her do some timid head-patting. "And maybe Patrick here will show you his dogs."

"They're not all mine," Patrick said. "I just walk them." He pointed them out one by one. "The black lab is Pedro. He likes to chase squirrels. The border collie is Kristi — all she wants to do is catch Frisbees. The little pug is Napoleon, the old schnauzer is Asta, the weimaraner is Marmalade, and this brown mutt is Buck. Go ahead and pat them if you like. Except Pedro. He doesn't like people much."

Alexandra made her way through the dogs, patted each one on the head, steered clear of Pedro, and finished off with Buck, who licked her hands and made her laugh. "I like Buck the best," she said to Patrick.

He grinned. "Me, too. Buck's my dog."

Alexandra restarted her petting circuit, and Jane said to me, aside, "Now she won't mind so much that I dragged her along this morning. Thank you. And your friend."

I almost explained that Patrick wasn't my friend, but didn't know how to without sounding rude, so I watched Alexandra instead. The encounter with the dog congress had softened the expression on her face, made her look different, happy, like someone who could care less about grade five in-groups and out-groups. I said to Jane, "If Alexandra would like to come with me to the park sometime to walk Tup, she'd be welcome."

"Thank you," Jane said, "but I don't know. She's a little shy with strangers."

Alexandra said, "I'd like to go. When?"

We made a date for the next day, Sunday, in the afternoon, Jane and family hustled back into the library for Red Riding Hood, and I went ten steps down the sidewalk with Tup before I thought of saying goodbye and thank you to Patrick. I turned back to do so, but he was already a block away, walking in the other direction, his book stuffed into a back pocket, the dogs trotting at his side.

~

At home, I read through the architectural guide in a few hours and found out about several Rose Park houses I'd never noticed before. One house in particular caught my fancy, a small peak-roofed cottage on Green Street that the guide identified as an example of the Gothic Revival style. I'd have to go see it some-time, see if its charm was more than photograph-deep.

I cracked open Mary Elizabeth Bishop's account of her life and rambles next, and learned that she was the only daughter of a prosperous brewer who lived on William Street. I also learned that her high-spirited and repetitive account of her daily walks through the area's sylvan glades was skimworthy, at best. When I came to about the twentieth mention of her faithful terrier Jock

— the rabbit-chasing scoundrel — I called an eager Tup, slipped the architectural guide and a new sketchbook I'd bought into a backpack, and set off on a ramble of our own.

Our usual walk destination was the Rose Park sports park — a lively place that was home to tennis courts, a children's playground, and a football field, and was located four blocks away. This time, I headed off in the other direction, east, to Cawley Gardens, where I took Tup off his leash, let him roam, sat on a bench, and started contemplating the site for its potential as a piece of Molly's puzzle.

The architectural book contained a 1901 photograph of the Cawley Gardens house, a massive château-style, three-storey, stone-faced mansion that boasted twenty windows on the front alone, multiple roofs dotted with towerettes, and a drive-through columned entranceway termed a porte-cochère. According to the short history on the page, the house reigned in splendour as a private residence for forty years, was sold to the government and used as a convalescent home after World War II, fell into disrepair, and was demolished — a white elephant — in 1960.

Not a sign of it remained. Not a brick, stone, or roof tile. Where the photo showed the house and paved forecourt to have been was now an expanse of thick grass studded with trees grown to heights and breadths sufficient to provide shade for park visitors and climbing opportunities for intrepid children. Where there had been outbuildings and formal landscaped gardens, more grass and trees. I looked around. There had to be some evidence remaining of such a significant house other than the historical society plaque nailed to a rock at the park entrance. Without some sign, how could Molly use the green scene before me for the puzzle book? What could she ask her readers to do? Count the squirrels, name the tree types, match the unleashed dogs with their owners?

There *was* the house's old driveway, or drive, still extant, in the form of the rutted roadway that bisected the park. The drive entered the park on the south, flowed over a rampart built to bridge the beginning of the ravine's slope, led to the tree-dotted lawn where the house's front had been, and turned west to exit on Highpoint Road. There, the roadway was barred to vehicular traffic by a waist-high steel gate painted in green and white stripes, the colours of the city parks department. Circa nineteen-sixty or seventy-something was my guess for the gate's vintage. Not any older.

I checked for Tup, spotted him moseying along toward the other end of the roadway, the south end. I stood up, followed him over, spied another green and white gate, and on the left side of it — was I seeing things? Or was that a square column standing off to the side? An old-looking square stone column, with no apparent purpose. It wasn't attached to anything, wasn't part of the adjoining property. Could it have been part of the old entranceway to the Cawley estate? A last remnant? Up close, I could see that the column consisted of three large sand-coloured blocks mortared together. There were badly chipped bevelled edges on top and bottom, and the stone itself had worn away on one side, to reveal a ribbed underlayer within. I touched the worn surface. I looked for lettering — a name or a number — but found neither, nor any indication of a light standard, no hole on the front or top of the column where a fixture might have been. I stroked the block surface, wanting it to be old and original. Though if it had been, wouldn't there be a matching column on the other side of the driveway, where there was now a drinking fountain, and, ten feet over, a mounded flower bed planted with petunias? In the place where another column might have been was air. And on the ground below the air, a square of concrete was set into the grass, a square that had to mark the former base of the matching column.

I pulled out the architectural book with trembling hands and turned to the Cawley Gardens page. The main photo showed only the house, not the drive, but an inset photo in the bottom right hand corner of the page had been taken from farther back, to convey the scope of the estate at its heyday, and it showed — be still, my hands — the gateway that had once controlled entry, including my column and its disappeared mate.

Two boys on bikes came along, deked around the green-and-white gate, and rode over the grass to the water fountain. They stopped to take a drink and took no notice of me, flushed with excitement, face pressed to a beat-up piece of stone. I stepped back, took out my sketchbook, and began to draw the column, tried to capture on the page its rough, uneven surfaces, its bits of decorative moulding, its ideal suitability to be a hidden but in plain sight feature for Molly's book. And for ten or fifteen minutes, I forgot to be sad.

When my drawing was done, I packed up, found Tup grazing on a discarded chocolate bar wrapper near the bench, and headed him back across the park to leave, past a flagstone path, partly overgrown with weeds, that led underneath the rampart and into the ravine. Graffiti was spray-painted on the lower part of the rampart wall; the path petered out under the archway. Beyond it, the land dropped down into a dark quiet under the densely leaved tops of the trees that had grown up from the ravine floor.

The footpath was that way, and the site of the old lodge Molly had mentioned, but I didn't go down. I'd save that outing for another day, a day when unexpected rushes of emotion about sand-coloured columns wouldn't have rendered me so vulnerable to hearing a remembered echo of Hannah's voice in my ear, sharp and quick, chiding me to forget the past, to move on.

~

About a month into our friendship, I'd talked Hannah into helping me search Glenwood, top to bottom. My biggest hope for the treasure location was the lookout tower, a dramatic architectural detail that crowned the house and appeared far more promising from the outside than from within. A reporter from the neighbourhood newspaper had once speculated that Jeremiah Brown sat in the tower for hours at a time, searching for a sign on the road of the return of the two sons killed in World War II, but the first time I stepped inside the tower, I dismissed the reporter's notion — there was nowhere to sit. Access to the tower was via a wrought-iron-railed circular staircase that led from the master bedroom on the third floor. At the top was a small square room — basically a landing — big enough only for a single person to walk around and look out the four windows set into the plaster walls. There was no hidden vault up there, no secret room, or none that I could detect after I put my ear to the wall, tapped the plaster at six-inch intervals, and listened for a telltale hollow sound. In earnest, Nancy Drew style (Hannah: "She always irritated the shit out of me"), I looked at the stair rail through a magnifying glass to see if a hairline crack in its surface might reveal the presence within of a tightly rolled paper clue covered in spidery black handwriting. Nope. I would have checked the window frames for more potential hiding places, but Hannah pointed out that the windows were new, installed within the last ten years by the house's previous owners.

When I spotted a small trap door built into the tower's beamed ceiling, I ran downstairs all aflutter, brought up a step stool from the kitchen three floors below, and spent ten minutes finding a way to wedge it into the narrow space between staircase and window, only to discover that the trap door opened into an empty crawl space. There was no steamer trunk in the corner, filled with old clothing and a bundle of letters, no moth-eaten military uniform set up on a dressmaker's dummy with a clue-riddled antique postcard hidden in the breast pocket.

I abandoned the tower room at last and dragged Hannah through the rest of the house. We examined the original wood panelling in the dining room to see if a tug on a lamp sconce or the chandelier might swing a portion of the wall open. We poked around in the basement looking for cupboards with false backing, or a discolouration in the floor that might indicate the concrete had been disturbed. We completed every search technique I could think of — and there weren't many, with so much of the house done over — until I was forced to give up.

"It kills me," I said to Hannah one day at her kitchen table, the day we'd lifted a loose floor board in a closet, to no avail, "that we'll never know the real story."

Mrs. Greer walked in and set her coffee mug in the sink. "The real story about what?"

I turned to her. "Doesn't it kill you to think that these walls know the truth about the treasure, and though we sit within them, we'll never learn their secret?"

She said, "You have a unique outlook on life, Blithe. Has anyone ever told you that?"

Hannah said, "I don't believe for a second that walls can know secrets, but if they could, wouldn't it be the old walls that knew, the ones that were torn down when the kitchen was renovated?"

"You know what I mean."

"Maybe you should make it your life's work to solve the mystery, Blithe," Mrs. Greer said. "Your quest. Everyone needs a quest."

I didn't take this comment too seriously, since Mrs. Greer was at that time writing the sequel to her first big success: a fantasy novel about a time-travelling, quest-pursuing girl who voyages to fairy-tale lands full of knights, dragons, and swirling mists.

Hannah picked up her camera and focussed in on my glass of milk. "Or you could forget the past, forget all this treasure crap, and get on with your own life."

"Give up on the treasure without knowing what really happened? Is that what you're suggesting?"

She had held the camera still and snapped her picture. "That's what I'm suggesting."

~

I showed Alexandra how to clip and unclip Tup's leash to his collar, and how to wrap the end of the leash around her hand. I told her Tup would prefer to walk on the lawn side of the sidewalk because more interesting smells could be found there than on the curb side. And I let her lead the conversation.

She peppered me with questions about Tup. What breed was he and how old and did he sleep in my room, did he sleep on my bed? Had I owned a dog when I was her age? Had my parents made me look after it? We discussed the suitability of eleven-year-old girls as dog caregivers all the way to the park entrance, until she stopped and said, "Hey. Isn't that the dog-walker over there? That Patrick guy?"

A figure that resembled Patrick Hennessy stood in the middle of the football field and threw a ball to a dog that resembled the dog he'd claimed as his own the day before. "I think it might be."

Alexandra said, "Does Tup catch balls like Buck does?" She'd remembered the other dog's name.

"No, Tup likes to wander around and sniff the ground. That's his specialty."

"Oh." Disappointment all over her face.

"But Patrick might let you throw the ball to his dog if we asked him."

"You think so?"

"Why don't we go see?"

We started across the field. Alexandra said, "Did you tell Patrick to meet us here?"

"No. I only met Patrick yesterday for the first time. Five minutes before you did." Or had that been the first time? There was something familiar about him, about the way he carried himself.

"I thought maybe he was your boyfriend."

"No, I don't date. Anyone."

"Why not? Are you a spinster?"

I smiled. "I suppose I am. But how do you know an old-fashioned word like that?"

"I read a lot."

As had I, raised on classic English children's literature, full of words like hedgerow and lolly and governess and wardrobe. And spinster.

We had come within hailing distance of Patrick, close enough to hear him grunt with exertion when he threw the ball down the length of the field. He nodded hello at us. "You guys following me?"

In the manner of a spinster governess, I said, "Good afternoon, Patrick. You remember Alexandra?"

"Hey, Alexandra."

She looked at the ground. "Hi."

"Alexandra's never thrown a ball to a dog before."

Patrick tipped his baseball cap back, said to her, "You want to throw Buck's?"

Alexandra said, "Yes, please. "

Buck dropped a ball on a rope on the ground at Patrick's feet, along with about a cup of saliva, and Patrick said, "The trick is to hold the toy by the rope. That way you don't get dog spit all over your hands when he brings the ball back. Look, I'll show you."

On Alexandra's first attempt, the ball only travelled a few feet, but on her third try, the throw went far enough to make Buck run, and she whooped with delight. At throw number five, I sat down on the grass and let Tup off his leash, wished I'd thought to bring a book. At throw number eight, I thought about asking Patrick if

I could borrow the one he had jammed into a pocket of his pants, another mystery novel from the look of the font that spelled out the author's name. At throw ten, I said to him, "What happened to the book you were reading yesterday? Did you finish it already?"

The sideways glance he gave me was wary. "Yeah."

"Do you read a lot?"

Warier still. "Some. Why?"

"I just wondered. I don't meet adult avid readers very often."

Alexandra said, "I read one or two books a week, depending how long they are. How many do you read, Blithe?"

I could be terse, too. "It depends."

After four more throws, I said, "Did you go to Northside High, Patrick?"

He didn't turn around. "Yeah."

"I thought I'd seen you somewhere before. How old are you?"

"Twenty-six. That was a good throw, Alexandra. Nice arc."

Two years younger than me. "Do you have siblings?"

"Five. Two older and three younger."

"I beg your pardon? You come from a family of six children?"

"Yeah." He didn't say any more, but I could have sworn he asked if I wanted to make something out of it.

Three more throws, during which I realized where I'd seen Patrick, in an apron, more recently than in high school. "And you work at Bagel Haven now?" The incredulity in my tone made both Patrick and Alexandra turn around. Tup and Buck remained intent on ball-chasing and ground-sniffing.

Patrick looked back at the field. "Yeah. I do the weekday bake there. How'd you know?"

"I saw you there, last week."

He didn't reply, though I thought politeness would have dictated a reciprocal comment of some kind.

Alexandra said to him, "How come Buck isn't bringing the ball back this time?"

"Sometimes he gets tired and needs a rest, so he lies down. He'll get up when he's ready to play some more."

I unfolded my legs and stood up. "Come, Alexandra. We should go. We don't want to take up all of Patrick's afternoon."

"Okay," she said. "Bye, Patrick. Thanks."

"Yes, thank you, Patrick," I said, "and for yesterday, too."

He said, "You're welcome," sat down on the grass, and opened his book.

When we were out of his earshot, Alexandra said, "Patrick's eyes remind me of a plate we have at home that looks as if it's cracked all over, but it's not."

I'd seen guardedness and suspicion, and she'd seen a cracked plate. I said, "You'll have to show it to me later."

We walked once around the park perimeter, stopped for a drink at the water fountain, and sat down for a few minutes next to a tennis court where an intense game was in progress between two men. "Do you play tennis?" I said.

"No. I hate sports."

"I've never been too keen on them either."

Alexandra swung her legs back and forth under the bench. "What about when you're teaching, and kids in your class don't want to go to gym? Do you make them go?"

"I don't think I've taught a child yet who didn't like gym. Do you dislike it?"

"It's better since I learned to get out on purpose. Like in dodgeball. If you're out, you can sit on the bench for the rest of the class."

I saw Alexandra throwing her slight body in front of the ball — dreading the impact, but desiring it, too. I heard the other kids yell that she was out, saw the fierce feral expressions on their faces that elimination games so often provoke, saw her limp off to the bench, to sit and rub at the sore spot where the ball had hit her, to count the minutes until she could return to the safety of the classroom. I saw all this, and a pang of sadness for her sounded in my chest.

"Other kids love gym, though," she said. "Josh is only in kindergarten and gym is his favourite subject."

I thought I knew the answer, but I asked anyway. "What's your favourite subject?"

No hesitation. "Silent reading."

~

Jane was sitting on her front steps reading the newspaper when we came back. Joshua, in the driveway, shot a plastic puck with a hockey stick into a child-sized net. "How did the walk go?" Jane said. "Did you two have fun?"

Alexandra said, "Patrick was there with Buck and I threw a ball for Buck a bunch of times and he caught it in his mouth, and I didn't get any dog saliva on my hands, not once."

Jane smiled. "Gee, that does sound like fun."

Alexandra ran up to the door. "Can you wait a second, Blithe? I want to show you that plate I was talking about. I'll be right back."

Over the sound of Joshua's hockey stick slapping the driveway, Jane said, "Thank you so much for taking Alexandra out. That's two days in a row you've cheered her up."

"It was a pleasure. We'll have to do it again sometime."

"Thank you, but I couldn't impose."

"It's no imposition. I enjoyed her company. She's interesting and funny." And sad.

"That's kind of you to say."

Why should she think I was sincere, when we'd both been brought up to favour politeness over honesty, when the two were so difficult to distinguish from each other? I said, "I'm not being kind, I mean it. How about next Sunday, at the same time?"

"He shoots, he scores!" Joshua yelled.

Jane searched my face, seemed to come to a decision. "Do
you think you might be interested in babysitting Alexandra the
odd time? For money?" She rushed on. "I know you're too old
for babysitting and way overqualified and you're already doing
that research job and I wouldn't ask at all, but you two seem to
relate, which is not a common occurrence with Alexandra and
adults." She closed her eyes for a moment. "I'm so glad there are
only a few weeks left in the school year. Alexandra's teacher has
no sympathy for a child like her."

"A child like her being how?"

"Bright, but non-conforming. And not socially adept."

How could I say no? I didn't imagine myself an Annie Sullivan
to Alexandra's Helen Keller, but maybe if I spent some time with
her, I could help her feel less alone. Help myself feel less alone.

Jane and I had just set a time to meet the next Sunday when
Alexandra came back out the front door. "Here," she said. "Now
do you see what I mean?" She handed me a blue ceramic dinner plate, an artisanal piece made with a finely cracked surface
under a shiny glaze.

"Why did you bring that out?" Jane said.

Alexandra said, "Don't Patrick's eyes look like that? They do!"

Jane and I both stared at the surface of the plate for a
moment, then Jane said, "You're right, Alexandra. Patrick's irises
do resemble this finish. I noticed them yesterday."

Not that I much cared, but she was right.

~ Chapter 4 ~

When I discovered Patrick's secret baker identity, I wondered, for about a minute, if I should avoid Bagel Haven, so that he wouldn't be able to make another joke about me following him. But there was no good reason to allow the small-worldliness of Rose Park to circumscribe my movements. Not when I could tuck myself at a back table, not when I saw how infrequent and short-lived were Patrick's forays from the kitchen. I wasn't sure if he even noticed my presence at Bagel Haven the next few days.

Besides, after my afternoons spent engaged in puzzle book research, and my quiet evenings at home, I liked having a morning destination. I welcomed Arthur's cheery comments on the newspaper headlines and the weather; I enjoyed the consistency of the nine o'clock Bagel Haven scene. The retired man in the visor, whose name was Fred, was always there, at *his* table. The young mother with infant came often, looking less exhausted every day. And the three-man orange-suited maintenance crew, whom I'd privately nicknamed Curly, Earring, and

Goatee, could be counted on daily to supply a laugh track for my breakfast, to give me a window on the real world, versus the Rose Park version.

Though they gave a me scare the morning they stopped by my table.

"Excuse me," said the one I'd christened Curly. "Me and my friends are hoping you can help us settle a bet."

My face flamed and my shoulders hunched as if I'd been caught in mid-offence. As if I'd blurted out the nicknames I'd invented for them and hurt their feelings. I swallowed a large unchewed chunk of bagel. "A bet? About what?"

"Lorenzo, here," Curly said, and indicated the guy I thought of as Earring, "says you're the sister of a guy named Noel Morrison who was in our year at Northside High, but I say no way."

I answered quickly, without thinking. "Sorry. I don't have a brother. I'm an only child."

"I told you," Curly said to Earring. "She doesn't look like him at all."

I took a sip of juice and saw out of the corner of my eye that Patrick was standing in the doorway to the kitchen, behind a loaded trolley of bagels. The unaccustomed adrenaline rush triggered by the lie must have gone to my head, because I said, "You know, I went to Northside, and I don't remember anyone named Noel. Who was he?"

A timer in the kitchen sounded — bing, bing, bing.

Goatee said, "He was an asshole."

Curly nudged him. "Nice talk."

Goatee said, "I still say he brought Ryan down."

Ryan? Who was Ryan?

Curly said, "You don't know what you're talking about."

The timer binged on. From the cash, Arthur called, "Patrick, can you get that timer, please?"

"Now you've got me curious," I said. "What did this guy do that was so bad?"

Goatee turned away. "Nothing. Forget it. Thanks for helping us out."

Earring said, "Are you sure you're not his sister?"

"I think if I had a brother, I'd know."

Goatee pulled on Earring's sleeve. "Let's go. Look who's coming."

Patrick eased the bagel trolley out of the kitchen, navigated the turn. Patrick, one of six children, younger sibling to (now I remembered) a guy of Noel's age named Ryan, and possessor of the cracked-blue eyes I saw in sharp focus when he passed by, nodded at the stooges, and looked me full in the face with a glare so cold it could have air-conditioned the room.

~

I searched the memory banks for information about Ryan Hennessy en route to the puzzle book site I'd selected to visit that day: a house on Fairway Drive that had been the clubhouse, circa 1897, of the Rose Park Golf Club, when the blocks surrounding it had made up the course. The club had moved to a location several miles north in 1905; the greens had been divided into building lots and the clubhouse converted to a single family dwelling. The only sign of the house's origin was the two-storey, gingerbread-trimmed porch that had once afforded lounging members a view of the fairway. Or so I thought. I sat down on a curb across the street to give the place the once-over and see what else I could find.

Ryan Hennessy hadn't belonged to any golf club. The Hennessy house on Hillside Road had been modest, semi-detached, the sole family car an economy model. The father had owned a store of some kind in the east end of the city, hardware perhaps, and had died young, when I was in high school. I remembered that much, but I couldn't picture Ryan clearly. He might have been a certain tall, wavy-haired guy from Noel's year who favoured athletic jackets, or not.

I pulled out my sketchbook and started to make a quick drawing of the clubhouse. What could Goatee have meant when he said Noel had brought Ryan down? Down where? And how likely was it that Noel would have known Ryan during his one year at Northside High?

I had hated private girls' school after only one day, but from an early age, Noel thrived at the boys' version: Hounslow College, a prestigious institution that my father, grandfather, and great-grandfather had attended before him. For years, Noel was head this, house that, an honour student, a sports star, debating team captain, ad nauseum. Mom, Dad, and I were all surprised when he announced his desire to transfer to Northside for his graduation year.

"I need to walk among the *hoi polloi*," he said. "Mix with a broader spectrum of the population, enrich my life experience."

At the time, I thought Noel's decision to cast off the rep tie, blazer, and flannels in favour of more contemporary clothes was related to his desire to have sex with a wider range of women than those he met at the golf club or the ski chalet or the dances organized to bring together private school girls with their male counterparts. But now I think he switched out of boredom. And with a desire to see if he was capable of rising to the top of a bigger bottle of milk.

I peered at the gingerbread above the porch. Was that a golf ball motif worked into the carved pattern? It was. A stylized leafy vine design incorporated golf balls where one would expect an acorn or a pine cone. I'd found my hidden in plain sight feature. I snapped a picture with the cheap camera I'd bought for the purpose, made a rough sketch of the pattern in the sketchbook, and packed up.

Noel had had nothing to worry about. His Northside sojourn proved he was the richest of cream. Within two months of his arrival, he was the Morrison that everyone knew. He dated the prettiest girls, captained the rugby and tennis teams, pulled off a ninety average, was named valedictorian. Given his looks and talents, how could he not excel? He won over everyone he met — boys, girls, teachers, parents. Only I had been immune. And maybe Goatee.

~

The next day, I visited another puzzle book destination: the old two-room schoolhouse on Stewart Street, a building long since made into a residence, and expanded both up and back. The front of the structure held its original square shape, a pair of solid entrance doors and a set of wide wooden steps. The owners had even installed a brass school bell (fixed in place) in the small open-sided bell enclosure that rose above the center peak of the roof. I sketched and photographed the building, and imagined Molly's text for her illustration asking her readers to guess at the building's original function. The answer page could show the school in its prime, the small yard filled with children in antique clothes turning hoops, or playing ball with thin bats and undersized baseball gloves.

Another day, I checked out a restaurant called The Stables, located on the outskirts of Rose Park. The building, once an early Rose Park landowner's lavish stables, now filled its mahogany-trimmed, tiled horse stalls with diners sitting on built-in banquettes. Bridles and saddles and English prints of hunting scenes featured in the decor, roast beef (not fox, horse, or hound) was the specialty of the house, and the waitresses wore riding habits, including jodhpurs and boots. The restaurant had a loyal, if old-school, clientele — my parents were known to have eaten there —

but to me, at first, from the outside, it seemed too obvious a site for inclusion in the puzzle book, too lacking in anything hidden. Until I noticed an adjacent gas station called Smithy's, the small back building of which was constructed of old-looking brick. Or was it just dirty brick? Closer examination revealed the brick to be both old and dirty, and the matching old and dirty man who worked there confirmed my suspicion that the Smithy moniker came, not from any past or present proprietor's surname, but from the site's original function as a blacksmith's workshop. "There's not many around here knows that anymore," he said. I thanked him for sharing his knowledge, and rode home feeling quite the clever child.

On the afternoon my parents were expected back from England, I walked Tup, took him into the big house, left a welcome note on the hall table, and went solo to a four o'clock movie, an English period piece awash in gorgeous scenery, elegant houses, Empire-waisted dresses, and articulate, witty characters speaking in plummy accents. Afterwards, I stopped in at the Market to buy some watercress, white bread, and butter for my dinner, and ran into my mother standing in front of the prepared food counter. Her appearance gave no hint of recent airplane disembarkation — every hair was in place, her lipstick refreshed, her clothes unwrinkled.

I said, in a bad English accent, "What would Madam fancy for dinner this evening?"

She turned. "Blithe! How are you? How was Tup? You look pale. And you sound funny. Are you all right?"

"Tup and I are fine. How was London?"

"Marvellous. We had a wonderful time."

"Good. What are you buying?"

She pointed to the contents of her cart — a bag of prewashed lettuce and some mineral water — and patted her belly. "Just salad tonight for me after all those restaurant meals, but I think I'll take some chicken curry for your father. You know how he likes a nice curry." To the counter man, she said, "One serving of curry, please."

The man packed and weighed her order. I tried to think of an exit line that wouldn't sound abrupt, and she said, "Noel sends his love."

Doubtful. "How is he?"

"He took me to a lovely restaurant and gave me a superb lunch, and afterwards we went gallery-hopping — it was the perfect afternoon."

Of course it was.

"How was your week?" Mom said. "Have you gone out and met people?"

~

I went for a bicycle ride after dinner and deviated from my usual route around the neighbourhood to run along Hillside Road, the street where the Hennessy family had lived when I was young. The small house I remembered looked the same — neat and well-kept — as it had when I'd walked by it every day on my way to elementary school. Whether any Hennessys still lived there, or how many, I couldn't tell, nor was I very curious to know. I rode around a few more blocks, made my way home, and coasted into the driveway behind Dad and Tup, who appeared to be headed for the coach house. Dad turned when I called him, and held up a covered plate. "I've brought you some leftover food," he said.

I jumped off the bike and wheeled it up the driveway next to him. "Thanks. Good trip?"

"Busy. A little tiring. But productive."

I pulled open the garage door, flicked on the light, fiddled with my bike lock. "Have you got a minute to come upstairs? I'd like to pick your brain about old Rose Park. I've been doing some research on its history."

He held the plate of food toward me, seemed eager to hand it over. "Yes, your mother told me about your project. I'd be pleased to discuss it sometime, but now is not the most convenient moment. Mom's waiting for me with coffee."

"Maybe I should phone your secretary and book an appointment."

He passed over the plate at last and dusted off his hands more times than were necessary. "That might be difficult, too. I'm off this week to Boston for some meetings."

"I was joking. Call me when you have a few minutes. Or come by." I lifted an edge of the foil and smelled the curry.

"All right, dear. Goodnight." He started back to the house.

"Hey, Dad."

He turned and cupped a hand to his ear.

"One quick question: do you know anything about a lodge that used to be down in the ravine?"

"A lodge?" He put his hands in his pants pockets and rocked on his heels. "I don't know if I'd call it that. There was a rudimentary hut down there with an open hearth, yes, a place to take shelter. I have a photograph somewhere of my grandfather and his cronies standing in front of it in their younger days. But the thing was torn down years ago, long before you were born."

"I'd like to see that picture."

"I'll find it for you. Goodnight again. Come along, Tup."

~

I browsed the apartment bookshelf that evening for reading material and found my dog-eared copy of a classic mystery called *Brat Farrar,* by Josephine Tey. I'd analyzed it for an English paper I'd written in university about post-war English suspense novels, but I hadn't picked the book up since. I opened it, read the first page, sat down in my reading chair, and, in minutes, fell under its spell.

I stayed up late reading, slept till ten the next morning, read some more over my breakfast, and was close to the bang-up finish when my mother knocked on the apartment door. I thought about not answering, pretending I wasn't home, but she persisted, knocked rat-a-tat twice, and called out, "Blithe, are you up?"

When I opened the door, Tup charged through, followed by Mom, who walked five steps in, looked at my unwashed hair and pyjama-clad body, stopped, and whispered, "You *are* alone, aren't you?"

"Not anymore."

She made straight for the living room windows, opened them one by one. "Why aren't you outside on such a lovely day?"

I offered her coffee or juice. She looked at her watch, said no thanks, not at this hour, and sat down on the couch. "Would you care to join us for dinner tonight? We're having the Braithwaites and the Morgans over."

"No thank you. I think I'll stay in." I held up the book, which I ached to get back to. "And read."

"Suit yourself. I also wanted to tell you I've decided to go with Dad on his trip to Boston. So could you look after the mail and Tup again?"

"Sure."

She picked at the burn hole in the couch arm. "And Blithe, about your social life, seriously — you know you're welcome to entertain anyone you like in this apartment, at any time, don't you?"

"I know, thank you. Are you sure you won't have some coffee?"

"We could use a code." She walked over to the fireplace and picked up a small sculpted figure from the mantelpiece, a piece I'd found wedged into the back corner of one of the kitchen cupboards. It was a reproduction of a prehistoric fertility goddess figurine, about six inches tall, a primitive art piece with a featureless head, pendulous breasts, huge buttocks, and a swollen abdomen. Part of Noel's legacy, I assumed, though I didn't want to guess what use Noel might have made of it.

Mom said, "When you're not to be disturbed — for personal reasons — you could put this object on the window-ledge outside your front door and Dad and I would know not to knock. What do you think?"

"I think it's not an issue because I'll never have sex again."

Concern and embarrassment met on her face. "What do you mean by that?" And, in a lowered voice — in case Tup might hear, I suppose, "Did something bad happen with Gerald?"

Nothing that I wanted to discuss with her. "What I meant was, if I were ever to sleep with someone again, and that's a big if, I'm not sure I'd want you and Dad to be the first to know."

"Oh, I see." She turned the goddess around in her palm. "What is this thing, anyway?"

"A museum shop replica. Would you like to have it?"

"No. No, thank you." She put it back on the mantel, came and sat across from me. "Your eyebrows need shaping," she said. "I have an excellent esthetician if you want her number."

I counted to three, said, "Why didn't you ever tell me Tup had a dog-walker?"

"The Hennessy boy, do you mean? Why would I tell you when you were in California?"

She was right. There was no reason. "I've run into him a few times. He also works at a bagel shop I go to. He's the baker there."

"Really? I hope he washes his hands and removes the dog hairs from his clothes before he bakes."

"I'm sure he does."

"You should wash your hands after walking Tup, too."

I not only washed my hands after Mom and Tup left, I showered and dressed, ate the curry for lunch, tidied up, and sat down at the table to review the state of my puzzle book research progress. During the week, I'd ticked off another site on my list, a faded Georgian manor known as the Adams house. The property's unique characteristic was a three-foot-high unmortared stone perimeter wall, built in 1881 and maintained by all subsequent owners of the house. I liked the idea of over a hundred years of continuity and caring, and I'd been entertained by an outlandish claim made in the *Rambles in Rose Park* book about one distinctive white stone in the wall. According to Mary Elizabeth Bishop, the white stone was actually a piece of ancient Pentelic marble, brought home by a nineteenth century tourist from the Acropolis in Athens. Since Jane's warning about Mary Elizabeth, I doubted the story could be true, but the stone was an ideal hidden in plain sight feature that I had duly recorded.

Among the sites remaining to be surveyed was Glenwood. I'd visited it twice since Molly had left, to perform my housesitting duties. I'd waved at a gardener cutting grass and at an eavestrough cleaning man, but I hadn't stopped and studied the house with any concerted effort. Also still on the list was the Morrison manse, though when my parents were away would be the best time to examine it, unless I wanted to run into my mother and risk conversing about eyebrows and paleness and my sex life while I stood on the street and stared at the house, walked around it and checked its surfaces, and otherwise invited her curiosity and commentary.

The only other places yet to cover were the Field Street footbridge over the North Ravine and the lodge/hut in the same vicinity. I looked out the window at the cloudy afternoon. I had more than enough time to bike up to Field Street and over the footbridge, descend into the ravine, and make my way to the lodge site. I could easily ride the length of the trail on my bike and return to civilization through Cawley Gardens before dinnertime. Or I could delay that trip a little longer and go over to Glenwood, alone — there'd be no workmen there on a Saturday.

Glenwood it was.

~

In decorative detail alone, Glenwood had much to offer. There was the windowed lookout tower, crowned with wrought-iron fencing. Three different colours of tiles made up a flower-motif pattern on the roof, and rosette shapes had been cut out of the carved wooden trim that the architectural guide referred to as curvilinear bargeboard. Even the house's brickwork was of visual interest: some bricks stood on end, some protruded halfway out of the wall, others were set in at an angle to form eyelash-like patterns over top of the arched windows and doorway.

I sat down on the park bench opposite the house, opened my sketchbook, and started to draw. Molly could take her pick of which detail to highlight in the puzzle book: the yellow roses in the stained glass panels over the front door, the heart shape in the wrought iron weather-vane that sat atop the first roof line, or one of the brick configurations.

When I'd finished my drawing, I lifted my pen off the page, stretched my arms up above my head, took one last look at the house, and froze in place. I'd seen something — a movement, a flash of colour, a face? — in a second-storey window. When there should be no one inside, when Molly and Dr. Greer weren't due home for several days, when all the work Molly had organized was for the exterior of the house, and only I had the key.

Could what I'd seen be a trick of light and shadow, a reflection in the glass of a passing cloud or a bird in flight? I watched the window, tried to tamp down the instantaneous physical reaction that had overtaken my body. One glimpse of the unexplained, and blood pumped at top speed to my extremities, a nauseous fearful feeling seized up my stomach, and I started to sweat. I rapidly considered possible explanations for a foreign presence in the house: maybe Molly had forgotten to tell me about a cleaning lady. Maybe the curry contained a hallucinogen. Maybe the ghost of Jeremiah Brown was making its first-ever appearance. Ridiculous notions all. But wait, what was that? I jumped at the sight of a flicker of motion, convinced against all reason that the house contained an ill-intentioned intruder. Except an intruder wouldn't stand at a window and stare out at me, would he? Would he?

The image moved, the window swung open, my breath caught in my throat, my courage pooled in my leaden feet. A bare arm waved, and a voice I knew, Hannah's voice, called out, "Blithe Morrison, is that you?"

~ Chapter 5 ~

Hannah looked the same, but more so. Her hair, still ear-length and tousled, was chunked with sun-induced golden highlights. Her skin, always tawny, was tanned darker than the fashion, which made her teeth look that much whiter. She wore no makeup, and her costume, er, outfit — an indigo-dyed cotton shirt, pocketed walking shorts rolled up high on her long legs, necklaces and bracelets of beads strung on leather cords — seemed like something from a magazine ad for a scent called Jungle, or Desert, or maybe War Zone. Except that Hannah's clothes, her tan, her hair, were all real.

She invited me into Molly's living room, offered me white wine from Molly's fridge, told me she'd made an impulsive decision to come home for some rest and relaxation between assignments, instead of jaunting off to Sardinia. "How about you?" she said. "I hear you're staying with your parents for the summer. What hell is that?"

Not hell. More like purgatory. "It's just for a few months. And I'm not actually under their roof. I'm in the coach house."

"That would still be too close for me." She squirmed in revulsion at the thought. "But you seem to tolerate that whole parental age bracket better than I do. Like how you're working with my mother on her Rose Park book."

There was an unspoken question in her voice that I didn't understand. In an attempt to answer it, I gave her an overly detailed progress report on the puzzle book research I'd conducted so far. "I'm almost finished," I said, after telling her about the school bell, the smithy, and the golf ball motif in the clubhouse's gingerbread trim. "About all I have left are the sites in the ravine."

An amused glint came into her eye. "Ah yes," she said, "the ravine. Your favourite place."

There was no need for her "Ah yes," no deep, dark secret about me and the ravine. I found its wildness unsettling, was all. The ravine wasn't even wild compared to real woods or bush, since civilization was always within view, in the form of the houses perched on the hills above. But it was wild enough. Small, harmless snakes were apt to dart in front of you if you walked on the ravine path. Snails lay in wait to be crunched underfoot. Loud or big (or both) insects — dragonflies and crickets and grasshoppers and cicadas — abounded, along with a surplus of ordinary but no less off-putting mosquitoes and ladybugs and horseflies and aphids. In summer, the plant life became overgrown and bushy, and small rodents ran rampant. In fall, there were burrs everywhere. And always, there were thickets. Not the safe Bambi type of thicket, but the more sinister kind, perfect for hiding dead bodies.

When I was a child of about ten, I used to go for walks in the ravine, by myself. And sometimes I saw lone men here and there, stopped up or down a slope, peeing. Urinating, my mother would say. Never the same man, and never anyone I recognized. I didn't think much of it until one afternoon when my father and I took our dog Angus into the ravine for a walk and saw a peeing man from a ways off. Dad swore under his breath at the sight — as rare and sure a sign for him of wrath as the Angry Eyebrow — and hustled me out of there. He took my arm and marched me in a quick-step back up the path toward home, lecturing all the while about how civilization had encroached on the ravines, but parts of them would always be untamed. I guess he thought that if he talked fast and long, I wouldn't notice his alarm, his concern for my safety, the sharp way he called Angus in to us, the speed of the pace he set. But I was nothing if not observant.

After that incident, my parents made me promise I wouldn't go into the ravine alone again. By the time I met Hannah in high school, I hadn't been down in years and wasn't eager to go. She was. "It's like entering a whole other world when you walk into those woods," she said. "A world where uptight old Rose Park doesn't exist."

I humoured her sometimes, and went near with her — we'd sit on one of the bridges, and she'd smoke. Or we'd climb a tree in Cawley Gardens, one of the crooked ones that overlooked the ravine, and try to get comfortable on the knobby branches, and talk. But I avoided going all the way in.

Now, Hannah said, "You still don't like the ravine, do you?"

"I'm not too fond of it, no."

"Well, if you want to see the site of that old lodge for my mother's book, you have to go into the deepest part."

"And find the right spot." The map Molly had given me, a copy of a decades-old town plan, was far from clear.

"Do you want me to show you the site?"

I did and I didn't, would have preferred to find it on my own.

She said, "We could go right now."

Now? "I can't. I promised my mother I'd help her prepare for a dinner party she's having tonight."

"Tomorrow, then?"

"I'm babysitting tomorrow."

"Babysitting? Aren't we a bit old for that?"

Another lie: "I only sit for one family that pays me exorbitant rates."

"Good for you. Milk the bourgeoisie whenever possible, that's what my dissidents tell me."

I couldn't keep a disapproving frown from wrinkling my forehead. "*Your* dissidents?"

"The ones I photograph."

Had she always been this tiresome? I smoothed my forehead and stood up. "I should be going. How long are you in town?"

"Not long. This place is deader than I remembered. I don't suppose you'd want to make the bar scene with me tonight, after dinner, would you? Now that you're single again?"

No, I did not want to play the ugly stepsister to her Cinderella. "I don't think so."

"Not ready to date yet, huh? At least you're free of that corporate wage slave you married. I had to wonder when I heard he was an accountant."

As opposed to an unbound-by-societal-chains free spirit like her, whose work was published in newspapers and magazines owned by capitalist media tycoons.

"About the ravine, though," she said. "Why don't I take you down tomorrow? You're not babysitting the whole day, are you?"

I had run out of excuses, could find no reason not to meet her at eleven the next morning. "Great seeing you again," she said when we parted, and I nodded and smiled and lied and said the same.

~

I spent the evening imprisoned in the flat, unable to go out in case I might run into Hannah. There was nothing interesting on television, I'd finished *Brat Farrar*, and I couldn't fetch Tup from my parents' house for company on a clandestine walk around the block, because if I did, I would have to mix and mingle with my mother's dinner guests, who talked and laughed far too loudly with my parents in the garden until one o'clock in the morning.

I should have been relieved when they left, when the braying of banal conversation and the peals of drunken laughter ceased — finally, I could lay my weary head to rest — but I was too upset to sleep, too frenzied, having used the evening to immerse myself in a deep pool of dislike, to reflect and obsess and churn in it, to spit out spumes of metaphorical anger at my parents, their dinner guests, anyone who gave or attended parties (particularly parties with an outdoor component), Hannah, Noel, and, oh yes, Gerald, my ex, whom I'd met in someone's backyard, at a summer party. In the days before I fully understood that all social interaction was doomed and pointless.

The party in question was given at the tail end of teachers' college, by a fellow graduating student named Sonja. Sonja was older than the rest of us, was married with kids, lived in a family-centred neighbourhood full of minivans and kids playing street hockey, was embarking on a second career as a teacher (she had formerly produced television commercials), was one of those outgoing, high-energy, gregarious people you can't help liking even if you're the opposite.

On party night, I walked through her open door, almost tripped over a pile of kids' shoes and baseball bats in the vestibule, and side-stepped into a front hall filled with a capacity crowd. I squeezed through to the kitchen, greeted Sonja — who was acting her vivacious self, was mixing up a vegetable dip in a bread bowl while guffawing at someone's joke — presented her with a bottle of wine, and accepted a glass of sangria in exchange from her husband.

I didn't mind the chaos, the clamour, the signs that mess-making humans inhabited the house (the atmosphere made a refreshing contrast to that of my parents' place), but I was still at a party. Ergo, once I'd pushed past the kitchen throngs into more throngs in the backyard and lacked the bravery to tap people I knew on the shoulder and interrupt their conversations, I took up a wallflowery position leaning against a bare stretch of fence, sipped my wine, and tried not to look as uncomfortable and alienated as I felt.

Gerald appeared at my side not ten minutes later. That is, a stocky man with a young face wandered out, looking more lost than I hoped I did, and beelined for the bit of fence beside me. I said hi, and, ever the scintillating conversationalist, "This is a good leaning spot."

He said, "Particularly if you know no one and are wondering how soon you can leave."

"Or if you're wondering why you showed up at all."

He looked at me a moment, not up and down, but in the face, searching for further signs of a kindred soul, he told me later. He must have detected one or two, because he smiled, which made him look much nicer, and said, "I'm Gerald Lang. I'm an accountant. I live next door. Sonja and Tony invite me to all their parties so I won't complain if they get noisy later, which they usually do. Why are you here?"

We talked a bit, I went in to freshen my drink (I'd been taught to limit cocktail chatter to five minutes, tops, per person), saw no one I wanted to fill the next five minutes with, came back to the fence, and talked to Gerald some more. An hour later, we decamped to a nearby coffee shop, where I found out Gerald was four years my senior, had grown up in a small town northwest of Toronto, was single, and had a subscription to the local symphony concert series. "I mention the symphony," he said, "so you won't think I'm a complete nerd without any cultural interests."

"Why I would think that?"

"Because apart from the interest I take in classical music, I am a complete nerd."

He was unpretentious and quick and self-deprecating. He liked to eat out, to try new and different restaurants of the inexpensive kind I favoured, was not inclined toward couple-dating or large-group socializing. He was content to spend evenings at home, working while I read, content to engage in quiet, unpretentious lovemaking.

We stayed content for two years, during which I laboured, not without doubts and struggle, at my first teaching job, a grade one/two class in a small midtown public school, and Gerald worked hard and long at the big accounting firm where he was partner. We had just begun to talk about maybe moving in together when he was offered an unrefusable, lucrative, career-enhancing transfer to his firm's L.A. office. California was far away. Moving there would be a big upheaval. Those circumstances somehow led us to consider marriage, my mother got carried away with the concept, and I used up so much energy downscaling her wedding plans — a dress not a gown, fewer guests, simpler flowers, no skirted chair covers, please, and why couldn't we have plain white china and silver plate for the reception instead of gold-rimmed and sterling — that I didn't devote sufficient attention to the issue of whether mutual contentment was enough to base a marriage on. Or to whether I should permit my mother to invite Noel to the wedding.

After many hours spent reviewing, analyzing, and picking apart the pieces of my marriage, I've become certain Gerald and I were doomed to failure anyway. If I try to accomplish the impossible feat of being objective where Noel's concerned, I might concede that he didn't cause the breakup, just hastened it along. But the hastening in itself was reason enough for some of the enmity between us. And the way he did it reason for more.

~

Late night in the garden with their laughter-mad friends or not, at least one of my parents rose early the next day. When I awoke after a night of fretful dreams, I found a large manila envelope had been slipped under my door, with my name written on it in my father's neat handwriting.

Inside the envelope was an old photograph of five men standing on the steps and porch of a small wooden cabin. They were dressed in antique hunting clothes — fedora-style hats and tweed jackets belted cross-wise with wide leather straps. They held guns, and a few brandished what looked like dead ducks. The cabin could hardly be seen behind the men — all I could make out was that it was small, and loglike, and seemed to actually exist. I flipped the photograph over. On the stained backing, an old-fashioned hand had written, "The Lodge, 1935," and a list of the men's names, including my great-grandfather, Douglas Scott Morrison, and, two hunters over, a man — most of whose face was in shadow — identified as Jeremiah Brown.

~

"How'd dinner with your parents go last night?" Hannah said. We were walking down Field Street to the footbridge.

"It was a bit too talky and noisy for my taste. What about you? Did you go out?"

"Yeah, to the Ranch House." The Ranch House was a raunchy bar near Northside High, had been a notorious fake-ID hangout in our high school days. "That place sure hasn't changed," she said.

I examined her with the careful regard of a scientist observing an alien life-form. "Did you enjoy yourself?"

Hannah ran her fingers through her curls. "I got bored, so I drank too much and danced a lot and was driven home by a young guy with a pickup truck." She waggled her eyebrows at me, but I felt the disgusted frown forming again. I looked away before she could see it.

We'd reached the footbridge. Hannah said, "Hey. They've changed this thing." So "they" had — a new bridge had been built of steel and concrete, nowhere near as charming as the arched wooden one had been.

"And in the last couple of years," I said. "That picture you took of the old bridge wasn't taken very long ago, was it?"

"What picture?"

"Molly gave it to me, with some others you took of the sites for the book."

"Oh, yeah." She leaned over the side of the bridge and spat onto the valley floor. "Look," she said. Two women were walking below, their heads down. "Should I?" She horked up some more saliva.

"For god's sake, Hannah, don't."

I left her leaning over the edge and I walked slowly across the bridge. I examined it end to end in search of a distinctive anything, but the structure was so modern and utilitarian, its surfaces so unmarked and smooth, there was nothing to see. I came back to Hannah. "Let's go down, try a different angle."

A steep pathway ran down the hillside beside the bridge. A path worn from footsteps, but sprinkled with rocks and gravel and tree roots. We made our way down the path — Hannah nimble and sure-footed, I more hesitant — and arrived at the bottom, where a wide, unpaved trail ran through the center of the ravine. We walked along it fifty feet or so, stopped and turned around, looked back at the bridge. From that angle, I could see that the design of the steel buttresses and supports formed a linked row of A shapes, like the sample printing inside an elementary school exercise book cover. "There's our hidden in plain sight feature," I said.

"Where?"

"The A's, do you see?"

I pointed up, but my eye was caught, under the bridge, by the sight of Patrick, with Buck, coming down the trail towards us.

Hannah muttered, "Shit." And, "Just what I need right now." But she made a big over-the-head waving motion to Patrick and yelled hi in a friendly fashion that would have fooled me.

I said, "You know him?'

"He's the guy who drove me home last night. Talk about awkward." She raised her voice, yelled, "What are you doing down here?" Half-playful, half-hostile.

"What are *you* doing down here?" he said. "I walk in the ravine every day."

Buck loped up to us and Hannah spoke to him in a cutesy form of puppy-talk that made him jump on her and lick her face. She laughed with apparent delight at this treatment, but Patrick told Buck to get off her and apologized. When Buck had dismounted, Hannah said, "Sorry, guys. I haven't introduced you. Blithe, meet Patrick."

Patrick and I exchanged an impassive glance. "We've met," I said.

Hannah looked from one to the other of us. "Now I know I'm home. The only people I've talked to all weekend and you know each other?"

Patrick kept his eyes on Buck. "You two out for a walk?"

Hannah said, "Blithe wanted to come down here but she was too scared to come alone. I'm her bodyguard. And guide."

I couldn't quite hide my annoyance. Or didn't bother to. "So guide away, then," I said, and to Patrick, "Excuse us. We should get going."

Patrick said, "Me, too. I have to be somewhere."

Hannah said, "Where? Where do guys who hang out on Saturday nights at the Ranch House go on Sunday mornings?"

He looked down the trail behind him, and I found myself hoping he wouldn't answer, would leave her hanging. But he said, "My mother expects me for Sunday lunch."

Hannah threw a not-so-playful punch at his arm. "Don't tell me I was two-stepping all night with a guy who still lives at home."

He rubbed at his bicep, and an unbecoming shade of pink stained his face. "I don't live there. I just go for lunch on Sundays."

Hannah said, "Ah. A dutiful son. Isn't that sweet?"

I said, crisply, "Shall we, Hannah?"

Patrick and Buck headed up the slope, and Hannah and I set off down the trail. When we'd passed an elderly couple, four cyclists in full bike regalia, and a pair of joggers, I said, "You met Patrick at the Ranch House?"

"Yeah. He's a great dancer, if you know what I mean."

I couldn't picture Patrick dancing. I could picture Hannah, though, her arms held high above her head, all sensuous and come-hithery. "He doesn't seem like your type," I said.

"What do you mean? Young, nice butt, can dance? He's exactly my type. For a one-nighter."

For a repugnant second, I tried to picture that, too.

Hannah yawned. "Oh well. We all make mistakes. I'm just glad I'm leaving town tomorrow."

We walked on through the shafts of sunlight that penetrated the canopy of tall trees. Thickets and snakes aside, the scenery *was* pretty.

Hannah said, "It's probably best if you don't mention me to Patrick. The sooner he forgets about last night the better."

My spinster governess persona put in an appearance and said, "I barely know him and I have little occasion to speak to him."

"Good. Hey. I think the lodge site is just up ahead here, around that curve."

"Hold on." I stopped, took from my pocket the folded-up photocopy of the town plan, opened it up. "Where are we now?"

Hannah stood close to me and held onto an edge of the paper, and I caught a whiff of fresh body odour on her, unless it was on me. "There," she said, and pointed. "See how the map shows a curve in the creek? That's the curve right there, in front of us."

I looked up from the plan, from the stiff surveyor's printing, the intersecting lines and confusing notations, the careful charting of the creek's course, and tried to reconcile it with the natural vista in front of me. "Are you sure?"

"Positive."

We walked along the curve of the trail. I said, "Did you ever know Patrick's older brother, Ryan Hennessy? He would be Noel's age."

"I don't think so."

"I guess you couldn't have, come to think of it. He left Northside before you started there."

"The name doesn't ring any bells. Look, there's where the lodge was. On that flat bit of land."

Flat bit? We drew up to a patch of semi-level ground about fifteen feet square, populated with the usual trees and rocks and plant life. "This is it?"

"As near as I can tell."

I mentally superimposed on the scenery the image of my great-grandfather and his buddies standing on the porch of the so-called lodge. "You'd never know there'd been a cabin of any sort here."

"You could say the same for the Cawley Gardens house and it was a hell of a lot bigger and meant to be more permanent. And this was more like a shack, wasn't it? A place to warm up and clean one's gun."

I heard a rustling noise in the undergrowth near my feet and jumped back onto the trail.

"Relax," Hannah said. "It was just a mouse."

I shuddered, recovered, said, "The problem is, as far as the puzzle book goes, this section of the ravine looks exactly like any other section of the ravine. Uninhabited."

"I don't know," Hannah said, and looked around. "What's that over there?"

Over there was a sturdy tree with a birdhouse nailed to its side. The wood of the birdhouse was so weathered its colour matched the tree bark. We walked over to it and I said, "Do you think this might date to the time of the lodge?"

"I doubt that men who wanted to kill birds would provide a place for them to nest."

"You're right."

"But I don't see why you couldn't use it as your special feature."

"Molly said as long as the item is permanent."

Hannah gave the birdhouse a tug. "It's on good and solid. It's been here for decades, I'll bet."

"Okay, done." I took the cheap camera out of my bag.

Hannah sat down on a tree stump out of range. "Since when have you taken up photography?"

"Since never. I just point and shoot and hope for the best." I took two pictures of the birdhouse, stepped back a few paces, snapped a wider shot, checked the indicator. "I've got one shot left on this roll. Should I take it of us?"

"Sure." She came up beside me, placed her face beside mine, cheek-to-cheek, took hold of the hand in which I was holding the camera away from our heads and adjusted the camera position. "This angle's more flattering," she said. "Now quick: press the shutter before our smiles turn fake."

~

Later that day, I stood in Jane Whitney's vestibule. "I thought Alexandra might come over to my place this afternoon to play

Scrabble and make cookies, if she'd like. Though we'd have to walk to the store first with Tup, and buy some ingredients."

Jane said, "What do you think, Alexandra?"

"Junior Scrabble or adult Scrabble?"

"I only have an adult set. Which kind do you prefer?"

"Adult."

Jane nudged her. "Please and thank you."

"Please and thank you," Alexandra said, and sat down on the floor to tie her shoes.

Jane said, "How's your research for that book going, Blithe?"

Images came to mind from my morning in the ravine: Hannah spitting over the bridge, punching Patrick on the arm, and tugging on the birdhouse. "Fine, thanks. I'm almost finished."

"Was the *Rambles in Rose Park* book any help?"

"Yes, yes, it was. Though I remembered what you'd said about Mary Elizabeth Bishop's reliability when I visited the Adams house and saw the white stone in the wall, the one she said was marble brought from the Acropolis in Athens."

Jane leaned against the doorframe. "Do you want to hear a secret about that?" She looked a little guilty, but not too. "I snuck over to that house once — years ago now — chipped off a sliver of that white stone, and sent it away through my museum connections to be dated and analyzed. In case Mary Elizabeth could be right."

"And was she?"

Jane helped Alexandra up. "No. As I suspected, the stone was run-of-the-mill North American marble, and not terribly old. The truth was less interesting than her fiction, I'm afraid."

Alexandra and I walked to the Market, tied Tup up outside, made our purchases without having to run out and stop him from barking, and turned back for home. Halfway there, I spotted three girls a block away, coming towards us. They looked close in age to Alexandra, but they wore what I considered to be age-inappropriate outfits of tight tank tops and short shorts, to go with the age-inappropriate lollipops they sucked on. Did Alexandra know them? Probably. Would they snub her? I hoped not. I switched the bag of groceries to my left hand, freed up my right in case it would be needed to perform a yet-to-be-determined defensive action. So I could grab Alexandra's hand and run, if necessary. We came near, I tensed up, the girls sang, in chorus, "Hi, Alexandra." And was I projecting my childhood onto hers, or did I hear a hint of mockery in their pitch?

Alexandra muttered a hi back, and pulled Tup on. I tried to stare the threesome down with my best strict-teacher face, but they didn't notice, were too busy laughing and conspiring, the suckers hanging out of their mouths like the cigarettes they'd be smoking in a few years.

Safe in my driveway, I said, "Those three girls we saw back there — are they in your class?"

"Yeah."

"Are they your friends?"

Vehement head shake. "No."

I didn't ask who *were* her friends. In case she didn't have any. "How many days until school's out?"

"Four and a half." Not that she was counting.

"And what will you do for the summer? Does your family go away?"

"No, Mommy thinks cottages are boring. She'd rather stay home and work. So I get to go to a bunch of different day camps."

"What kind?"

"There's a science camp and an art camp and a computer camp — stuff like that. It'll be mostly geeky kids and no one I know, but I don't care."

It had taken me twenty-eight years (almost twenty-nine) to figure out that life's easier to endure and happiness less elusive if you don't care about anything, if you don't make the mistake of pinning your hopes, of having expectations. But I didn't think Alexandra needed to understand that sad truth yet, not already, not at age eleven.

We climbed the stairs to the flat. I said, "How do you feel about peanut butter cookies?"

"My Grandma Whitney makes good ones that are soft and crumbly. Can we make that kind?"

"We can try." I showed her in, uttered a few silly jokes of the Cowardice type, took out the cookie ingredients, gave her an apron. She tied it on, washed her hands at the kitchen sink, said, "The first step is to cream the butter, right?"

She would find her way, wouldn't she? Books might continue to sustain her and give her solace in the difficult year or two ahead, but in the wider worlds of junior high and high school, a kindred soul or two would surely appear — brainy, verbal kids like her who could become her friends. She would learn how to be liked and how to like back. She'd find a niche — she could take an interest in drama, maybe, or marine biology, or French — and nestle into it, make it fit. Couldn't she? And have a romantic life if she wanted, or not, and go to university and pursue a career in a field she enjoyed.

I took the softened butter out of the microwave and scraped it with a spatula into the mixing bowl, handed her a wooden spoon. It was just as likely she'd emerge successfully on the other side of youth as not. More likely. But there was little point in telling her that now, when she felt like the neighbourhood misfit who can't relate to anyone her own age. Not any more point than when my mother had told me that if I smiled more, hid my boredom better when people made small talk, and mastered the art of entertaining, I could meet and marry the right man, and carry on living the lifestyle I deserved, the one I'd grown up with.

If I'd known Alexandra better, I might have hugged her when she pulled back her hair into a scrunchie and asked if she could crack the eggs. Instead, I told her to crack away, I suggested we press a chocolate chip into each cookie (though I've never been fond of peanut butter and chocolate together), and I let her eat some cookie dough, raw.

~ Chapter 6 ~

Patrick and I sat at right angles to each other on a four-sided bench that enclosed a large maple tree. The dogs — his group and Tup — grazed and gambolled nearby. For all of three minutes we sat and I waited for him to speak, to explain the reason for the cloak-and-dagger routine that morning at Bagel Haven, when he'd stopped at my table, blocked the light with the bagel trolley, and said, "I need to talk to you." His eyes had been hidden under the brim of his cap, his mood behind a poker face.

"What about?" I'd said.

He'd looked left and right. "Not here."

I'd almost laughed. "Where?"

Still spy-like: "Meet me at Cawley Gardens at eleven o'clock."

So here we were now, on the square bench, and I was discomfited enough by his silence to break it, to say, "What did you want to talk about? Not Hannah, I hope."

He kept his face and eyes turned away. "Why not?"

"Because I have nothing to say about her. This weekend was the first time we've seen each other in years."

He picked up a large stick from the ground and started to break twigs off of it. "Is she a good friend?"

"No, not anymore." If she ever had been.

Pause. "I didn't like it when she said we'd been two-stepping all night."

I picked up a stick of my own. "I thought the euphemism a little hackneyed, myself." He said nothing, but made a face that suggested both exasperation and resignation.

"What?" I said.

He called Buck and threw the stick for him to fetch.

I said, "Are you going to say anything else, or is this strange conversation over now?"

The cracked blue eyes met mine for a second, then moved away. "Nothing happened between me and her."

I shrugged. "It makes no difference to me what you do."

"We talked at the Ranch House, and she wanted to dance, so we did. Then she got drunk and I drove her home. End of story."

"I have to say, I can't quite picture this alleged dancing."

"Is that a family trait or something? To talk the way you do?" His tone wasn't biting, exactly, but there were a few teeth in it.

"What do you mean?"

"The way you work pretentious words into every conversation. I understand what alleged and hackneyed and euphemism mean, you know."

What the hell? "Did I say you didn't?"

"And entourage."

"Who said anything about an entourage?"

"You did. At the library, when you introduced me to that little girl. Who is she, anyway? Your cousin?"

I was much too occupied trying to recall under what circumstances I might have used the word entourage to ponder the implication of his remembering I had. "Alexandra and I aren't related. I babysit her sometimes. She's lonely."

"Oh, come on. What's the real reason?"

I dropped my stick on the ground. "What do you care why I babysit Alexandra?" And why did I feel under attack?

He leaned back on the bench. "I don't care why you babysit. I just wondered if you were telling the truth. You and Hannah seem pretty quick with the lies."

My blood, which had started to simmer a few paragraphs back, jumped to a boil. "What's that supposed to mean?"

"It means I don't know why Hannah wanted you to think I slept with her, and I don't know why you pretended to those guys at Bagel Haven that you weren't Noel Morrison's sister."

Oh, that. My head started to ache, which, taken with the boiling blood, made a sickening combination. I said, "I can't and won't speak for Hannah. But my relationship with my brother is no one's business but my own. Certainly not yours or your friends'."

He didn't look at me. He didn't speak. He stood up, walked off, and marshalled his dog entourage — of course. That's when I'd used the word before, to describe the dog pack. He walked off and I sat and gazed at the green space where the proud old Cawley Gardens mansion had once stood, and I felt a wave of sadness wash over me, a swell of self-pity that stung my eyes and brought a flow of mucus to my nasal passages.

He came back, stood on the grass, facing me, ten feet away, and said, more neutral now, "Was it true what Hannah said about you being afraid to go in the ravine?"

"Why?" The word came out sour.

"Forget it." He turned his back.

"WHY?"

He didn't answer. He just walked away, with the dogs, down the path, into the darkness under the trees.

~

Gerald and I were married on a Saturday at four o'clock, at my parents' church, reception to follow at the golf club. On the Thursday evening prior, my parents, Noel, Gerald, and I sat in the parents' drawing room, nursing our drinks and our various states of edginess. Noel had flown in from Europe earlier that day, and we were scheduled to meet Gerald's family for dinner at a restaurant.

Noel was into his second martini when he said, "What, no bachelor party? You must be joking. What's a wedding without a bachelor party?"

Dad chuckled. "I sure remember mine."

Too loudly, I said, "Gerald doesn't want a bachelor party." I was proud of Gerald's uncoerced and long-ago stated views on the subject — he hated stags, they made him uncomfortable.

Noel walked over to the bar, poured himself another drink. "I'll organize something small for tomorrow night," he said. As if I hadn't spoken. "An intimate, tasteful evening for Gerald and some close friends. We'll play cards, drink single malt, smoke a few cigars." He winked at Gerald, and disquiet spread within me. What was Noel up to? Did he even like Gerald? I hadn't expected he would.

I opened my mouth to tell Gerald he didn't have to accept Noel's offer, but I shut it when I saw the happy grin on his face: the sign that Gerald had fallen prey to Noel's conspiratorial man-to-man charm. He gave Noel the names and phone numbers of four pals, and told me later, when we were alone, that he was looking forward to the Noel-led night out.

I said, "I thought you hated stag parties."

"You heard him — he'll organize something tasteful. I thought he was very gracious to offer, actually, and to insist. None of my friends insisted."

On the morning of our wedding day, Gerald called — I had slept the night at my apartment — and told me, no big surprise, that the party had gone late, he was a bit hungover. Despite a slight greenish pallor off the top, he showed no profound ill effects during the ceremony and reception, and there seemed to be no further repercussions from the night before, other than that his friends avoided meeting my eye when they wished me congratulations, and Noel's all-in-good-fun toast came across, to my sensitive ear, as a put-down of accountants in general, and of Gerald in particular.

Within a week, Gerald and I had finished packing up our separate households, sent our various belongings to storage — his house was rented out to a corporate transfer coming the other way, my high-rise apartment given up altogether — and set off for California, where he worked long hours at the accounting firm, I taught at a small private school, we occupied a rented house filled with rented furniture, and we were so harried and exhausted that I thought it understandable we rarely had sex.

A few months into our stay, Gerald came home one night, a little too drunk to have been driving, after an evening out with some of his new colleagues. He trudged into the bedroom where I lay in bed reading, sank down in an armchair, made no move to undress, and told me that the guys had headed on to a strip bar after dinner, and had urged him to join them.

I said, "A strip bar? What kind of people go to strip bars?"

"Lots of people."

"Not our kind of people."

"You're wrong. They're people just like me. Precisely like me. I should have gone with them tonight. I wanted to go with them." His voice was glum, his posture hang-dog.

I smelled something rotten and doomed in the air that I hoped was the stale beer and cigarette smoke from the bar he'd been in. I heard a dull pounding in my ears that I didn't recognize as the death knell of our marriage. "If you wanted to go so badly," I said, "why didn't you?"

He twitched around in the chair. His head was sweating, though the room was not warm. "I want to tell you what happened at my bachelor party," he said. "I need to tell you." So I put my book down, pulled up the covers to my chin, and heard all about the night with Noel in the hotel suite downtown. About how the party spun out of control when Gerald and his four accountant friends drank too much, and lost a lot of money, mainly to Noel, who turned out to be quite the card player.

I saw five soused accountants, ties loosened, glasses knocked askew, and Noel laughing behind his hand at what easy marks they were. I said, "How much did you lose?"

"About a thousand each."

"You took a thousand dollars in cash to a poker game?"

"During the game, we went down to a bank machine in the hotel lobby and made some cash withdrawals on our credit cards."

I thought: it could have been worse.

Gerald said, "And that's not the worst part."

Around midnight, he said, two hookers showed up with a supply of cocaine and ecstasy. They'd been summoned by Noel, who was full of interesting suggestions for how the hookers might entertain the group, en masse, and who, being the evening's big winner, offered to pay for the entertainment.

I covered my ears. "I don't want to hear anymore."

"I don't know what came over me." Gerald's voice was charged with emotion, and the beads of sweat on his temples had turned into rivulets. "Over all of us. It was like living a scene in a porn movie. The drugs, the women, the depravity. I've never done anything like that in my life. I never would have thought I *could* do anything like that."

He went on, and revealed how wrong he'd been when he'd said the drugged orgy was the worst part of the story. When I'd heard more than I could bear — he felt compelled to paint a detailed, vivid picture of everything he'd done — he told me the sad and sordid punch line: that ever since, he'd thought of nothing but how much he wanted to do it all again.

~

The Morrison house is a stolid, squat presence on the landscape, with its centre hall plan, its plain brown brick, its three floors that are wider than deep — no frou-frou'd bijou here. The oldest house in Rose Park continuously occupied by the same family has a façade so unremarkable it had not merited a mention in the architectural guidebook. And though it had been standing for about fifty years when Mary Elizabeth Bishop set off on her rambles, she'd seen no reason to write about it either.

I came home from my meeting in the park with Patrick, stood in front of the house, looked at it for a few minutes, tried to clear my mind of turmoil, and looked at it again. Maybe if I moved my feet, I could concentrate better. I started a tour around the perimeter, began a visual inspection.

The wood trim on the upper floor windows needed to be repainted. A few roof tiles were missing, a few more broken. Pigeons were cooing in a sheltered alcove under the eaves — did my parents know they were nesting there? I came around the back, walked past the glassed-in conservatory. Maybe it could rate as the house's distinctive feature. No. It wasn't exceptional enough.

I completed my revolution, wandered up the front walk, zeroed in on an old plaster relief of the family coat of arms that the original Morrison ancestor had installed when the house was built. I'd forgotten the thing because of its obscured position above the front door of the house, under the peak of a small porch roof. I wasn't keen on the crest's connotations of nobility, but its hand-carved look, its antiquarian symbols — fleur-de-lys and a shape that could have represented either a battle-axe blade or a phase of the moon — lent it a homey appeal. It also satisfied the hidden requirement, being noticed only by tradesmen, mail carriers, or gas meter readers waiting on the porch, and only if they looked up. Most of all, its irrelevance, its Ozymandias-like quality — take that, Patrick — pleased me.

I sketched and photographed the coat of arms, and knocked on the front door, as much to explain to my mother why I'd been lurking around outside the house as to socialize. She invited me in for coffee, poured us both a cup, and offered me a plate of chocolate-covered digestive cookies.

I said, "Mom, would you say I use big words when I talk?"

"You didn't just then."

"In general, I mean. Would you say I indiscriminately throw hundred-dollar words around?"

She placed her index finger on her chin. "I would say that you speak like the well-educated, well-brought-up young woman that you are."

"So my speech *is* riddled with ostentatious Latinate terms?"

Mom frowned. "Why are we talking about this?"

"Someone sort of accused me of being a verbal showoff today."

"Who?"

"No one important. A guy at the bagel place I go to."

"Sounds like someone was flirting with you. What kind of guy?"

The lie rolled right off my lips. "An old guy. Around seventy. One of the regulars. And he wasn't flirting, he was being critical."

"He may be older, but I wouldn't be so sure he wasn't flirting. You know how boys are, how they throw snowballs at the girls they like."

I rolled my mental eyes up to a mental ceiling. Maybe when she'd grown up, young males had signalled their amorous intentions with violence. In my day, the snowballs had been aimed at the losers and sissies. "I wanted to ask you something else, too:

do you remember ever hearing any neighbourhood gossip about Ryan Hennessy, the older brother of Patrick the dog-walker?"

"Ryan Hennessy? Are you joking? Of course I heard about him. Who didn't hear when he was arrested?"

"Arrested? For what?"

"You can't have forgotten the Rose Park Burglar. Goodness, it was such a relief when Ryan Hennessy was caught and we could all sleep at night. You especially, hiding out in my dressing room, scared to death."

I put down my cup. "I remember the Rose Park Burglar, but I don't remember hearing he was Ryan Hennessy."

She assumed the finger to chin thinking position again. "Come to think of it, you may not have known he was the burglar. The whole affair was dealt with hush-hush because he was underage. It was his mother who turned him in, when she found some of the stolen goods in their basement."

I imagined an angry mother in Dickensian long skirts, a linen dishcloth in her hands, yelling at the teenage Ryan, cuffing him about the head. A young Patrick in a muslin shirt cowered in the corner with his hands over his ears and his eyes shut, next to wailing babies in bonnets and gowns.

Mom said, "It's possible charges weren't even laid — your father would know. But Ryan returned what he still had in his possession and paid most everyone else back, with money and labour, doing yard work and so on. Noel helped him a few times, raked some leaves with him, out of the goodness of his heart."

"Noel, my brother Noel?"

"If that's the kind of sarcastic tone you used with the man at the bagel shop, no wonder he was annoyed."

Funny how that kind of comment can shorten a mother-daughter visit.

Mom walked me to the door, opened it onto a framed view of the verdant lawn and sculpted bushes. "When Dad and I are back from Boston," she said, "we should talk about your birthday, about how you'd like to celebrate it."

My twenty-ninth birthday was two weeks away, a reminder I didn't need of the inconsistency between where I ought to be in my life trajectory and where I was. "How about we ignore the birthday this year?"

"I could gather together the Morrison relatives for a dinner, and invite some of your teacher friends along, if you like. Do you still keep in touch with any of them?"

Not much, not since I'd left for California. And I'd never liked to combine non-Rose Parkers with family anyway, for fear of the money-coloured glasses through which friends might view me after seeing my parents' house, and grounds, and manner. I said, "I don't think I'm up to any kind of public party."

"Nonsense. We have to do something. Decide what you'd like, and let me know."

Yes, madam.

~

I made myself popcorn that night for dinner, sat down to eat it, played back the day's events on the film reel in my mind, and paused at the scene where Patrick had called me a liar. I wasn't a liar. *Was too.* Was not. Not the bad kind. I didn't bend the truth to make people like me, didn't indulge in empty flattery to get ahead, didn't falsify my accomplishments for boasting purposes. I only lied when I had to, to be polite, or when I was under attack. By Curly, Earring, and Goatee, for instance, on the subject of Noel. Or by my mother, when she was pushing me too hard on the socializing issue. Or by Hannah, when she scoffed at the notion of me babysitting, as if she were so much further advanced in life.

I lied all the time, in other words. *Did not.* I hadn't lied once to Molly or Jane or Alexandra, for example. Nor to Patrick, in the few conversations we'd had.

I tried to put his accusation out of my mind, which meant I could think of nothing but. When I could stare no longer into my cold, dead fireplace, I grabbed a small backpack and went out into the warm, dark night — it was close to nine o'clock. I took out my bike, rode through Rose Park, across a bridge and up a substantial hill, down a valley and up another long incline, and came to a lively uptown intersection alight with movie marquees and stores and restaurants open for business.

I locked my bike outside a twenty-four hour drug store, went in, bought some shampoo and a new toothbrush. How refreshing it was not to know a single person I passed in the aisles of the store. How liberating to realize how very few of the people on the streets thereabouts had grown up in Rose Park, had parents from Rose Park, or cared a whit about anything to do with Rose Park.

I walked into a big, bright bookstore, browsed through the new releases, saw nothing of interest. I moved on past the candles and vases and picture frames, and rode the escalator upstairs. Several couples and small groups of people, all of whom undoubtedly had cozy circles of intimate friends with whom to celebrate their birthdays, sat in the café partaking in lively conversation, fitting in, enjoying an evening out.

I turned a corner and came face to face with a shelf titled "Classic Mysteries." I bent down, ran my finger along the T's, stopped at the lone copy of *Brat Farrar*, an inexpensive mass market edition with a plain cover. I pulled the book off the shelf, straightened up, flipped through the pages, read the jacket copy, and stood, thinking, with the book in my hand, for about a minute before I took it to the cash.

The book came with me to Bagel Haven the next morning. I'd struggled at home the night before, tried to come up with the perfect comment to write inside it, and floundered over these drafts:

Speaking of brothers,
Blithe

I am not a liar.
Blithe

The way I see it, there's lying, and then there's lying.
Blithe

At midnight, I inscribed the book with:

Patrick:
I thought you might like this book.
Blithe

which had the virtue of containing only monosyllabic words.

I didn't have the guts to present the book in person. On my way out of Bagel Haven, I asked Arthur to hand it to Patrick in a spare moment, and implied the book was not a gift, but belonged to Patrick already, that he'd left it behind somewhere. Did Arthur deliver it? I didn't know. And I didn't see Patrick at Cawley Gardens to ask him when I took Tup out there around noon, after my parents had left for Boston.

I might have happened to drop by the park again later in a humiliatingly transparent manner, but Jane called me, frantic, at one o'clock, to say that Joshua had fallen off the monkey bars at school and possibly broken his arm. She'd taken him down to the emergency room for who-knows-how-long and her husband was out of town on business, her sitter sick, her mother unreachable. She wouldn't call if she weren't desperate, but might I be able to pick up Alexandra from Rose Park Elementary at three-fifteen, take her to my place, and keep her until Jane could get home?

I could, and welcomed the distraction, too.

~

I arrived ten minutes before dismissal time and sat down on a bench in the school yard. An assortment of nannies and mothers, some with toddlers and babies along, waited in segregated groups. The upscale moms with highlighted blonde hair and trim physiques stuck together, the nannies clustered by continent of origin, and a few plainer women commiserated off to the side.

The first kids out of the school were younger than Alexandra — grade one or two boys who ran and shouted, little girls who walked out in pairs and threes. Big kids and medium-sized kids followed, and within a few minutes there was enough of a press that I stood up and moved closer to the entrance, leaned against a spindly tree, kept my eyes focused on the doors, and felt a stir of worry. I hadn't missed her, had I?

A group of girls of about Alexandra's age came out. They wore tank tops or tight T-shirts, bracelets and hairbands, and low-rider bottoms that exposed their thin midriffs. Some walked arm-in-arm. In among them could have been the three girls Alexandra and I had seen on the street. Must have been, given the attitude spoken by their body language. One girl, dressed in a mint green tank top and matching short shorts, and possessor of an eye-catching golden shade of hair colour she would spend her adult life trying to replicate, broke free from the group, ran up to a capri-panted mother who stood near me, and said, "Mom, I invited four more people. Is that okay?"

The mother smoothed her daughter's hair. "Sure. I ordered extra party sandwiches anyway. Now, if everybody's here, let's go. The bouncy castle's all set up and waiting in the backyard."

They swept by me, the happy confident girls, the happy confident mother, and my heart ached and cracked for Alexandra, who wasn't going to the party, who straggled out of the school alone a minute later, weighed down by her backpack and her wild frizzy hair and her differentness.

I said hi brightly, tried to hide the overdose of empathy I was feeling. "Did you get the message from your mom that I was coming?"

"Yeah. Is Josh's arm broken?"

"They don't know yet." I took her backpack from her. It was so heavy, I almost dropped it on the ground. "What's in here?"

"We did a desk dump today."

We walked toward my mother's car, which I'd parked across the street from the school. "What's a desk dump?

"It's where you dump everything that's in your desk on the floor and then you have to clean it up and take stuff home or throw things away."

"And in here is everything you have to bring home?"

"Yeah. I told Mrs. Semchuk it was all garbage, but she said not to be difficult, not today."

"Oh."

"Mrs. Semchuk's a bit of a control freak."

Most teachers were. I said, primly, "One of the challenges of school is learning how to manage different kinds of people."

"Did you learn how to do that when you went to school here?"

I dropped the teacher act, let show the me that used to be her. "Well, no. I tended to retreat and withdraw. During recess, for instance, I hid out and read books."

She looked at me with her wide eyes, checking to see if I told the truth.

I turned back to point at the spot on a hill near a bush where I had often burrowed in to read, and found myself facing a deserted school yard. "Where did everyone go so fast?"

"Probably to Haley's end of school party."

You would think I'd have learned, in all my years of post-secondary education and teacher training, a useful tactic to employ in this situation, but there is no effective method I know of for dealing with childhood social exclusion. Or with adult social exclusion, for that matter. I said, "Who's Haley?"

"A girl in my class."

"Did you get invited to the party?"

"No."

"Do you wish you had been?"

She shrugged. "I don't know."

I opened the trunk of the car, threw in Alexandra's two-ton backpack and some caution. Inside the car, I said, "You know, once, in high school, I was invited to a very cool party. I'd never gone to a big bash before, and I was only invited to this one because the host was dating my friend."

Alexandra put on her seat belt, said nothing.

I started the car. "Should I go on? Or am I boring you?"

Another shrug. "Go on."

"I didn't tell my friend or anyone else how much I looked forward to the party, but I picked out something special to wear and blew-dry my hair and put on lipstick and was altogether very keen."

"What happened?"

"Nothing horrible. But the party was not fun, not in any way. The conversations were boring, people got drunk and threw up on the lawn, my friend started, uh, flirting with her boyfriend's best friend, the two guys had a fist fight, and a neighbour called the police."

Alexandra stared straight ahead.

I said, "My story doesn't seem to have achieved the desired effect."

One for me — she smiled. "Sorry, but there were a few things wrong with it."

"Such as?"

"Such as you're not supposed to talk to eleven-year-olds about teenagers getting drunk and making out."

"I know that. But you seem more mature than the average eleven-year-old. And I didn't talk about making out."

"Wasn't the girl you knew making out with her boyfriend's best friend?"

One thing I *had* learned from teaching was the importance of being alert around bright kids. "Well, yes, she was."

"The other thing is that last year another girl at school had a party with a bouncy castle. She's moved away now, but her mother made her invite everyone in the class, so I got to go."

"And?"

"It was the best party ever."

"I see." A block passed. I said, "So what did you do in school today other than the desk dump?"

"We did mnemonics."

There was a high-priced word. "Did you now?"

"Mrs. Semchuk makes us do them every week on our spelling words. But today's were just for fun. I did one for the word 'tabulate.' Want to hear it?"

"Please."

"Tup And Blithe Up LATE. Get it?"

"Sort of."

"You'd understand it better if you saw it written down."

I pulled into my parents' driveway. "I get it. And I'm flattered you used Tup and me."

I offered Alexandra a snack and suggested that after it, we could stroll with Tup over to Molly Greer's to deal with the mail and the flyers. She said okay, whatever, and puttered around my living room, picked up the Rose Park architecture book from the coffee table. "Is this what you're reading now?"

"That's a library book I borrowed to help with my research."

After a minute, she said, "Do you want to hear a mnemonic for the word library?"

I passed over a plate of peanut butter cookies. "Can't wait."

"Live In Books. Read And Read all Year."

I repeated it back to her. "It's good, but aren't there one too many a's?"

"The one for 'all,' you mean? You're allowed to do that — put small words in the middle. As long as the mnemonic helps you remember."

I wasn't so sure. "Do you want more milk?"

"No thanks." She moved the architecture book aside. "Is this the project you talked to my mom about? The one with the white stone in the wall?"

"Yes. I'm helping out a writer named Molly Greer who lives in Rose Park. She writes children's books. Have you ever read her?"

She hadn't, so I pulled a couple of works from the Greer oeuvre off my bookshelf, suggested she borrow a Michael and Matilda twin detective novel, and, on the way out and to Glenwood with Tup, explained the puzzle book concept in more detail. I could tell from the attentive way she listened, from the questions she asked, that she found this topic far more interesting than my tales of teenage revelry.

I said, "Molly Greer's house is going to be included in the book too. It's that yellow and red brick one up ahead with the tower on top." And with the workmen swarming over its front. A truck parked in the driveway had "Richardson's Tuck Pointing" painted on its side, and two workmen on scaffolding were doing something — scraping? filing? cleaning? — to the brick. A heavy-set, red-cheeked man in a hard hat and work clothes stood on the lawn watching. He introduced himself as Bob Richardson when I said hello and told him I was the housesitter.

"We got started late on this job," he said, "so we won't finish today. We'll have to come back tomorrow morning early. Is it okay if we leave some equipment and supplies in the garage overnight?"

I said fine, no problem, tied Tup up to the porch, went inside, turned off the alarm, and took Alexandra to Molly's study, where we looked up tuck pointing in a dictionary and learned it had to do with the fixing of mortar between bricks. Knowledge stored, we watered the house plants — Alexandra wielded the watering can — picked up the mail, and went back out. We were looking at the bricks to see if we could tell which ones had been tucked and pointed when Alexandra said, "What's that block with the letters on it?"

"It's a cornerstone that shows the year the house was built."

"In Roman numerals, right? I only know those up to twenty. What's M-D-C-C-C-L-I-V stand for?"

"Let me see now. M is a thousand, and C is a hundred. And D ... D must be five hundred, plus the three C's would make it eight hundred. One thousand, eight hundred, and L equals fifty, and the I and the V make four, so —1854. I think."

Alexandra said, "I could make a good mnemonic for that."

"If your teacher only knew how you've taken these mnemonics to heart."

"I'll try, then you."

"You first."

"Okay. Here's mine: Mothers ... Don't ... Cook ... Chili ... for Children ... Lately... In ...Venezuela."

I smiled. "That's good. Funny."

"Your turn."

"Must I?"

"Yes."

"All right. How about this: My ... Dalmation ... Sees — get it? the three C's makes the word sees? — Large ... Intelligent ...Vegetables."

"Large Intelligent Vegetables?"

"You've never encountered any of those? All right then, how about: My Dalmation Sees ..." I searched my vocabulary for a better L-word than large, and came up with the one-dollar word "light." "How about this? My Dalmation Sees Light ... In ... oh my god."

"Why 'oh my god'? There's no V in oh my god."

I couldn't speak to answer her. I was too transfixed by a mental image of Jeremiah Brown's clue, the letters formed of wispy smoke, floating in the air above the cornerstone like a cheap special effect — *a Man with a Dog who Sees Light In the Valley.* "Could you wait here a second, Alexandra? I'll be right back. I have to ask the tuck pointing man something."

I ran over to Mr. Richardson, turned on a semblance of charm, and questioned him about his trade. He warmed to his subject, was happy to explain that the traditional hand tool used to remove mortar was a chipping hammer, that yes, with enough chipping one could probably ease a brick right out, but that wasn't the standard procedure, no. I stopped listening when he explained how to redo the mortar. All I needed to know was if removal of the cornerstone was a job within my grasp.

I untied Tup, said goodbye to the tuck pointing gang, told Alexandra I'd just remembered something I had to do, apologized, and jog-walked her home, where, I said, we would probably find her mother, back from the hospital. And did I consider telling Alexandra about the treasure clue, about what her interest in mnemonics had made me realize? No, I did not, I'm ashamed to say, not for more than a second. I was too entranced with the idea of me me me finding the treasure, alone, and getting all the glory.

Jane *was* home with Joshua. His wrist was only sprained — he sported a sling but no cast. Jane was profuse with her thanks for my time, and invited me to stay for ordered-in Chinese food, but I declined, and did my best to contain my excitement, managed not to blurt out my suspicions, or rather, wild guesses, about the Glenwood treasure's whereabouts. I examined Joshua's arm as if I were in no rush, expressed sympathy, dashed home, packed a bag, and sped back to Glenwood.

The sun was still bright in the sky when I started in on the cornerstone with Mr. Richardson's chipping hammer. I almost chipped off a few fingers in the process, but after much swearing, sweating, and exertion, I had loosened the stone enough to ease it out of the wall. It was heavy, heavier than Alexandra's backpack. I set it down on the ground with a thump, reached inside the dusty cavity left behind in the wall, felt all around. Felt nothing.

What if the real meaning of the clue was that the treasure was buried in the ground below my feet?

I sat and stared at the hole in the wall. I made a motion to kick the stone, realized that my foot would suffer more damage than the stone if I did, settled for a hard push, rolled it over. And exposed to the light a long, narrow slit that had been cut into the back side of the stone, above and parallel to its bottom edge.

I tried to see inside the slit, but couldn't. I swung my body around, lay face down on the ground, and peered in. Still too dark. The sun had dipped below the tops of some tall trees. The crevice was deep and narrow.

The chipping hammer wouldn't fit into the opening, so I let myself into Molly's house, retrieved a letter opener from her desk and a bread knife from her knife rack, and ran outside with them, worked away with both tools until a dusty square corner of some kind of paper peeked out of the opening. With my breath drawn, I unfolded a document that was undoubtedly an old surveyor's plan, or an engraver's certificate, something irrelevant and inconsequential, yet another false hope.

Except that it wasn't. What I held, against all expectation, was a hand-drawn treasure map, a worn but legible document that consisted of a large X drawn pirate-style, a paragraph of small squared printing I couldn't make out in the late afternoon light, and a simple diagram of a road or a river.

The noise of a heavy door closing across the street made me jerk my head up in alarm. A woman and a teenage boy in a baseball uniform got into a car, backed out of the driveway, and drove off. They did not stop, open a car window, and demand to know for what nefarious reason I had removed the cornerstone from Molly's house, but they could have. Time to get out of there.

I slipped the map carefully into a pocket of my backpack and, with much huffing, puffing, and scraping of knuckles, wedged the cornerstone back into the brick wall. Then I packed up, wrote a note for Mr. Richardson asking him to please secure the cornerstone, slung my precious cargo over my shoulders, and hurried home.

~ Chapter 7 ~

S afe in my kitchen, with the blinds drawn and the door double-locked, I examined my prize.

The aged piece of paper could better be described as an annotated drawing than a map. Off to the left side were written the words "Glenwood Ravine." The river-like shape was labelled "Mud Creek." The X was situated at a spot two inches to the right of the creek. And underneath the drawing were these words, neatly printed:

> The treasure is buried in the old underground game locker situated fifty feet due east from the doorway of the old hunting lodge. The locker is brick-lined and covered with a wooden trap door into which is set an iron ring. Two old willows guard the site. May the money bring more happiness to the finder's life than it has to mine.

There was no signature.

I memorized every inch and mark on the paper and, for a few crazed minutes, considered running out the door that instant and down into the ravine. But it was too late, I was too unprepared. The treasure could wait one more day. Tomorrow I would go, first thing. Tomorrow I would go, and, and, do what? How thick was the forest cover east of the lodge site? How would I pinpoint the location of the lodge's door? What tools would I need? I poured myself a tall glass of water, drank it down, imagined myself in the ravine the next morning, with the map and a shovel and a measuring tape, digging in the ground while curious joggers and walkers asked me what on — no, in — earth I was doing.

My head was jumbled with thoughts, the flat too small to contain them. I hid the map among some papers on my desk, took Tup out for a walk, and began to devise a simple plan to cover my true purpose.

I walked fast, tugged impatiently on Tup's leash when he lingered too long over an intriguing scent, calculated the what and the how and the when, and tried to extinguish the fantasies that had crackled into being the second I'd removed the paper from its hiding place. I stomped on the flaming pictures of me as celebrated treasure hunter, being interviewed on national radio, having my picture in the newspaper, appearing on the local television news. I threw buckets of cold water on the heartwarming notion that Noel and my parents and every person who'd ever ignored or passed over me might soon stand in awe of my achievement.

The outcome of my hunt, of any search for glory, was far likelier to be heartbreak and disappointment, I knew. But the prospect of finding the treasure was so enticing that I was as high as the oak tree outside my window when I came home to the sound of a ringing phone with my mother's voice on the other end, calling from Boston.

"I forgot to tell you," she said. "I'm expecting a courier delivery tomorrow of a large parcel. Can you look out for it?"

Huh? "Okay, sure."

"Thank you. How are you? What's new?"

Everything. "Since yesterday? Not much." Pause. *Ask her something.* "How's your trip going?"

"Good. I spent a pleasant afternoon touring Boston with the conference spouses, and Dad's meetings have gone well."

Dad, Dad. There was a treasure-related issue I'd thought of during my walk to ask him. "Is he there? May I speak to him?"

"I'll put him on."

She set down the phone and asked Dad to take it. In the background, I heard him say, "She wants to talk to me? Now? Whatever for?" Then, "Hello?"

"Hi, Dad. I have a quick legal question for you about the Glenwood treasure. Because of that book I'm working on."

"Well, your mother and I have already begun Happy Hour, but you can try me anyway."

"Do you know what the law is about finding treasure? If the Glenwood money had actually been hidden all this time, and someone found it now, could that person keep it? And what would be the tax implications?"

"Oddly enough, I did some research into that subject a few years ago. I can't remember what caused me to do so, but I definitely had one of the associates look up the case law and the statutes pertaining to this matter."

I made a cranking motion with my hand. "And?"

"Were the treasure to exist, one could argue with some confidence that it would be the rightful property of the finder, in accordance with Jeremiah Brown's written statement of his intentions for the money."

"So the finder could keep it?"

"Not necessarily. A case could also be made by the major beneficiary of his will, which was, you may remember, an organization that benefitted war widows and orphans."

"Oh."

"And Brown's distant relations, the descendants of his cousins or some such, might also try to make a claim, and force the matter to arbitration. But whoever was granted ownership of the money in the final proceedings would have to pay taxes on it, yes."

My visions of fortune dimmed, but I could still pretend not to hope for fame. I thanked him, hung up, paged through the puzzle book file, and found and dialled the phone number of the rented house where the Greers were staying in Nova Scotia, a number Molly had given me in case of emergency. A new tenant answered — she'd just moved into the house for a few weeks' stay and knew nothing about the Greers, who were probably on the road for home.

I was alone on the treasure hunt, then, for at least a day or two. Fine. I could do alone. I located Dad's old photograph of the lodge, compared it to the treasure map and the town plan, took out paper and pen and ruler, made some painstaking measurements, performed some calculations, wrote lists. I laid out every detail of my plan and recorded it on a steno pad, took a break to cut myself some strawberries and a banana and eat them standing up by the sink, sat down, and reviewed my notes thrice more.

~

My first stop early the next morning was Bagel Haven, for a toasted bagel and a bagel sandwich, both to go, the sustenance I needed to get through the day ahead. I was in the lineup at the cash to pay for it when Patrick came by and said, "I liked the book. Thanks."

Book? "What book?"

"*Brat Farrar.*"

The book I'd given him the day before, in my previous life. "Oh, good. I mean, I'm glad. I liked it, too."

"Can I believe my eyes, Blithe?" Arthur said. "Is that a sandwich you clutch? The end of the world must be nigh. Patrick,
do you see? Blithe has varied her order."

Patrick smiled and retreated to the bake room. I played
along with Arthur for the time it took to pay and left right after,
bagged bagels in hand.

Tup was waiting for me outside in Mom's car. Our next
stop was the nearest garden centre. I made the purchases written on my list, drove back to Rose Park, and parked near
Cawley Gardens, where I loaded up an old red wagon I'd
brought from the garage with Dad's shovel and the newly
bought supplies. Navigating the wagon down the slope was a
bit tricky — the wagon bumped the back of my shins five times
and the shovel fell off twice before I thought to walk beside the
wagon instead of in front of it, and to hold the shovel in my
hand. But I reached the bottom without the loss of equipment
or dog, and started down the trail to the spot Hannah had
shown me past the curve in the river.

The day was sunny and breezy and not too hot, perfect for
a walk in the woods, which must have been why I passed ten
people going the other way in my first five minutes on the path.
They were grouped in ones and twos, with and without dogs
and bikes, their presence a mixed blessing, a reason to worry less
about my traditional thicket-based ravine fears and more about
how to deal with witnesses to my intended groundbreaking.

I rounded the creek's curve; the site loomed up ahead. I eyed
the tree line and tried not to be discouraged by the lack of any
willow trees in the vicinity. Fallen trees were everywhere in the
ravine, felled by lightning or rot or age. The willows must have
died since Jeremiah's day. I drew up near the birdhouse, pulled
the wagon off the path, and began to unload, a task that would
have been easier if my pulse hadn't been pounding in the bridge
of my nose, if my breathing hadn't been so rapid. I could no

longer distinguish the anticipation from the apprehension, but I didn't care — I'd rarely felt so alive.

Tup began his usual sniff and wander routine. I bent down and unloaded the garden centre booty — the four saplings I'd bought, along with a bag of topsoil, a trowel, and a special measuring tape the clerk at the store had assured me was what one used when laying out flower beds or patio layouts. Or, in my case, when measuring distances on the ground that corresponded to markings on maps.

In a lull between passersby, I took out the town plan and the tape, extended the tape to where, according to my figurings, the lodge had stood, and marked the spot with a rock. Further measurements and rocks thrown down established where the doorway to the lodge had been. From there, I measured out the fifty feet to the game locker's location, which appeared to be in among some thin young trees and thicker older trees and various tall and short plants that could have been wild grass or milkweed or loosestrife or something else altogether. (Plant identification had never been my strong point, as student or teacher.)

I'd hoped that the locker would be visible. I'd hoped that if my measurements were correct, I could stand on the designated spot, look around, and see the locker door, in plain sight. I'd imagined the rusty iron ring on the trap door catching my eye, and the only struggle being to get the door open. No such luck. I stood on the spot, I stared at every inch of ground in close range, moved around a few degrees to the right, stared some more. Step by step, I made a complete circle, strained my eyes, and saw nothing but greenery.

Had I misidentified the locker location? I walked back and forth on either side of the designated spot, kept my eyes on the ground. Two middle-aged women in exercise clothes came by, and one of them asked if I'd lost something. "I'm just interested in the ecosystems down here," I said, with a big smile. This ridiculous response seemed to satisfy — they smiled back and walked on, as if I were normal. Or as if I weren't, so the sooner they got away from me the better.

My backup plan, if I couldn't see the trap door, was to dig. Maybe, like some of the flagstones that had once formed a diagonal path across the lawn between my parents' front door and their driveway, the trap door had become buried under what I prayed would be a thin layer of soil. I would dig shallow holes all around where the locker was supposed to be, until I struck something wooden or metallic or brick. And if anyone asked me why I was digging, I'd say I was planting trees as part of an environmental project of the type I'd always handed over to the school science specialist.

What the plan hadn't allowed for was the hardness of the ground, the amount of effort required to dig at all. After half an hour, I had dug a hole four inches deep and six inches wide. An hour and a half more, I was exhausted, and the yield of my efforts was two more small holes which had unearthed rocks, hordes of crawling insects, and a tree root.

In the course of my digging, cyclists had whizzed past and ignored me, also a couple with two dogs. An elderly man walked slowly by and said good morning but nothing else. No one cared what I was doing; the baby tree purchase had been a waste of time and money. "I've lost my mind," I said, and as if in reply, Tup emitted a low growl. He smelled the dogs coming before I heard the jingling of the collars and chains that heralded the arrival of the first one around the bend, followed by five more, and by Patrick.

He stopped next to where I knelt on the ground. "Hi," he said. The dogs roamed around him and sniffed at Tup.

I shaded my eyes against the glare of the sun above his head. "Hi."

"What are you doing?"

Head back down, I spaded up a clod of earth. "Planting trees."

He checked behind him to see if the hundreds of trees usually in the ravine were still there. "Why?"

"It's Plant-a-Tree Day, didn't you know?"

The dogs panted. I made earth-scratching noises. When I looked up again, Patrick was still there.

"Do you want some help?" he said.

"No, thanks. I work better alone. And I'm going to take a lunch break soon, anyway."

A jogger ran by. Patrick said, "You came down here by yourself after all."

"Yes, yes I did. On a sunny day like this, the ravine feels quite" — I'd been about to say tranquil — "calm."

"Yeah. It's like a whole other world down here."

"That's what Hannah used to say."

No reply.

"Don't let me keep you," I said. "The dogs probably want to keep going." Though three of them had jumped into the creek and were cavorting about in the water as if they could play there forever.

Patrick said, "I'd like to talk to you about that *Brat Farrar* book sometime." He gestured to my planting paraphernalia. "When you're not busy."

"Yes." I shaded my eyes again. "Let's do that, sometime." Sometime when I could recover the ability to think about anything other than one obsessive, all-consuming goal, when I wasn't in the grip of treasure fever.

~

I didn't find the locker. I didn't find the treasure. I didn't find a damn thing, though I spent most of the day in the ravine. Afterwards, I went home, ran into the courier delivering Mom's package — he was about to stick an "I was here and you weren't" notice on the front door — and received a large, flat, heavy box addressed to Mrs. C. Morrison. I laid it down in her front hall, retreated to my flat, rechecked my notes, slept fitfully if at all, and returned the next day to the ravine to dig in an area ten feet away from my first locus. In case my original estimation of the lodge size — based on the square drawn on the town plan map and its dimensions relative to the height of the men standing in front of it in Dad's picture — had been incorrect. But still nothing.

At four o'clock on the second day, I conceded defeat, dragged my weary body home, peeled off my clothes, took a shower, put on pyjamas, lay down on the couch, and fell asleep.

The ringing of the phone woke me. I let the machine take it and eyed the angle of the shadows cast across the living room by the setting sun. The kitchen clock read eight-twenty, late enough that I could stay down for the night if I wanted. I closed my eyes, floated on the surface of sleep, and was roused again by Tup licking my hand and breathing on my face. I groaned, hobbled my stiff body up and over to the door, and opened it for him.

He leapt out, knocked over a small cardboard box sitting on the mat, stopped to sniff at it. I bent down — a move that made me painfully aware of which muscles I'd used to dig — picked up the box, and told Tup to go spend two pennies, an old family joke.

The box was tied up with a narrow blue ribbon. A tag attached to the ribbon read, "B: I thought you might like these, P." Inside, underneath a neat square of parchment paper, were four blueberry-filled oatmeal squares. I picked one out of the box, popped it into my mouth, let the sweet, blue taste linger on my tongue. Delicious. I put the kettle on, called Tup back in, returned to the couch with a mug of tea in my hand, and ate the rest of the squares straight from the box.

The light on my phone was blinking. I picked it up, listened to a cheery message from Molly, back from Nova Scotia and returning my call of two days before. Also a message from Mom,

left earlier that afternoon, to say she and Dad were home, and
had I thought any more about my birthday.

I hung up, rubbed my face, pushed my dirty hair off my
forehead. When would I learn? I'd gone through life hoping I'd
be picked for the lead in the grade six play, that the boy I had a
crush on in junior high would like me back, that my high school
English teacher would return my exam paper first, with the
highest mark. I'd hoped that my mother would give up her
social ambitions for me, that I could find some minor occupational field to be better at than Noel, that my husband and I
would live happily ever after. And even after all those hopes had
died unfulfilled, I'd entertained the most preposterous hope of
all — that I'd live a fairy tale and find a buried treasure.

I could keep on hoping for any number of impossible
dreams if I wanted to experience defeat and disappointment and
shame and strong doses of self-hatred when I failed. Or I could
stop doping myself with the hope drug, avoid the highs and
lows, live out my days in an unaltered, consistent state that
allowed neither joy nor heartbreak, but something sober and stable and much less upsetting in between.

I turned on the television, flipped around, and came across
an old black-and-white movie that I could tell — from the soft
lighting, the cut of the costumes, the valiant demeanours of the
hero and heroine — would end in good triumphing over evil,
kindness being its own reward, the meek inheriting the earth. I
flipped away from that escapist fantasy and stopped at a reality
television show, one that gloried in and indulged its perform-
ers' basest natures. I sat and made myself watch it, and let my last
tears of self-pity (so I vowed) roll down my sorry face.

~

"There must be a reasonable explanation the treasure wasn't
there," Molly said.

We were at Bagel Haven. She'd asked to meet so I could hand over the completed puzzle book research. And at my table in the back, I'd told her about my treasure-hunting exploits.

I said, "I'll reimburse you for the extra tuck pointing charges."

"Don't be silly. But this confirms what I've thought all along — there never was a treasure."

"I can't believe that Jeremiah Brown would go to the trouble of making and hiding the map and then not bury anything."

"Do you think someone else found it, then?"

"Someone who destroyed the game locker? I don't know what to think. I'm sure the lodge location is right. I double-checked the site Hannah showed me with the town plan."

Her brow wrinkled. "When did Hannah show you this? When she was here last week on her surprise visit?"

"Yes. I gather you didn't know she was coming?"

"No, I didn't. Not before her visit, nor during it. Though she was kind enough to leave a note informing me she'd left the sheets and towels she'd used in the dryer."

Molly looked so grumpy I didn't know whether to sympathize or join the attack. I said, "I'm sorry you missed her."

"She hasn't been home in years, and she shows up when Larry and I are away?" Molly balled up her napkin, threw it on the table, and stood up. "If I'd known she was coming, I could at least have made her go through her junk in the basement." She departed for the washroom, muttering.

When Patrick passed by a minute later, I thanked him for the blueberry squares. "They were lovely, and they came at just the right time. Did you make them yourself?"

"Yeah. Glad you liked them."

Molly walked into the awkward silence that followed, nodded at Patrick, and said to me, "Why don't we go down to the ravine right now, take a look around?"

I gave her a warning glance, said okay, and started to get up. Patrick said, "You doing more tree-planting today?"

"No. Just going for a walk."

Molly swept some crumbs off our table. "Lovely day for it."

Patrick said, "You should water those trees if you want them to grow. Take a pail down and use water from the creek, maybe. I could do it later, if you like."

I edged toward the door. "It's kind of you to offer, but you shouldn't trouble yourself."

Outside, Molly said, "What was that all about?" and I told her about Patrick's appearance in the ravine during my digging session.

"Do you think he suspects what you were up to?"

"I think he's written me off as the local lunatic."

"Too bad. He's cute. Is he single?"

I looked at her askance. "I don't know."

"Would you go after him if he were?"

I gave her another look. "Would you, if you were single?"

"Me? Heavens, no. I'm too old for him. But you know who would pounce on him in a minute?"

"Who?"

"Hannah. She'd try to hook up with him for sure."

"Hook up?"

"Isn't that what kids say nowadays? I used that expression in my latest book."

"How contemporary of you."

"Of course, Hannah would only go after a guy like — what was his name again?"

"Patrick."

"Hannah would only go after a guy like Patrick as a plaything, to be used and discarded. Hannah's always had a predatory side."

I said nothing, because it was true.

Molly said, "The one time I thought she might have met her match was in your brother."

"What do you mean? Noel and Hannah never dated."

She frowned. "No? I thought they had. I must be mistaken. Hannah had so many boyfriends, and she never introduced me to any of them. Never mind. Lead me to the treasure place."

We entered the park at Cawley Gardens, followed the ravine path, came to the lodge location. We walked back and forth, we remeasured with our feet, and we checked out the treelings, which did seem a mite droopy. We examined the ground all around them — Molly knelt down and probed the earth in several places with a sturdy stick, a search technique I hadn't considered. We spent half an hour there, but came no closer to finding anything.

On our way back, I said, "You believe I didn't find the treasure, right?"

"Yes, why?"

"It occurred to me that you might think I found the money and am telling you this fake story to cover up my discovery."

"I might think that of others, but not of you."

"Well, thanks. I didn't want you to wonder." Or to know how much mental time I'd devoted to twirling around in the treasure's spotlight.

"I'm just sorry you didn't find it. If anyone deserved to, you did."

"Yes, but think of the valuable life lesson I've learned from this experience."

"Let's hear this."

"From now on, I'm going to take the low road, not stick my neck out, keep my expectations low. I'm going to treat my emotional well-being like a financial investment: the less I risk, the less I have to lose. "

A pause, then a skeptical, "I see."

"For instance, now that I've finished the puzzle book research, I plan to laze about for the rest of the summer and do nothing."

"And you don't think you'll be bored?"

"No, I'll be peaceful, a model of equanimity. Did I pronounce that word right? I don't think I've ever spoken it aloud."

"Yes, you did, and you did a fine job on the research, too. I hope you didn't find *it* disappointing."

"Not at all. I enjoyed doing it. Did you notice the Field Street footbridge, behind us, by the way?" I turned and pointed. "See how the frame of the bridge forms a line of A's?"

She looked up. "How clever of you to have found that. And how unclever of me not to have known the old bridge was replaced. I wonder when that happened. Shows how long since I've been down here."

We started up the steep narrow path into Cawley Gardens, Molly in the lead. Ten feet up, she stopped short in front of me, and placed a hand on her chest. "That's where I saw them!" she said. "On the old footbridge. I'm not insane."

"Saw who?"

"Hannah and your brother."

What was she saying? "When?"

"Years ago. When did your brother move away?"

"He would have left for college a month or so after you moved here."

"But I saw him with Hannah long after that. I know, because I didn't set foot in the ravine until at least a year after we came to Rose Park. Did he come home for weekends or holidays?"

"Occasionally. When he wasn't invited somewhere else more exciting."

"It must have been one of those times that I saw them, then. I knew it. They *were* a couple."

They couldn't have been. Not without me, the master observer, the all-seeing one, knowing. I said, "Even if you saw them — or people who looked like them — standing on the bridge together, that doesn't necessarily mean they were dating."

"It was them all right, and they weren't just standing. They were necking. Passionately, as I recall. Or should I say making out? Do people still use the term necking anymore?"

~ Chapter 8 ~

I spent some mind time that evening filtering my friendship with Hannah through a so-she-dated-Noel screen — I remembered the weekends when she'd cancelled our plans at the last minute, citing an unconvincing bout of illness, or an uncharacteristic desire to be alone. Weekends when Noel had unexpectedly arrived home from Harvard.

I cringed when I recalled the occasions I'd confided to her my animosity for Noel. They weren't excessive in number, but I'd complained at sufficient length and depth that I suffered now from hindsighted mortification, writhed in retrospect at the memory of one particular day, when Hannah and I had sat in a coffee shop near Northside, drinking cappuccinos, and I'd lamented being an unwilling player in Noel's one-upmanship games. "You know what he's like?" I said. "Like the cutthroat competitor in a beauty pageant mystery, the contestant who wants to win so bad she'll kill to wear the crown."

Hannah lit a cigarette with her Zippo, flipped the lighter shut. "What the fuck is a beauty pageant mystery?"

"I swear — the last time he was home, for Thanksgiving, I walked by his room when he was in there alone, and I heard him muttering and cackling and hatching plots."

"Plots? What kind of plots?"

"Schemes for world domination, no doubt."

Hannah exhaled smoke and laughed at the same time, broke up the plume into small sardonic puffs. "You have to learn to curb that imagination of yours, Blithe. He was probably talking on the phone."

Probably to her.

"Anyway," she'd said, "what do you care what he does? Get over this childhood shit. Live your life."

Hannah's advice had been easy to follow once Noel moved to Europe. For years, Noel had been absent, our contact minimal. Before the wedding, my attitude was one of good riddance. Since, things were even simpler: I planned never to speak to him again.

I hadn't forgiven him for the role he'd played in corrupting Gerald, but when I stopped to weigh his level of heinousness on my personal scale, the revelation that Hannah had numbered among his sexual conquests didn't increase it any — there wasn't much that could make me hold Noel in less regard than I already did.

I *was* newly angry with Hannah, though. For falling for Noel. For not telling me. For not having been my true friend, when I, in my naïveté, had thought, for a short time, that she was.

~

I sat on my bench in Cawley Gardens and read the books section of the Saturday paper. Tup rambled nearby. Something — a noise, a movement glimpsed in my peripheral vision, a wind shift — made me look up, at Patrick, approaching the park entrance from across the street. The angle of his cap brim and the lope of his gait were unmistakable. So was Buck, at his side.

I waved, and when he came closer, I said, "You're every-where I go." Not complaining.

Patrick gestured over his shoulder. "I was at my mother's house, helping her clean. Her arthritis is bad today."

I invited him to join me on the bench. He removed a paperback from his back jeans pocket so he could sit, and showed me, when I asked to see, that it was another Josephine Tey mystery, *The Franchise Affair.*

I said, "Are you enjoying it?"

"It's not as good as *Brat Farrar.*"

"It's not as resonant, I guess."

"No evil brothers in this one, you mean?"

"I was thinking of my evil brother. Do you have one, too?" Let him tell me about Ryan if he wanted to.

He moved his neck from side to side, as if working through a crick. "Sure. Ryan. The black sheep of the family. He lives in Niagara Falls."

"What makes him a black sheep?"

"The fact that he's been in jail a few times."

"In jail?" I pictured a bulkier, older version of Patrick, with stubble on his scarred face, tattoos on his arms, and broken teeth, leaning on a prison yard wall. "In jail for what?"

"Don't look so shocked. He's not that bad. All of his crimes were non-violent. Possession of stolen goods, cross-border smuggling, minor offences like that."

"Oh, well, then."

He allowed me a small smile. "But why don't you like your brother? He always seemed like a popular guy."

"You knew Noel?" Did everyone?

"I knew who he was. He played rugby with Ryan at school. Were you joking when you called him evil?"

No. "Let's just say that Noel is not very kind, or nice. Period."

Patrick took his usual long time to respond, but this time, his silence struck me as thoughtful rather than rude. After it, he said, "Your guy was kind and nice, though, wasn't he?"

My guy? He couldn't mean Gerald, could he? "Who?"

"Brat Farrar."

"Oh, Brat. Yes, Brat is very unlike Noel. Because though Brat has flaws and makes mistakes, he's essentially good."

A description I liked to think could also fit me.

~

"What are we going to do today, Blithe?" Alexandra said. "Where's Tup?"

"Tup's at my parents' house. Would you like a scone? I made them myself."

"No, thanks. What are we going to do?"

On a rainy Sunday afternoon, Alexandra was at my apartment, touching the objects on the mantel. She opened and closed a box of wooden matches, uncurled the wick of a scented candle Mom had given me that I'd never lit, picked up the fertility goddess figurine and carried it back to the couch with her, sat down with it in her lap. "This thing is cool," she said. "It's like the opposite of Barbie. Does it have a name?"

"Not at the moment. Would you like to name it?"

She turned it over in her hands. "How about Trixie?"

I gave an involuntary laugh. "Does it look like a Trixie to you?"

"What do you think it should be called?"

"Trixie's as good a name as any. Do you want to play cards?" I opened one of the kitchen drawers and looked inside for a deck.

"The one in Mom's magazine is called Earth Mother."

"Sorry?"

"The thing like this in my mom's magazine is called Earth Mother."

I found the cards, brought them to the table. "What magazine is that?"

"It's about museums. The article I saw had a picture of a doll like this in it and some other stuff you don't have."

"That's not surprising. Trixie's the only museum replica in my possession." I shuffled the cards. "Do you know how to play poker?" I did. A film student I'd dated in my first year of university had taught me. "No? I'll teach you. We'll use pennies and play for money."

We were on about our fifth hand, embroiled in the intricacies of seven-card stud, when the pitter-patter of my mother's nails was heard at the door, mixed with the sound of the rain on the roof.

"Dad and I are just back from lunch at the Donaldsons'," she said, when I'd let her in, "and I saw your light was on." She noticed Alexandra, and switched to a gushy voice. "Hello, there, young lady. You're from across the street, aren't you? I'm Mrs. Morrison. And I'm afraid I've forgotten your first name."

Alexandra mumbled, "It's Alexandra," and brought her cards up in front of her face.

"Alexandra's not much of a gabber," I said. "And we're in the middle of a poker game. She's up twenty cents."

Mom said, "I won't keep you, then. I just wanted to finalize the plans for your birthday party."

"I didn't know there were any plans to finalize. I'll raise you five cents, Alexandra."

Mom leaned against the kitchen counter, after first checking it for signs of dirt. "Come now, Blithe, everyone should have a birthday party. Don't you think, Alexandra?"

Alexandra said nothing, picked up Trixie, rolled her around on the tabletop.

I said, "How about if just you, Dad, and I go out for dinner?"

"At last, we're getting somewhere! Shall we go to the golf club? I could get Antoine to make us a beef Wellington. Do you still like beef Wellington?"

She had me by the taste buds. Beef Wellington was one of the few accoutrements of my parents' lifestyle I adored, even in summer. We set a day and time for dinner, and she left with a cheery bye-bye to Alexandra and me both.

As soon as the door closed behind her, Alexandra started with questions. What's beef Wellington? How did my mother get that white streak in her hair? What's a gabber? And why had I said she wasn't one?

I explained all, finished with, "Because you're not, not with strangers, anyway. Wouldn't you agree?"

"Yeah, I guess."

"Do you mind I said that?"

"No, but I wondered how you knew."

"I'm the same, that's how."

She shuffled the cards not at all well. "Is that why you don't have any friends to invite to your birthday party?"

"I have friends," I said. Though I couldn't think of any, other than Hannah, also known as a snake in the ravine, my employers Molly and Jane, Arthur — everyone's friend — at Bagel Haven, and maybe Patrick, who thought I was a lying word snob. "Birthdays are different for adults, anyway. Not such a big deal."

"It's okay," she said. "I don't have many friends either." Her sympathy moved me. Stung a bit, too, but my inner adult prevailed, reminded me I was supposed to be a positive role model. I said, "I think socializing is overrated, anyway. There's not enough said about the joys of spending time alone."

"You get more reading done when you're alone, that's for sure. How many cards do you want?"

Later, when I re-offered the scones, Alexandra took one with butter and raspberry jam, and pronounced them good.

"But not as good as the ones my Grandma Whitney makes. No offence."

"No offence taken."

She wiped her mouth with her napkin. "Hey, do you have another book by Molly Greer that I could borrow? I liked that first one."

Was she trying to win back my favour after the scones and friends insults? Or had she really liked Molly's book? And did her motivation matter? I went to my bookshelf and found Molly's first, *The Enchanted Castle*, handed it over.

When Jane came by at pick-up time, Alexandra said, "Look, Mom, look what Blithe has." She held up the goddess figurine. "Her name is Trixie. She's just like Earth Mother in your magazine but she's a replica."

Jane took the figurine from Alexandra, looked it over, top to bottom, back to front. And again, slowly. Said, "Isn't that funny," but as if it weren't.

"And Blithe's having a birthday party next weekend," Alexandra said.

Jane set Trixie down on the table. "Does that mean you can't babysit, Blithe?"

"No, I'm fine to sit. And it's not a birthday party. It's just dinner with my parents on Saturday night."

Jane asked me if my impending birthday was of the milestone variety, I said no, it wasn't, Jane threw in that she'd spent her fortieth in quarantine with Joshua in the full throes of chicken pox, and they left with the usual thank yous and goodbyes and see you next weeks. Though not before Jane had taken a last quizzical look back at Trixie, lying on the table in all her large-breasted, swollen-bellied glory.

~

On Monday morning at Bagel Haven, Patrick said, "The rain

was good for your trees. They look much healthier now. Have you seen them?"

"No, I haven't. I overdid the ravine's charms last week."

"You should go down sometime, take a look."

I searched out his eyes under the brim of his baseball cap. They looked friendly. Not hostile, anyway. I said, "Tell me: do you *ever* take that hat off?"

He shook his head and walked away, but he might have smiled before he went.

On Tuesday morning, during a quiet moment, Patrick said, "Do you know of any other good mystery books?" He made the hand gesture for quotation marks in the air. "'Resonant' ones?"

I saw Arthur glance over at us from his spot at the cash, and in a lowered voice, I told Patrick I'd think of a few titles for him, bring a list the next day. I don't like to give reading recommendations as a rule — it bothers me when people tell me they disliked or were indifferent to a book I loved. But I was willing to make an exception, since Patrick had taken to *Brat Farrar*.

On Wednesday, I gave him the names of four more English post-war suspense novels, all available at the library. "I can't guarantee resonance," I said, "but I'll say this: they all feature well-woven plotlines, and tea."

"I'll look them up," he said.

On Thursday, he came over when I stood in line waiting to pay. "I read one of the books on your list last night," he said. "The one called *The Ivy Tree*."

Where had he read it? Sitting in a recliner in a gloomy basement apartment, probably, wearing a faded polyester paisley dressing gown over a T-shirt and boxers, under a pool of light from a beat-up floor lamp. I said, "Did you like it?"

"Yeah, I did."

I felt a surge of I didn't know what — gratitude? vindication? affection? — somewhere between my head and my heart, combined with hunger for breakfast. "Good."

"Are you walking your parents' dog this afternoon?"

"Yes, why?"

He pushed back the brim of his cap with the back of a cornmeal-dusted hand. "I thought maybe we could meet at the park, and talk about the book."

We met at Cawley Gardens, walked through the ravine with his dogs and Tup, and talked about what we'd liked and disliked about the book, about what was credible and dated in it, and what was not. And when we'd exhausted that topic, I told him the history of the Cawley Gardens house, a story he seemed interested in and claimed not to have heard before, not in any detail.

The next day, he said he'd started to read another of the recommended books the night before, but he did not suggest we meet to discuss it. Neither did I. In keeping with my no-hope, low-road, when-in-doubt-stay-home-alone approach to life.

On my way out of Bagel Haven that morning, I stopped at the condiment counter to dispose of my trash. Arthur was there, replenishing supplies. I nodded a hello, and he said, "He grows on you, doesn't he?"

"Who?"

"Patrick. He's a good kid. He has a good heart."

I think I blushed. I know I shrugged and unconvincingly pretended unawareness of Arthur's motives. I also reached over and started to organize the sugar packets.

Arthur said, "The girls from the beauty school down the street are more interested in his looks than his heart. You should see them at lunchtime, all tarted up in their makeup, stopping in here just to watch him walk back and forth with the bagels."

I stammered that I didn't know there *was* a beauty school in the vicinity, and was glad I was such a firm adherent of the expect-nothing credo, because if I weren't, Arthur's comments might have made me ill.

"Mind you," Arthur said, "Patrick seems unaffected by the girls' attention. I think he's looking for someone more mature."

I was about to ask where the beauty school was, and what kind of programs did it offer. Or I could have pointed out that the cream jug was empty. Anything to bring the conversation back to safe, flat land. But when I looked up from the neat row of sugar packets I'd formed and into Arthur's face, his expression told me not to change the subject, but to *jump in*. A fierce knitting motion of his eyebrows seemed to suggest I *seize the day*.

I might have read into his facial contortions, but I had the feeling he wasn't too big on equanimity and, given half a chance, would advocate the high road over the low.

~

On Saturday, my actual birthday, my parents dropped by at nine o'clock in the morning. I was on the couch when the knock came, engrossed in rereading the book I had discussed with Patrick, *The Ivy Tree*, by Mary Stewart.

"We've brought presents!" Mom called out from the porch.

I let them in, said they shouldn't have, that they could have waited until our dinner date that evening.

"Birthday presents should be given at breakfast time," Mom said. What I hoped was her last pronouncement on birthday rituals.

"Here you go," Dad said, and placed two items on my kitchen table. I suspected the bigger, fussily gift-wrapped box contained a piece of clothing of my mother's choosing — a cashmere sweater, perhaps, or a Burberry scarf. The other parcel looked like a book. Probably a new biography of Churchill, or Jane Austen, or Mary, Queen of Scots.

Mom clapped her hands together. "Open my present first. The bigger one."

I picked up the box. It was heavy. Not a scarf. "So what time are we meeting tonight?"

"Seven. And wear something nice."

I rolled my eyes in Dad's direction. His reply was a wink, which made me wonder how often he listened when Mom spoke.

"Don't worry about the paper," Mom said. "Rip it."

I tore off paper and ribbon, and uncovered a large, bubble-wrapped wooden picture frame. Mounted inside it was a work of oil-stick on paper, a madly colourful landscape of rolling rural hills with a Mediterranean flavour. "It's beautiful," I said, and meant it. The picture was sunny and happy and quiet and expansive all at once.

"Do you really like it? I hoped you might. I didn't want to buy you jewellery — you so rarely wear the pearls we bought for your twenty-first. But after the year you've had, we wanted to give you something special. Didn't we, Dad?"

He murmured a noise that Mom interpreted as assent.

Mom said, "The artist is a friend of Noel's, a talented young woman he introduced me to in London."

Oh. "Is she young and attractive?"

"Yes. A gamine type with a pixie cut. How did you know?"

"Lucky guess." I carried the picture over to the mantelpiece, moved Trixie to one side, and leaned the frame against the wall. "I like it very much." Unfortunate associations or not.

"I'm glad," Mom said. "Happy birthday, sweetheart." She leaned down and kissed me.

Dad cleared his throat. "I have a small gift for you, too."

I picked up his package, which was wrapped in brown kraft paper and tied with white string.

"It's not much," Dad said, "but because of this work you've been doing with that Greer woman — "

"Her name is Molly," Mom said. "Molly Greer."

"— I thought you might be interested in my father's old journal from the year he worked on Jeremiah Brown's file, so I had it spruced up for you."

I unwrapped a burnished leather-bound notebook, opened it and read the first page.

January 1, 1963

A quiet day indoors except for a bracing New Year's Day stroll in the neighbourhood. Cold roast beef for dinner.

"Thanks, Dad," I said. "This is unique."

"It was tucked in amongst R.T.'s effects — I have several boxes of his files in the spare room. I used to keep his papers in the library until your mother redecorated. It took me quite some time to locate this particular volume."

"Charles," Mom said, "get to the point."

"I was at the point — that the journal provides a valuable chronicle of a time gone by."

I thanked Dad for his brand of thoughtfulness, and kissed his dry cheek.

"We'll go," Mom said. "We've got errands to run. Will you be all right for the rest of the day? Are you going to the hair salon?"

"Don't think so, no."

"Have you arranged to meet some friends for lunch, I hope?"

I planned to go for a bike ride, alone, down to the beach. "I'm having lunch on the waterfront."

"Wonderful. See you tonight, then. We'll leave here at seven. And do look pretty. For me?"

~

I'd forgotten that a visit to the golf club entailed running the hi-how-are-you circuit with the sexagenarian set. My cheek was soon wet from the several avuncular-style birthday kisses I received on our arrival. I moistened my throat to match with the excellent champagne my father ordered. A quick look around the dining room when we'd entered had shown me I was the only adult present under age forty, but I didn't mind — I was too tired to mind much after the long downhill ride to the lake, and the equally long uphill ride back. And I wasn't averse to company, after an afternoon spent watching various parent-child and gay and straight and old and young couples promenade on the boardwalk, all apparently unaware of the joys of solitude, everyone in a happy pair. I'd showered on my return home, and blown dry my hair, and put on a dress, applied some makeup, searched out my pearls and clasped them around my neck, was grateful now for the burgherish pleasure to be found in an old-fashioned dinner.

The beef Wellington was a perfect pink throughout, the pastry butter-rich and flaky, the horseradish freshly grated, the Merlot mellow. The middle-aged waitress, whom my mother addressed by first name, seemed content with her lot in life, was not the oppressed and angry sort I dreaded being served by in Establishment haunts, not one to be flipping the bird at the gentry or spitting into the drinks behind the kitchen door. And the many interruptions of our conversation by the parental friends gave Dad no opportunity to drone on at excess length, Mom no chance to bring up the dating subject.

So smoothly did the evening flow that I agreed when Mom suggested we eat our dessert in the lounge, a clubby area where cigar smoking, cognac drinking, and leather furniture were encouraged. I allowed her to lead me first to the ladies' room — all gold brocade wallpaper and bamboo-look chairs set in front of gilt-framed mirrors — to freshen up. I was so relaxed I obeyed without objection when she instructed me to reline my eyes and reapply lipstick.

"Well, look who's here!" Mom exclaimed, in her best stage voice, when we entered the lounge and found Dad in conversation with Mom's golf buddy Marge and a man in his thirties who was presented to me as if he were the ultimate birthday gift. Or at minimum, a superior treat to the piece of chocolate layer cake I'd expected.

He stood up when I entered the room. He was tall, trim, attired in dressy casual clothes. His hair showed a touch of grey. His smile was warm, his eye contact faultless. He wished me happy birthday, and asked if I'd care to take coffee with him on the terrace. (My parents and Marge stood behind him, made run-along gestures, and mouthed "Go! Go!")

Outside, he treated the waiter politely, and did not smoke a cigar. He said he'd heard I was a teacher, spoke a few respectful words about the profession, commented on his children's schooling in the tone and manner of a semi-involved parent, made a not unfunny joke. He was Phil the lawyer, the recently divorced and perfectly pleasant son of Marge.

I responded in the polite cadences of my upbringing, and chilled my warmed-with-good-food-and-wine spirit with a bleak vision of a hypothetical future with Phil. To take up with one of his kind (with one of my kind), would be to sail and ski and cottage with him, to provide a gracious home where his children would be welcome, to give and go to dinner parties with his friends and colleagues — parties at which we'd drink too much and people would talk too much about politics. I'd be expected to travel with him and make corporate nice at important business conferences, to volunteer at his children's private schools, to plan around his golf games, to dine once a month with our parents at the club, to attend church services at Christmas and Easter, to organize lavish and special parties for his milestone birthdays, to endure a lavish and special party for my own. A life with Phil would be a repeat of my mother's life, in other words, a continuation of it, and might be Mom's idea of the low road, the straight and narrow, but was not what I wanted. Not now or ever.

No, despite all my resolutions and avowals, it seemed that what I really yearned for was to take a different path, a route of my own. What I wanted — attendant dangers be damned — was to careen around roads of a higher altitude. With someone more like, exactly like, Patrick.

~ Chapter 9 ~

"Come on in a minute," Jane said. "Alexandra wants to give you a birthday present."

I stepped inside the house. "I should never have let on I was having a birthday."

"Don't worry, it's nothing big."

Alexandra came downstairs with her hands behind her back. "Here. Happy birthday." She pushed a small, tissue-wrapped package toward me.

I unwrapped the delicate paper, pulled out a doll-sized hand-knitted pink sweater, and held it out in front of me by the long sleeves. "This is very cute," I said, though I had no idea why she'd given it to me.

"It's for Trixie."

"Trixie the fertility goddess?"

"Trixie the Earth Mother."

"How considerate of you to think of dressing her. She does have that odd habit of going around naked."

Alexandra said, "This way her private parts will be covered."

"Excellent idea." I looked more closely at the garment. "Did you make this yourself?"

"Yes. My Grandma Whitney taught me how to knit."

"Is that the same grandma who bakes? She must be a woman of many talents."

Jane said, "My mother is a *domestic* goddess."

"I'll go get your present for Blithe, Mom," Alexandra said, and ran off to the kitchen. Jane said, "My present's just a token, too. I hope you don't mind the fuss."

"On the contrary, Trixie and I will treasure our sweater forever."

"Actually, I wanted to talk to you about Trixie, later."

Alexandra came back and handed me a book-sized gift. "Here you go," she said. "From Mommy. Hey, we didn't sing." She looked at Jane. "Should we sing?"

"I don't think so, honey."

"Can I help you open it?" Alexandra said, and I let her rip open the paper, show me that it contained a faded first edition of Mary Elizabeth Bishop's classic *Rambles in Rose Park*.

"For my very own?" I said.

Jane smiled. "There were still a few copies in my mother's attic, and I figured you might be the only person left in Rose Park who would appreciate it."

I thanked her, put my gifts aside to take home later, and was about to leave with Alexandra for the park when Jane asked her to go upstairs and brush her teeth before leaving. Alexandra asked why, Jane said because, and Alexandra sighed and gave in. When we'd heard the bathroom door close upstairs, Jane said, "About Trixie: you mentioned she was a replica. Do you mind my asking where you bought her?"

"I didn't. I found her in a cupboard in my apartment when I moved in. My brother must have left her behind years ago."

"Where's your brother now?"

"He's a diplomat, posted in London. Why?"

"This'll sound crazy, but a similar figure was stolen from a museum in Berlin several years ago, and never recovered. That's what the article was about that Alexandra saw: stolen artifacts."

"You can't think Trixie is genuine?"

"I don't think so, but would you mind if I borrowed the figure and had a colleague take a look at it?"

"Like you did with the white marble?"

"With the owner's permission this time."

"Certainly you can. I'll bring her over later." Serve Noel right if Trixie turned out to be valuable and he'd left her behind.

~

There was a phone message from Patrick waiting for me when I came home from babysitting. He wanted to know if I'd like to go to a movie with him that night, and have dinner after. His voice on the tape sounded normal, unruffled, as if he had no fear of being refused, and wouldn't be devastated if he were. As if his request were reasonable.

The time was just after five. The night was young and so were we. Was he, anyway. I lay down on my bed and looked out the window at the cheery blue sky, and inside at some dust motes drifting in the afternoon sunlight, and I thought about the folly of having hope. About Gerald, and the treasure, and Marge's son Phil, and about Alexandra and the loneliness of the school yard.

I could lie on my bed and daydream for hours if I wanted, and not have to explain what I was doing or why. I could put on my pyjamas at six o'clock and eat chocolates and a bunch of grapes for dinner. I could not speak to a soul, not answer to anyone, not say or do anything that I might regret, that might come back to haunt or embarrass me later. I could cut myself free from the despair of wishing, stay home and not set myself up for a fall. Or I could do what I did: sigh softly, breathe in and out a few times, pick up the phone, and call Patrick.

~

The movie was a romantic suspense story about a charming bank robber, a gentleman crook of the kind found in movies that star big-name, fortysomething actors who choose beautiful twentysomething women to play their love interests.

I said, "Too much about that movie didn't make sense."

We were sitting in a trendy restaurant a few blocks away from the theatre — Patrick's suggestion. I'd ordered pad thai, he, steak frites.

"Like what?"

"Like when the robber shoots the security guard after a lifetime of pacifism. Or whatever the term is to describe peaceful bank-robbing."

"He had to shoot him to make the story work."

"Exactly. An unlikely but necessary plot development — I hate those. And what was with the woman? If she was supposed to be a bank manager, why were her clothes so skimpy and revealing?"

Patrick smiled at me over the wine and water glasses and the flame of the votive candle. "You're funny."

He was hatless, for once. He had good hair, light brown, wavy, longish. He hadn't been hiding a tacky haircut or a receding hairline under his cap. And he'd dressed up — he wore chinos, not jeans, and the neckline of his T-shirt formed a V instead of a scoop.

I drank some water. The "you're funny" remark I took to mean I sounded shrill. I pitched my voice to a lower register. "What did you think about the movie?"

"The robber character reminded me of my brother Ryan. How Ryan would like to think of himself, anyway."

"Is that affection I hear in your voice?"

"More like acceptance. He is the way he is."

"And how do you deal with that?"

He shrugged. "How do you deal with *your* brother's criminal past?"

"He hasn't done anything illegal yet, but give him time."

The light eyes flashed at me a second, then away. "Sorry, I must have misunderstood."

The waitress — a young woman with a geometric haircut, an exposed midriff, and a pierced nose — brought our plates to the table. I inhaled a not unpleasant bouquet of peanuts, fish sauce, and charred beef, and my befuddled-by-dating brain jumped, a little late, to a conclusion. "Has he?"

Patrick picked up his fork and knife. "Has who what?"

"Has Noel done anything criminal that you know of?"

Down went the silverware. Another flash of the eyes in mine. "I'm sorry. I thought you knew."

I demanded he tell me what I hadn't known — that Noel had been part of Ryan's break-and-enter gang.

"The Rose Park Burglar was a gang?"

"There were six or seven of them," Patrick said, between mouthfuls of steak. (I'd told him to eat while the food was hot.) "Ryan was the mastermind, but he spread out the work to various people, including your brother."

"My valedictorian, graduate-of-the-year brother."

"You don't believe me."

"No, I do. That's the trouble."

The waitress came by, filled up our water glasses, said to me, "You're not eating. Is the food okay?"

"It's fine," I said, and Patrick said, "Please eat."

I picked up my chopsticks, tried a mouthful of noodles — they weren't bad — and as soon as she'd gone, urged Patrick to continue.

"There's not much more to tell. Noel's job was to identify which houses in Rose Park contained the most goods worth stealing. And I think he also found the best entry points."

I could just see Noel, at age seventeen, pleasing my parents by making an appearance at a party in the neighbourhood, one of the endless round of celebrations organized to mark a wedding anniversary, or the start or end of a new school year, or the advent of the holiday season, or the arrival of a new shipment of fine wine. The same parties I avoided, he attended, in his navy blazer, yellow and navy striped tie, and yellow shirt — the better to show off his yellow hair. He came and accepted the single cocktail offered to underage teenagers by adults of my parents' class. "A small rum and coke would be great," he said, when he intended to have two or three. He stayed sober long enough to case the joint though, to notice the location, number, and portability of easily fenced assets like high-end stereo components and large pieces of antique silver, to make a quick estimate of the appraisal value of the jewellery worn by the hostess. To inquire with flattering interest when the family would be going away next on holiday or to the cottage, and to notice which side or back door was routinely left unlocked, which ground floor window easiest to slide open. I said, coldly, "Think of the excitement if he were the one who'd been caught."

"Ryan didn't rat on anyone else involved," Patrick said. "Part of the robber's code. Would you like some of my fries?"

"You're very calm about this."

"It's old news to me."

I stopped eating. "Wait a minute. How do you know so much about the gang? Don't tell me you were a part of it too."

"No. I was only thirteen when my mom found Ryan's hiding place for the stolen goods. I wasn't old enough or big enough to join up, but I heard about the whole scheme from

Ryan afterwards. Even after he was caught, he boasted about his crimes. Like he was some legend in his own time. The ass." Again, his voice held no trace of anger or resentment.

"But Noel had nothing to do with Ryan being caught, right? Noel didn't bring him down in any way?"

"How would he do that?"

"I don't know, but I heard one of those guys in the orange coveralls who come in to Bagel Haven — Lorenzo, is it? — say something about Noel and Ryan once that made me wonder."

"Lorenzo's another ass. He was in the gang too, and he never liked your brother. He and a couple of others Ryan had recruited from the east end distrusted the rich boy. You know how that goes." Patrick finished eating, laid his fork across his plate, tines down, next to his knife, the way my mother had taught me. "Let's order dessert," he said. "The pastry chef here is supposed to be good."

I took a time-out to the washroom, where I told myself there was nothing terribly shocking or unpredictable about the story I'd just heard. Nothing about Noel should surprise me anymore. Or bother me. I washed my hands in the freestanding salad-bowl-like sink that was a feature of the trendy bathroom — no gilt here — ejected Noel and the past from my mind, and returned to the table.

~

Patrick and I saw each other twice more that week, both times in the afternoon. I accompanied him on his dog runs to the ravine, and he took me down some of its lesser-known byways, showed me the new path that ran to a long-abandoned slate quarry on the other side of the creek. There hadn't used to be access from the ravine to the quarry, but the city had recently refurbished the area as a nature park, run some gravel walkways through it, built a few ponds and filled them with fish, planted bulrushes and swamp grasses, and declared it a meadow habitat, open to the public. The dogs roamed through, we sat on a bench and admired the view — hills and tree-lined ridges all around, the meadow before us — and Patrick told me about his childhood, that his mother had struggled to bring up the family on her own after his father died, that his first job, at age thirteen, had been as a dishwasher at a donut shop.

We walked on William Street and I pointed out where Mary Elizabeth Bishop had lived, explained about her rambles. We turned down Green Street, and I showed Patrick the Gothic Revival house with a peaked roof that I'd discovered doing research for Molly.

"But it's so small," he said. "Smaller than my mother's house."

"Look at its lines, though. They're so pleasing. Like a story-book cottage. Do you see?"

We walked and talked and he took my hand and held it in his cool, calloused one, and his touch felt natural and right.

On Friday evening, we went to another movie — a smart-mouthed romantic comedy that featured neither robbers nor brothers. On the way out of the theatre, Patrick said, "I should go home and feed Buck. Do you mind coming along?"

"Not at all," I said, as if the invitation didn't mean what I thought it meant. Hoped it meant.

He lived in a midtown, middle-class neighbourhood called Cooperdale, a mix of retail and restaurants and residential about ten minutes north of Bagel Haven. Not a bad area by any means, though we still might be headed for a dingy basement.

We drove in Patrick's pickup, an undistinguished grey vehicle. I filled the short drive time with natter — I congratulated him on living away from Rose Park, told him about the high-rise apartment I had in waiting, said, "I wish I could move in sooner than September. Living in my parents' coach house just perpetuates my image as the underachiever in the family."

"How is a teacher an underachiever?"

"It's a matter of context. In my family, there's Noel, then there's me. Where do you stand in your family hierarchy?"

He grinned. "Oh, I'm the big man in my clan. My older sister is married with kids, there's Ryan, my younger brothers are still in school and living at home, and I'm the guy with the three jobs who's on a first-name basis with the dog-owners who live in mansions."

"You have a third job beyond baking and dog-walking?"

He flicked on his turn signal. "In the winter, I plow snow." He pulled into a laneway behind a row of stores, parked at the back of a dry cleaning business, led me to a steel door illuminated by a plain light fixture, unlocked it, and showed me inside. A clean and well-lit set of stairs covered in speckled white tiles led to the second floor. At the top of the stairs, he unlocked another door and pushed his way past a happy Buck to invite me in.

He didn't live in a basement apartment. His place wasn't dingy, either, but clean and tidy, more so than my flat. And bigger than I expected. The entrance door opened into a modern kitchen — all white appliances and cupboards and a Scandinavian-look wood table, two chairs. Straight ahead was a large living room that fronted onto the street. It was furnished tastefully with a couch and easy chairs and an area rug and a coffee table, and was dominated by a wall unit that held a large television and an array of electronic components.

I looked them over from the kitchen doorway, said, "You have everything but a computer."

He was standing at the counter, filling Buck's dish. "I never got into computers. I was too busy making a living with my hands."

"Your three jobs must pay well — this apartment is very nice. You should see the mismatched mess I live in."

He put Buck's dish on the floor. "I bet your place has character."

"That's one word for it."

He washed his hands in the kitchen sink. With soap. "Are you hungry?"

I gulped and nodded.

"What do you feel like eating? There's a decent Italian restaurant down the street. Its desserts are overpriced, though."

My concerns were more about the where than the what — call me a loose woman as well as a resolution-breaker, but I wanted to eat in. Without making it obvious why. What would the heroine of an English suspense novel do in my situation? "Have you any eggs?" I said. "I could make us an omelette."

He had eggs, and butter, and ham, and some asparagus from the greengrocer on his block. There was also a loaf of brown bread from the nearest bakery, and a chunk of aged white cheddar from the cheese store. We had everything we needed for an English-style supper, including some white wine to wash it down with. We were only missing the blazing hearth to eat in front of, which we wouldn't miss in the heat of summer. We already had the dog lying on the rug.

We ate, he complimented me on my omelette-making skills, I praised his toast-making abilities, and we took our plates into the kitchen, where the trickle of nervousness I'd felt since we entered the apartment picked up speed, and threatened to become a shower. Before it could soak me right through, Patrick said, "I'll do the dishes later," took my hand, led me back into the living room, and sat down with me on the couch.

"Want to hear some music?" he said. He pushed some buttons on a remote, turned on some soft jazz, and moved close enough to me that our legs and sides touched. I tried to relax into the couch cushions, but relaxation was difficult, what with my nerve endings screaming, "Someone's touching us! Someone's touching us!" and threatening to throw the entire body into a swoon, and the organizational sector of my brain demanding to know what was next on the agenda, so it could plan the rest of the evening.

I ordered the nerves and brain to be quiet and laid my head on Patrick's shoulder, closed my eyes, regulated my breathing. So that when his free hand came around and stroked my cheek and the tender skin on my throat, all I needed to do, before I passed out from pure pleasure, was turn my face, lift my chin, and press my egg-and-wine-flavoured mouth to his.

~

Somewhere in the next twenty-four hours, I mustered the wit to call my mother and tell her I'd gone away for a few days, to visit a teacher friend who lived out of town. On the Sunday afternoon, I crawled out of Patrick's bed (a queen size dressed in bed linens both newer and more stylish than mine) and made my scheduled appearance to babysit Alexandra, during which I successfully impersonated a functioning adult who was not besotted and bedazzled. I did not sway on my feet when Jane whispered to me she'd had no word yet on Trixie's origin — the expert she wanted to consult was away on vacation. And I not only listened, but responded intelligibly when she asked if I'd like to join her family and friends for a potluck picnic party at the park the following weekend, to celebrate the beginning of summer. "I'd love to come," I said, "and I'll be sure to bring something tasty." Maybe Patrick. Maybe some of his baking.

I spent several afternoons and evenings of the week that followed at Patrick's place, in a lovely, disappointment-free, undepressed haze of bliss and infatuation. Because Patrick had to rise each morning at five to bake, I slept at home every night, but when my parents left the next Saturday to spend the long weekend at my uncle and aunt's cottage, and took Tup with them, I invited Patrick for an overnight visit chez moi, and to let his apartment air out a little.

I tidied my place beforehand, tried to bring it up to Patrick's level of cleanliness, a labour-intensive task, what with books and clothes and chocolate wrappers strewn about. Also my birthday presents, stacked up on a chair by the fireplace. I stowed Trixie's pink sweater in my underwear drawer where it seemed to belong, and tried to squeeze my grandfather's old journal into my overcrowded bookcase, but there was no room. I stood on my tiptoes and placed it on the top of the shelves, behind a three-inch lip of decorative moulding. I picked up the Mary Elizabeth Bishop book next, and tried to toss it up too, misjudged the distance, failed to break its fall, heard a crack.

Oops. I picked up the book and turned it over. The tumble had broken its spine, made a clean, full-length split between pages 178 and 179. My eyes dropped to the page, and I read:

> *On days when cloudbursts catch Jock and I unawares, we are glad of the bridges that span the ravine at intervals along the path where we ramble. The closest bridge runs atop Brock Road, the farthest under Field Street, and between is the King's Bridge, most pleasant of all because beneath its struts are not only two tall willows that provide canopies under which we may cower, but also a small roofed lodge where we can sojourn during a heavy downpour. Jock doesn't mind the wet, but I am glad of the lodge's protection, except in hunting season, when we are likely to find it overrun with gentlemen bearing guns!*

I coughed and spluttered (I'd swallowed a large, astonished gulp of air), sat down, read the passage through again, followed

by the next page and the one after that. But there was no further mention of the lodge, no better siting of a location some
two hundred yards away from the spot I'd searched.

I ran to my desk, opened the puzzle book file, pulled out
the photocopy of the old town plan that I'd used to locate the
treasure site, to find the lodge, to do every mistaken and for-
saken thing I'd done in the ravine. I stared at the photocopy,
and noticed — imagined? — that the square which marked
the lodge site on the plan seemed to be drawn in a darker,
thicker line than any other on the page. I closed my eyes, tried
to envision the path under the bridge, retrace my steps. And I
let a lust for the treasure overtake me once more.

~ Chapter 10 ~

Patrick's hat was still on, though it was late, though we were seated at my kitchen table, though it had taken me twenty minutes since he'd arrived with Buck, a backpack, and a cake tin, to relate the complete treasure saga.

"Well?" I said. "Say something."

"I like that picture on your mantelpiece. Where's it from?"

"My mother bought it for me in England. But what about the treasure? What do you think?"

"This new location could be another false lead."

"You're right. It could. Or not."

He scratched his head under the hat brim. "And those trees you planted?"

"I'm afraid they were just a cover story."

"I thought you cared about those trees. I've been looking after them."

"I'm sorry. And thank you. But I couldn't tell the truth at that stage of the game. I didn't tell anyone what I was doing. Not even Molly, not until after I'd failed. You understand that, don't you?"

He tipped his chair back, opened the fridge door, put the cake tin inside, let the door swing closed.

"You shouldn't have told me the truth now."

"Why not?"

"Because what if we go tomorrow morning and dig in this new location, and we find the treasure? It should be yours, but what if I decide I have a right to a share because I helped you take it out of the ground? What would you do? Have you thought of that? Shit, Blithe. You should know better. You should know people can't be trusted."

I had a blazing headache. "What are you talking about?"

He stood up, came over to me, put his hands on my neck, and started to squeeze — no, that's not what happened. He came over, rested his hands on my shoulders, and said, "You should be careful, that's all."

Yes, but I could trust him, so what was his point? Before I could vocalize the thought, he released me — lifted his hands and his mood — and said, "So what time should we hit the ravine tomorrow morning?"

We stayed up till midnight planning and packing. I was too wired to sleep much, and woke before six, before the alarm. We were out the door with Buck at six-ten — no shower, no coffee. We'd secured the digging equipment in the red wagon the night before, so we arrived at Cawley Gardens at six-fourteen.

On our way into the ravine, we saw a lone woman with a golden retriever coming up. It was too early for conversation, and I doubted anyone fool enough to enter thicketland at that time of day would think much of a couple with a dog taking their tarp-covered wagon for a walk anyway. We went for the averted-eye nod and the muttered good morning and passed by.

We followed the footpath, accompanied by birdsong and creek gurglings, the rattling of Buck's dog tags and the squeaking of the wagon wheels, walked under the first bridge and past the false site marked on the plan. When King's Bridge came into view, I had to fight the impulse to run.

As per pre-arrangement, I kept an eye on the wooded area to the right side of the path and Patrick covered the left. Because we couldn't help ourselves, we both looked on both sides. But I was the first to spot the two huge willow trees to the east. They were three storeys tall, and spaced fifteen feet apart, just south of the bridge. I jogged in to them through the undergrowth, stepped underneath the drooping branches of the closest tree, stared at the ground at my feet. I was standing among patches of some tall grassy material. Underneath was a leafy ground cover, also sparse. There was moss and sticks and small stones around, and about two yards away, on a diagonal from my left toe, what could be the edge of a moss-covered iron ring. I pounced down on all fours, grabbed hold of something cold and furry and wet with dew.

Buck came up beside me, bumped me sideways, sniffed around my hand. I pushed him away, and summoned Patrick over. "Look," I whispered. "Here."

He squatted down and touched the surface of the ground on either side of the ring, tried to scrape away some of the mossy stuff with his fingernails. He pulled out a Swiss army knife we'd found in a toolbox in my parents' garage, opened it to its biggest blade, and scraped some more, uncovered a tiny patch of wet and weathered wood.

We unpacked our tools — two trowels, a spade, and a shovel — and set to work. We scraped the surface around the ring in ever wider concentric circles, worked our way out to the edges. We didn't speak, other than to say, "Go to your left more," and "Hand me the knife for a second." And once I wondered aloud how long the amount of plant material we were rubbing off would take to grow.

When most of the surface of the trap door was exposed, we saw that its four edges were half-buried under a quarter-inch of hardened topsoil. So we spent another twenty minutes scraping and digging and spading until our tenth or twelfth exploratory tug on the iron ring gave a slight sign of yield. Followed by a further bout of work until we'd uncovered all the edges.

Even then, when no earth held the door down from above, Patrick's strong-armed pulls on the ring did not budge it up — some force sealed it at the sides or below. I tried inserting a trowel under one of the door edges and prying, but I just bent the trowel's blade. I sat back on my heels and swore. Patrick's turn to try. He picked up the spade, inserted it slowly and strategically on one side, and lifted a corner of the door clear of the ground by a half-inch.

It still wouldn't open all the way. Patrick wiped the sweat from his forehead with the bottom of his T-shirt, said, "You want to take it from here?" I said no, you go, and he carried on, moved the spade over a few inches, lifted the door a bit, shifted the spade sideways, lifted a little more. He made me wield the tool when there was only one stubborn corner left. He stepped aside, held the spade handle until I took it from him, and stood back while I made the final push and freed the last bit. "Pull it open," he said.

I crouched down, pulled on the ring, opened the door, heard the wood creak, felt it shudder, and looked into a hole about three feet square and four feet deep, lined with dusty red brick. Inside were a few small heaps of black earth scattered on its floor, about fifty crawling bugs, several spider webs, some sandy material in the corners, a bit of garbage — a crumpled clear plastic bag. And nothing else.

I pushed the locker door all the way back — a hundred and eighty degrees — laid it flat on the ground, dropped my legs into the hole, sat gingerly on the rim, bent over, sifted through the dirt and sand with my trowel, picked up the plastic bag, felt the walls for any opening or loose brick or false bottom.

Nothing. Again. Always.

Patrick said, "What's that you're holding?"

Disappointment had seized up my chest, my throat, my voice box. I croaked, "A bag. Garbage." I crumpled the bag in my hand, felt something inside it — a small piece of paper.

With clumsy fingers, I opened the bag and pulled out the paper, a narrow strip of plain white bond, typed with one faded sentence. In a monotone, I read it aloud: "Ha ha — got here first."

"Asshole!" Patrick said, and threw his trowel on the ground, stalked away a few steps, took off his hat, ran his fingers through his hair. Buck, who lay panting on the ground nearby, pricked up his ears.

"Who's an asshole? Jeremiah Brown?"

"No, the jerk who found the treasure and left you that note. It's like he knew."

"Knew what?"

"He knew someone else would come along. He digs up the treasure and doesn't tell anyone about it, but he can't resist leaving the note behind to brag about being here first. Fucking asshole prick."

The force of his anger — the strength of his emotion in contrast to the impassivity he'd shown during the salvage operation — was sufficient to pull me out of the slough of despond I'd fallen into, to even my keel. I placed the paper back in the bag, and climbed out of the hole. "I don't know. I think I might be relieved by this turn of events."

"Relieved?" He still sounded angry. "How can you be relieved?"

"Because I solved the mystery, but I don't have to deal with all the complications of the money."

"Are you nuts?"

"Listen for a minute. Imagine what it would be like if the money were here. We'd have to remove it and hide it somewhere and decide whether to tell people about it. What about Molly? How could I not tell her? And my parents. And as you pointed out last night, I'd feel like I should be sharing the treasure with you, and with Molly and Alexandra for helping in the search, but in what proportion? And what if someone else tried to claim it? In no time, the treasure could become a huge burden."

He seemed to have calmed down, shut his indignation off. "Okay," he said, mildly. "I understand now. You *are* nuts."

I tried to match his tone. "And anyway, if I'd found the treasure, and we stayed together, I'd always think you only loved me for my money."

Damn. That hadn't come out right, that mention of love. I'd meant it in the hypothetical sense. And even if the term might not be hypothetical in my case, I knew that usage of the word love on day ten of a couple's life was not a good idea. Especially coming on top of a sleepless night and a few hours of manual labour for no reward.

But Patrick lurched at me, hugged me from behind with great depth of feeling and much arm pressure, and said in my ear, "I'd only love you for you, not for anything else."

I'd had enough drama for one coffee-free morning. I turned around in his embrace, said, "Ditto," wiggled out of the hug, and looked down into the hole. "I guess we'd better cover this back up."

We piled the earth we'd scraped off the trap door back on top of it, camouflaged the site with branches and grass and leaves scattered around, and saw no one on our way out. It was eight o'clock when we arrived home, and we were tired, but we didn't go back to bed. We made coffee, and drank it, and talked. We debated whether to announce our discovery of the empty locker (I said we had to, for history's sake, Patrick thought history would survive without our news.) Once I'd reiterated that

I couldn't not tell Molly, we resolved the issue in my favour, and moved on to the more vexing question about who could have found the treasure before us, and when, and most of all, how?

I could have sworn I was the first person since Jeremiah Brown to see the message in the cornerstone, and if the unknown treasure-absconder hadn't learned the location from Brown's map, how had he found it? By happenstance? Had he seen Brown bury it? Had he heard a death-bed confession? Furthermore, why hadn't he gone public with his discovery?

"Why would he?" Patrick said. "What crook wants publicity?"

"Why do you think the person is a crook? We could be talking about a fine upstanding citizen here."

"Yeah, right."

When we'd exhausted all possible theories and found no answers, we went to bed for a few hours and slept, side by side, in the morning sunlight. We woke just after noon, I said I was hungry, and Patrick said, "There are the lemon tarts I brought for the picnic, or are we still going to that?"

~

The group gathered at the park was larger than I expected — Jane, her husband and kids, and her assorted friends and relatives, all told, numbered about thirty. People reclined on blankets spread out on the grass, or stood in the shade of trees. Some of the older folks sat on park benches, and most of the kids ran around in an unorganized game of soccer. Except for Alexandra. When she saw us, she came over from the bench where she had been sitting reading a book, looked at Patrick, then at me, and said, "Are you two still just acquaintances?"

I said, "We seem to be dating now, but we weren't the last time you asked."

She pulled us toward Jane. "Look, Mom. Here's Blithe. With Patrick." She might as well have added a nudge and a wink.

I presented the lemon tarts to Jane, told her Patrick had made them. She thanked him nicely and directed us both to the main course picnic table, which was laid with fried chicken, potato salad, biscuits, cold cuts, coleslaw, wedges of a smoked salmon and dill frittata, and a huge salad made with designer greens, crumbled blue cheese, and toasted walnuts. "Please help yourselves," she said.

I exclaimed at the bounty, and Patrick said, "The biscuits are so tall. Who made them?"

"I did." A white-haired woman on the other side of the table extended her hand across. "I'm Gillian Whitney, Jane's mother. How do you do?"

We introduced ourselves, Patrick asked Gillian how she had achieved such impressive biscuit height, the two of them started talking about butter to flour ratio, and Jane moved me away and into the shade of a tree. "I wanted to tell you about the results of Trixie's tests," she said.

"Oh, yes. What happened? She isn't real, is she?"

"No. My colleague at the museum came back from vacation, took one look at her, and laughed me out of the lab. Apparently the figure's made out of plastic that's been moulded to look like polished stone. Though it's a very good reproduction of the stolen piece, he said, faithful to detail and size, and not something he knew of the exhibiting museum having issued. He wondered where it could have come from."

"I have no idea." And now that I knew about Noel's past experience with stolen goods, I was afraid to find out.

"Anyway, I'll drop Trixie over to your place later today, along with a formal apology for having doubted her origins."

"No apology necessary. Think how exciting it would be if you'd found the missing fertility goddess." Almost as exciting as if I'd found a buried treasure.

~

I picked up Molly at Glenwood late the next morning and led her on a walk into the ravine. "What's so secret you couldn't tell me on the phone?" she said.

"I'll explain everything in a second. Thanks for coming out."

"I shouldn't really — I'm behind on my work. But you've piqued my curiosity."

"Okay. I'll make it fast."

I'd spent the morning at the city archives office, asked to see the file copy of the original town plan from which my photocopy had been made, and found the true lodge location to have been crudely obliterated with white-out, the fake site drawn in with what looked like a felt-tip pen. When I drew these markings to the attention of the clerk, he glanced at the document, opined that the alterations weren't fresh, and could have been made years or decades ago. They might have been the work of a misguided archivist predecessor seeking to make a correction, he said, but he didn't seem to care how or when the changes were made. His job was to store and keep track of the archived material, not to defend its integrity.

I told Molly this, and about the Mary Elizabeth Bishop book, led her to the weeping willow site, swept aside our camouflage, opened the trap door and showed her the empty locker. From my backpack, I produced a copy of the note that had been inside.

She sat down on the edge of the locker the way I'd done the day before, took the paper from me, read its message, said, "Wow."

"I know."

"Wow, and oh dear." She was flushed and sweaty, and breathing hard.

I bent forward. "Are you all right?"

"Just hot, and tired." She wiped some sweat off her upper lip. "And sorry your search ended this way."

We rehashed all the possible explanations for the absence of the treasure, or I did. She just sat in the locker and listened.

I said, "Now I'm wondering if this note is what Jeremiah Brown intended treasure-hunters to find all along. Maybe the Glenwood treasure was not a hoax but a prank with a moral about the danger of valuing money too highly. Or something."

Molly clambered out of the hole, brushed some dirt off the seat of her pants. "I don't know what to think. About anything."

I re-camouflaged the locker, and we headed back, trudged on in silence. Until she said, "Did you do all the work yourself? The digging and scraping?"

"I had help. Remember Patrick, the baker at Bagel Haven?"

"Do I?"

"You said he was cute and Hannah would hook up with him given the chance."

"Oh yes, him."

"We're seeing each other right now, and well, he helped me."

Molly stopped walking, grabbed my arm. "You have a new boyfriend?"

"So it seems."

She patted me on the back. "Good for you!" The degree of her enthusiasm, the width of her smile, made it clear how little hope she'd had for my romantic future. "What happened to your pledge to lay low and keep your neck in?"

"Rather quickly abandoned, wasn't it? Proof my word can't be trusted, I guess."

Her voice came back gruff. "Far from it. Proof of your open mind and generous nature."

She was quiet again after that, but when we'd climbed the final hill and stopped to rest at the top on a bench, she said, "You know what you should do? You should write a piece about your discovery for the *Rose Park Monthly*."

"Why?"

"People love local history stories. And it would be great advance publicity for the puzzle book, if I ever get the thing written. How about I call the editor and set it up for you?"

"But I don't know anything about newspaper writing."

"You'll do fine. And anyway, this is *your* story, has been for years. I remember you talked about it when you were a teenager."

A picture came up on my mental screen, in sharp focus, like a slide projected on a white wall — a still photo of Hannah and Molly and me in the kitchen at Glenwood, a glass of milk on the table shot through with sunlight. I said, "Do you remember when you suggested I make the search for the treasure my life's quest?"

"Did I? That was stupid advice. I should have told you to find a job you can stand and a good person to love and to hell with foolishness like the treasure."

I heard the crispness in her voice, attributed it to the hard going in the warm weather, the pressure of her work waiting at home. "I don't know," I said. "Maybe if I'd been more single-minded about the pursuit — "

"You'd have found out sooner that someone else got to it first." She pushed herself off the bench, and offered me a hand up. "So can I call that editor?"

~ Chapter 11 ~

On the second day of the summer's first real heat wave, Arthur greeted every customer with, "Hot enough for you?" followed by, "Gonna be another scorcher." The arrival of Fred, the older man with the visor, inspired him to add to his repertoire, "But I'll take the heat over the cold anytime," a sentiment with which Fred claimed to concur.

Not me. I was looking forward to a day spent sealed up in my air-conditioned apartment, was delaying my departure for the steamy bike ride home. When I could do so no longer, when I'd eaten every crumb of my bagel and sucked up every drop of juice with my straw, I carried my plate and cup to the counter, said goodbye to Patrick, and received back a curt nod I tried not to interpret as another example of the slight coolness he'd shown me since I'd told Molly about finding the locker.

"I understand why you had to tell her," he'd said, "but why would you agree to write a story for the newspaper?"

"Why not?"

"Because when it's published, the whole world will know what's going on."

"But the whole world — the neighbourhood, anyway — already knows about the treasure. The paper prints a local history feature on it every few years. My article will just be an update."

"Still."

"Still what?"

"You'll be calling attention to yourself."

"A minor, low-profile kind of attention."

"You just don't understand, do you?"

No, I didn't. I also didn't understand why he was so snappy with me later that same day at my place, when I surprised him looking at the Mediterranean landscape. I'd ta-taed off to take a bath, left Patrick reclining in an apparent state of torpor on my couch, the remote in his hand, the television tuned to some sporting event. But in the seconds it took me to realize I'd forgotten to bring my reading material into the bathroom, and to open the door to go get it, Patrick moved. Was standing by the fireplace when I came out, his back to me, holding the Mediterranean picture in front of him, at arm's length. He turned, and was about to set the picture on the coffee table when he saw me, and nearly dropped it.

"What are you doing?" we both said. My tone was curious, his downright accusatory.

I strode over to the bedside table and picked up the novel I was reading. "Getting my book."

He said, "I wanted to take a closer look at the picture. Do you mind?"

"You don't have to sound so snippy about it."

"You scared me."

"I'll have to make sure I don't scare you again if this is how you react," I said, and retreated in mid-dudgeon to the bathroom, not sure what the incident had been about — were we spending too much time together? did he need more "space"? — but determined not to make too much of it, not to dwell.

So at Bagel Haven that overheated morning, I resisted the temptation to ascribe any heavy significance to Patrick's curtness, and told him I would be home most of the day, working on the newspaper story, which, as far as he knew, was proceeding apace. What I really hoped was that I could use the air-conditioned time to wrestle my clunky first draft into a second one that I wouldn't be too embarrassed to call my own.

I waited to see if a mention of the story might set him off, but it didn't appear to. He said he'd call me later, would spend the afternoon with his married sister who lived in the suburbs and was home with her kids for the summer, going crazy. I told myself that I imagined the eagerness with which he returned to work, I quelled the fear that he would any day now tell me our relationship was doomed because I was too wordy and not built like a Brazilian underwear model, and I walked out into the soupy air.

At home, I read over my draft, made helpful notes in the margins such as "awkward," "no," and "fix," sat down at the computer, worked for an hour, and tied all my sentences in knots. I took a break, called Molly. "Help. So far the piece sounds about as fascinating as a university essay."

"You're probably trying too hard. Start over and write in your own voice, your speaking voice. Think natural, think informal, wield your sense of humour. If that doesn't work, call me back."

I hung up the phone, dished out a scoop of orange sherbet, and ate it slowly, let each mouthful soften on my tongue before I swallowed it. When I returned to the keyboard, I abandoned the verging-on-pedantic tone of my earlier draft and tried a more informal approach, as if I were telling the story to a friend. By four o'clock, I had written a thousand new words, of which perhaps six hundred felt close to right. The piece still needed sprucing up and splicing, but the essence was there.

So when I walked into the Market soon after, my step was light. Even the stroll to the store in the intense humidity hadn't fazed me; during it, I'd seen black storm clouds to the west. Maybe the weather forecaster's prediction that the heat would break with evening rain would come true. I picked up my few items — a piece of feta, some shrimp, tomatoes, and a package of orzo, lined up at the cash, and mentally began to reword a tricky subordinate clause in the second sentence of my article. I came to attention when the woman in front of me in line turned and said hello. It was Jane's mother, Gillian, buying butter and eggs.

She said, "Do you remember me, dear?"

"Of course. You're Gillian Whitney. You taught Alexandra how to knit and you baked biscuits for the picnic."

"I've heard a lot from Jane and Alexandra about you, too." She eyed me intently, as if I reminded her of someone, and I feared she would mention the Morrison name, say she knew my uncle or played bridge with my aunt. But she said, "Weren't you at the picnic with the young man who bakes bagels?"

"Patrick? Yes, he's — he's a friend. He brought the lemon tarts."

"I tried one — it was very nice. He has a light touch of the kind one rarely encounters these days. I told him that today when I saw him downtown."

My social smile faded. "Sorry? You saw him where?"

"At a restaurant supply store. We talked about cookie sheets and rolling pins at the picnic and I told him where I bought my equipment. The conversation reminded me I needed a few things, so I went downtown this afternoon, stopped by the store, and bumped into your Patrick. But that's this city for you, isn't it? Everywhere I go, I run into people from Rose Park."

Including people who were supposed to have spent the day with their married sisters in the suburbs. "Was he alone?" Or had there been a Brazilian underwear model at his side, towering over a revolving display of whisks?

"As far as I could tell. He bought a cookie sheet. We only talked for a minute. He has very distinctive eyes, doesn't he? That variegated blue of the iris? I've only seen that once or twice before."

"Yes, they're unusual." A Brazilian underwear model in her underwear.

"Anyway, dear, nice to see you again. Oh! Look at that rain!"

I turned where she pointed, toward the shop windows, to the sight of heavy rain pouring down from a dark sky.

~

There was a phone message at home. Not from Patrick. From Molly. "I'd be happy to proof your newspaper piece before you submit it, if you'd like. Or if you'd rather I didn't, that's fine, too. And guess what? I e-mailed Hannah about your discovery in the ravine and she replied right away instead of waiting her usual week to get back to me. I told you people would find the story interesting!"

There were no other messages.

I sank onto the couch, felt some rainwater drip off my hair onto my lap, stood up, grabbed a towel, draped it on my shoulders, sat back down. My worry about Patrick was reflexive, an old habit, baggage left over from my expect-nothing attitude, an attitude I wasn't altogether ready to give up, recent relationship euphoria notwithstanding. I still needed to be ready, if — that is, when — the inevitable let-down came, to avoid the humiliation of being hoodwinked on top of the usual devastation and bereavement. If Patrick were going to act distant, I'd prepare myself for the worst. So at least — and what a threadbare, tattered scrap of pride I would be clinging to — no one could say I hadn't seen it coming.

The phone rang. I picked it up on the second chime.

"Hey," Patrick said. He sounded happy, upbeat. "How'd your day go?"

"Good. I made some headway on my newspaper story. How about you?" I shut my eyes. "How was your sister?"

"She'd already made plans for the day, so I did some errands downtown."

Eyes open. "What kind of errands?"

"The shopping kind. I picked up a gift for you."

"Why?"

"I heard you had a birthday recently."

"Oh, no."

"Can Buck and I come over and give it to you?"

~

The gift was not a cookie sheet. (He'd bought that for himself.) It was a scale model, made of wood, of the little house on Green Street, the one-storey Gothic Revival cottage with the ginger-bread trim. I could hold it in the palm of my hand. "It's beautiful. Where did you get it?"

"From a company that makes architectural models. I took in some photographs and rough measurements. Your friend Jane Whitney told me about the place."

"Jane? How'd you get talking to her?"

"I had the idea, and I remembered you said she worked at the museum, so I called her and asked if she knew of a model supplier."

Not only thoughtful, but resourceful, too. "Well, I love it. Thank you." I set the little house on the mantel, in pride of place, and came back to sit with him on the couch, to lie in the crook of his arm, and lay my hand on his T-shirted chest, and listen to the rain pelt down on my roof. "Let's stay in tonight," I said, "and sleep here."

"What about your parents? Are they away?"

"No, but I don't care. I'm tired."

"I'm not tired. I feel good. Like it's a new day and I'm starting over."

I yawned. "Starting what over?"

"Life. You relax. I'll make dinner."

~

Patrick woke at six the next morning and took Buck out for a stroll in the unending rain, came back to bed, fell asleep. The ring of the phone woke us both. "What time is it?" I said.

"Eight thirty-seven. You going to answer that?"

"No. I don't feel like talking."

Patrick rolled over. "I should get up. I have dogs to walk."

"In the rain?"

The phone stopped ringing.

"Dogs don't care about rain."

I adjusted the pillows under my head. "I should get up and work on my story."

The phone rang again.

Patrick sat up, swung his legs over the side of the bed. "Do you want eggs for breakfast?"

"No food till later. I want coffee, but I'll make it."

He pulled on some clothes. "You really not going to get that phone?"

I pulled the sheet over my head. The ringing stopped.

He leaned down and kissed my shoulder. "I'll be back."

The phone rang for the third time after Patrick had gone, before the coffee had dripped through. I swore and picked it up.

Mom's voice said, "Blithe? Is that you? Are you all right?"

"I'm fine. How many times have you called?"

"Why didn't you answer before?"

"Are you calling about something urgent?"

"I was worried about you. That grey truck parked on the street all night, and then at breakfast, Dad told me he saw a scruffy young man going up the stairs to your place at six-thirty this morning, and you didn't leave that pot-bellied figure on your porch so I didn't know what was going on."

She'd checked the porch? "There's nothing to worry about. I had a friend over, that's all. And I never agreed to use your signal."

"I wish you would. What friend?"

Might as well tell her now as later. "Patrick Hennessy."

She took a few seconds to choke down this news. "Dad thought so but I told him he must be mistaken. How old is that boy? He seems so young — a teenager."

"He's twenty-six."

"Twenty-six? Is that so?"

"Why were you calling again?"

"Why? Because Dad said I should tell you about Noel's visit — he's coming home next week."

Just in time to ruin my relationship with Patrick. I tucked the phone receiver into my shoulder and poured the coffee. "What brings him to town?"

"What do you mean? He's coming to see his family."

I added milk. "What's the real reason?"

"Oh, Blithe. Why are you always so negative? He's attending a meeting in New York and he's stopping over on the way." Though he'd never stopped over before when in New York. Mom had always flown down and met him there.

"Thanks for the warning, anyway."

"He's eager to see you. He specifically asked if you'd be here. And he wanted to know if you liked the picture he picked out for your birthday."

"He picked out the Mediterranean landscape?"

"As soon as we saw that painting, he said, 'You know who this would be good for? Blithe, in that apartment over the garage. Isn't her birthday coming up soon?'"

Could he have changed? No. "I find that story difficult to believe."

"I think we'd better talk some other time, when you're in a better mood."

~

Molly took off her reading glasses. "The piece is very good," she said. "The anecdotes about your personal history with the treasure work well, and give it a nice human interest angle. And I love the part about the little girl and the mnemonics."

"I'm hoping Alexandra will like that part, too."

We were sitting in Molly's kitchen. She'd invited me over for lunch and to read the draft of my newspaper piece. Dr. Greer was at the tennis club, waiting for a court to dry.

She got up and went over to the fridge. "There are a few small things you could fix up, there always are, but nothing major."

"What small things?"

"To begin with, you could change the order of some of the paragraphs, and improve the flow. Should I show you what I mean?" She brought over a platter of chicken salad and set it alongside a bowl of green salad and a basket of sliced olive bread. "Or have I gotten your back up already? I know from my own experience how thin-skinned writers can be about their work."

"Show me first, and I'll see how thin my skin and high my back afterwards."

We managed a short editing suggestion without me taking umbrage — how could I, when Molly's suggestions made complete sense? — and moved on to eat a lunch made delicious by the inclusion of mango chutney in the chicken salad, and toasted pine nuts and crumbled feta in the green one.

While we ate, Molly entertained me with stories about her work on the new twin detective novel she'd set in Santa Fe, where she'd lived briefly, twenty years before, and told me that she kept having to call the Santa Fe tourist information office to verify the location details she'd thought she knew. "My point is that I'm still behind schedule, so I'm wondering if you might do me a favour."

"You'd like me to go scout Santa Fe for you?"

"No, I'm wondering if you would consider collaborating with me on writing the puzzle book."

"Define collaborate."

"I mean *The Rose Park Puzzle Book:* text by Blithe Morrison, illustrations by Molly Greer."

Why would she suggest such a thing? Was she feeling sorry for me? "You must be joking."

"I'm not. I'm dead serious. At least say you'll think about it."

"Okay." I'd already started to think about it, was surprised by how strong an urge I had to say, "Yes, I'll do it!" I must have wanted this unconsciously since I'd started the research, despite the small obstacle that I had no qualifications for the job.

Molly began to clear the dishes. When I stood up to help, she said, "I'm okay. Sit and mull."

"I can move and mull at the same time."

"In that case, would you mind running downstairs and bringing up a jug of milk? There's none up here, and I'd like to steam some for our coffee. You remember where the fridge is down there, don't you?"

I ran down to the basement, walked through the laundry room to the fridge room, and stepped right into three inches of standing water, a monstrous puddle that spread from wall to wall. I made an *aagh* sound, opened the fridge door, grabbed the jug of milk, ran back up, and stood, one stair down, in the kitchen doorway. "Molly, there seems to be a problem."

"There's no milk in that fridge either?"

"Part of the basement is flooded."

"Oh no." She wiped her hands on a tea towel, took the milk from me, set it on the counter. "How bad is it? Let me see."

I followed her downstairs. "Have you been down since the rain?"

"No. Where's the water?"

"In the fridge room."

"Shit," she said, when she'd flicked on the switch in the fridge room so that we could see the overhead light reflected in the shimmering carpet of water below. "Double shit."

Two sides of the room were lined with open shelving that contained bulk household supplies like paper items and canned goods, but the lowest level of shelf was high enough off the floor to have escaped damage. Lined up on the wall nearest to us were the fridge, the washer, the dryer and a big laundry sink, all stand-ing in water. The remaining wall held several metal filing cabinets, only touched by the water at their bases, and a stack of cardboard archive boxes, the bottom one of which was partly submerged.

I pointed. "We should do something about that box. Are the contents valuable?"

"That's only Hannah's old stuff," Molly said. "God, what a mess."

"Have you got any rubber boots?"

"By the side door. There should be two pairs there — mine and Larry's. Could you bring them both?"

Molly found a plunger in the basement bathroom. I brought the boots. We each pulled on a pair and waded in. Molly went straight for the drain in the center of the floor, reached into the cold water with her hand, made a grossed-out face, removed the grill, stood up, and began to plunge. I sloshed through to the boxes, and carried them one at a time out of the room. The last was the waterlogged one.

Molly had her hand underwater again. "This feels so disgusting," Molly said, "as if I had my hand in ... wait. I think I've cleared it." The drain belched, and the water slowly started to move. She pulled out her hand, covered in brown goop. "Leaves," she said. "Dead leaves."

I gave her a thumbs-up sign from the other room and lifted the lid of the wet box, looked inside. It was filled with blue plastic binders, labelled with dates. The first one, from nine years back, contained black-and-white contact sheets placed inside clear plastic sleeves. The pictures were mainly of people. No one I recognized, nor any of the settings. They were probably, given the time frame, friends from Hannah's art college.

I pulled out more binders, laid them on the ground. The covers of the binders from the bottom of the box were streaked with water. The bottom-most binder was wet inside, too — the plastic sleeves were slick with moisture, stuck to each other. And the photographs? I pulled out the edge of one of the contact sheets — a page of people-less outdoor scenes this time. It was dry. I slipped it back into the sleeve and was about to turn the page when I recognized one of the pictures halfway down the first row — the rain-swept image Hannah had taken of Cawley Gardens.

I turned to tell Molly I'd happened onto Hannah's old puzzle book pictures, but she was splashing and swearing in the other room, better not disturbed. I put the binder down, reentered the wet room, took an unopened package of paper towels off the shelf, said to Molly, "I'll see if I can dry off some of Hannah's photographs."

"Thanks." She didn't look up from steering the water into a slow-moving vortex around the drain.

I used a sheet of paper towel to wipe off each side of the sleeves in the wet binder, placed a dry sheet between each pair of pages, and moved onto the next. I wiped, inserted a dry sheet, and turned the page. Wiped, inserted, and turned.

The first picture of Noel, at about age twenty, his golden boy peak, showed up near the end of the book. It was a head and shoulder shot of him, in a polo shirt with the collar turned up, a cigarette hanging from the corner of his mouth. There followed a few different angles of the close-up, then some pictures taken from farther back that showed he stood against a background of leaves, outdoors. The last row of contacts on that sheet were full-figure shots. Most of them were candid, but in one, he posed for the camera with a pleased-as-punch grin on his face, and leaned against a tree. I gasped when I saw that picture, and turned quickly to see if Molly had heard me. She hadn't — she was too engrossed with the flood water.

I removed the sheet from its plastic covering, laid it between two dry paper towels, carried it to the laundry room, held it up to the light. Under the extra illumination, I could make out that in the full figure shot, Noel held a cigarette in his right hand. I also saw that my gasp had been warranted — there was no mistaking that the tree Noel leaned against was one of the willows next to the burial place of the Glenwood treasure.

I didn't stop to think. Some sort of deep-rooted clan instinct drove me to slip the contact sheet under the back of my T-shirt and tuck it into the waistband of my skirt. I apologized to Molly, said I had to get going — I was due for a playdate with Alexandra in twenty minutes. "I'll let myself out. Where should I put Hannah's binders? The box is history, I'm afraid." Cue hollow laughter.

She said to leave everything where it was and she'd deal with it later. "Thanks so much for your help. I don't usually make my guests clean up the basement."

"I'm sorry I can't stay and do more. Thank you for the lovely lunch, and for the editing." I backed away, lest she see the edges of the contact sheet through my shirt.

"The newspaper piece will be great!" she called after me, made me feel more guilty than I already did about not showing her the photo, not telling her that Noel seemed to have found the treasure and Hannah knew. But I couldn't, could I? I couldn't say, "Look, Molly. These photographs indicate that my wastrel brother and your two-faced daughter have known about the treasure for years and never told anyone."

No, before I told her anything, I had to think the significance of the discovery through, ascertain who had done right and wrong and how much and to whom. But I wouldn't have time to think until after my stint with Alexandra, which really did begin in a few minutes. I was on time when I rang Jane's doorbell. And miles away.

Jane led me into the main floor family room, where Alexandra lay on a couch, watching a video. Josh was lying on the floor, his head propped up in his hands. Jane said, "Alexandra was up much of the night coughing — she has allergies — so we're looking at a quiet time indoors today for you two. I'll take Joshua out somewhere noisy."

What had Noel done with the money? How had he taken it out of the ravine, and to what bank? How had he explained the age of the bills?

Jane seemed to expect a reply.

"Uh, if Alexandra's up to it," I said, "we could play cards or a board game."

"Good idea." Jane picked up her purse and her keys. "Come on, Joshua, let's go."

I sat down on an easy chair facing the television, tried to find space in my crowded mind to process the bright technicolour images on the screen, said, "Is this *Sleeping Beauty?*"

"Yeah."

"Is it a favourite of yours?"

"Not really. Mom put it on hoping it would make me sleepy. She wants me to go to drama camp tomorrow, and not stay home."

"How are your camps going?"

"Okay. So far, I haven't been the geekiest person there."

"Geeky? You never struck me as geeky."

Her sigh was nasal and sick-sounding. "You're just saying that."

"Not at all. To me, the word geeky implies that the person being described is annoying. And you're not annoying. If anyone's geeky, it was the girl who was having the party the day I picked you up at school. What was her name, again? Hannah, was it?"

Alexandra started to smile. "Haley."

"Same thing. A two-syllable name that begins with an 'H' and an annoying, full-of-herself manner."

"You're wrong." She was still smiling. "Haley's like all the other girls. Didn't you have any friends like Haley when you were a kid?"

"Yes, I did. That's how I know to be suspicious of that sort of girl. As opposed to reflective, quiet kids like you."

She gave me a you-sure-are-different look that pleased me. Yes, I was different, damn it. And so was she.

She said, "I thought teachers were supposed to pretend they liked all their students equally."

"They are, but I'm not your teacher. I'm something else." I pointed to the television screen, to Princess Aurora's three fairy godmothers flying around. "I'm a kind of fairy godsister. Except without magic powers, unfortunately."

"I wish you did have a magic wand. Then you could cure my allergies."

And change the world so that the likes of Hannah and Noel wouldn't trammel over it, unchecked.

~ Chapter 12 ~

I sat Patrick down at my kitchen table, handed him a beer, and told him about Molly's basement flood. "So then," I said, "I turned the last page of the book, and found this!" I handed him the contact sheet with a flourish, and pointed at the offending frame. "Notice anything familiar about that willow tree?"

He looked at the sheet, put it down, and said, dully, "Your brother found the treasure."

"And Hannah's involved, too! That's why she showed me the wrong location for the lodge. She must have altered the old map in the City Hall archives, and made a copy for her mother's file. She may even have come home that weekend for the sole purpose of leading me astray!"

My exclamations were not contagious. Still expressionless, he said, "And Noel left the ha-ha note in the locker."

"I should have recognized it right away as his type of gloaty gesture. But the existence of the note doesn't explain why Hannah would go to such lengths to keep me away from the real site. I would hardly have recognized the typescript as coming from Noel's old Underwood typewriter with the raised 't' key on it or anything. So why all the effort taken to prevent me from finding the locker?"

He hadn't touched his beer.

"Patrick?"

"What?"

"I asked you a non-rhetorical question. Why do you think they wanted me to stay away from the locker?"

He didn't look at me. "I've told you before — some people, me included, prefer their business to be private."

"And why is that?"

"I think it's called the need-to-know theory of sharing information."

I came around to his side of the table and sat down next to him. "If I believed in that approach, I wouldn't have told you about any of this, and then where would we be?"

He put his arms around me, spoke into my hair. "We'd be just you and me falling in love and not tangled up in your brother's mess."

I broke free. If I weren't so preoccupied with the treasure, I might have savoured his choice of words, but I did no more than squirrel away the sentence to deconstruct later. "How is this a mess? It's intriguing, a puzzle to be solved."

"You've solved it already. Your brother found the money, doesn't want anyone to know, and won't be happy when he discovers you're in on his secret."

"Maybe I should confront him about it. He's coming home for a visit soon, did I tell you? Maybe I should ask him in person what he did with the money, why he never told me or Mom and Dad about it."

Patrick took a long slug of beer.

I said, "Though there is Molly to consider. She'd be upset if she found about Hannah's involvement, I know she would. And if I bring it up with Noel and my parents, I'd end up having to tell Molly. So maybe you're right. Maybe the real story is better left buried underground."

He took off his hat and tossed it onto a chair. "I'm worn out."

"I'm sorry. I'm too hyper. I'll calm down. Come sit with me on the couch." I lowered a mental curtain down on act three of the treasure drama. A thick, red velvet curtain. "There. Now. How are you? How was your day? How's your mother?"

He nuzzled my neck. "She wants to know when she gets to meet the new girlfriend."

"Really?"

"Yes. I told her she'd like you." His mouth moved down to my collarbone. My body, already warmed up, rose and roused. My hands found his arms, reached inside his sleeves to touch his shoulders. When I spoke, my voice was unsteady. "Why'd you say that?"

His head was bent over me, his breath warm on my skin. "Because I like you."

I threw a few thoughts in the direction of the time of day, the lightness of the sky, the fact that my parents were home and Buck was lying on the floor by my front door, and pulled Patrick to me anyway.

~

Patrick was quiet afterwards, and said no thanks when I suggested we eat something. He'd had a big lunch at his mother's house, and he had to walk Buck, and he needed some rest before getting up at five the next morning to bake.

I said, "I have to work on my newspaper article tonight, anyway. It's due tomorrow."

He sat up in bed, swung his legs over the side. "And there'll be no mention in the article about who might have found the money, right?"

I reached over and touched the smooth, tight skin on his back. "No. And I won't bring it up with Noel, either. Better not to open up that can of vipers."

He pulled his T-shirt over his head. "Will you remember this?" he said.

My mind had already wandered off, was reciting the lead sentence of my newspaper story, testing its relevance in light of the Noel angle. "Remember what?"

"How good we are together."

I smiled and stretched. "At least until tomorrow."

He shook his head. I said, "What?" He said never mind, called Buck, and left.

Well, I was hungry. I had some tomatoes that Patrick had brought over the day before from the farmer's market, some dried tagliatelle in the cupboard, and olive oil, always. No fresh basil, unless I wanted to snip some from Mom's garden, which, given our latest testy exchange, I didn't. But enough ingredients for a simple meal. Enough to cook up in fifteen minutes and sate me for the rest of the evening spent at my computer revising my newspaper piece.

I replaced weak verbs with stronger ones, removed a few adjectives, and chopped some long sentences in two. I wasn't completely satisfied with the draft when I went to bed at eleven — there was a problem with the link between paragraphs three and four, and the rhythm of the ending wasn't quite right — but I was almost there. I could finish it in the morning, and still make the noon deadline.

Molly called the next day when I was looking over the piece one last time. "I wanted to thank you again for your help with the flood," she said. "You're a better daughter than my own sometimes."

As if I didn't feel bad enough about withholding information from her. "No thanks are necessary — I didn't do anything." Except pilfer some photographs. "Has the basement recovered?"

"It and me both. But the flood distracted me from convincing you to write the puzzle book. Have you thought any further about it?"

"Sorry, I haven't. I've been busy with the newspaper piece. I'm going to submit it this afternoon."

"Think of all the extra time you'll have free when that's done! Say yes to the book and you'll be guaranteed something to do."

My guilt spoke for me. "Okay, then. Yes. I'd love to give it a try."

I could hear her beaming over the phone. "That's my girl."

~

Patrick came over after my deadline, after I'd filed the article by email from home. The last sentence wasn't perfect, but I couldn't rework it anymore, was glad to send it off, have it done. And curious to see what was inside the small white cardboard box he carried.

"For you," he said.

"To celebrate me finishing the article?"

"For no reason."

I opened the box. Inside was a chocolate-drizzled pecan tart, sitting on a paper doily.

He said, "I've been experimenting. Let me know what you think."

"Can I try it now?"

"If you want."

"I'll just take a bite." I sat down at my kitchen table, cut myself a piece, and forked it in. The first mouthful tasted rich and sweet and eggy, but not too. The pastry was light, the chocolate of premium quality — I had to have more. "It's wonderful," I said, after a second taste had made me hungry for a third. "The best of your creations I've eaten to date."

"Thanks. I'll tell my baking teacher you approve."

"What baking teacher?"

"Gillian Whitney. I've only met with her once. She asked if I'd be interested in learning some of her baking techniques, for free. So she can pass on her legacy, she said."

"But why?"

"Why is she willing to teach me?"

"No, I assume she's taken you on because she thinks you have talent. But why are you wanting to learn more?"

"Because I don't want to bake donuts and bagels for the rest of my life." Unsaid: who would?

I thought about the desserts he ordered whenever we went to trendy restaurants. Ordered, ate some of, and analyzed. Why hadn't I seen it sooner? "You want to become a pastry chef."

A defensive shield went up right away. "Maybe."

"Why don't you take a chef's course at a college somewhere?"

"I can't afford to go to school full-time."

I took hold of his hand. The shield was still up. "Not that anyone with your talent needs a college diploma."

"Don't flatter me."

"I'm not flattering you, I'm being truthful: I'd put your tart up against any item from a fancy bakery, and declare it the superior item, without a doubt."

That made him smile. For what might have been the first time since I'd shown him the picture of Noel by the willow tree.

~

Patrick's moment of good humour was fleeting. For the next few days, he was loving, yes — he hugged me in an overly clingy way several times — but he was otherwise subdued. I tried asking a few times how was he feeling, but all he'd say was that he was tired — in addition to his bagel baking and dog-walking, he did two more baking sessions with Gillian Whitney, from which I reaped a gorgeous slice of ganachecovered chocolate cake and a delectable lime-mousse-filled, raspberry-topped napoleon.

I could have worried more about his gloom, but I had my own occupational concerns to deal with. Repeated failed attempts at drafting some child-friendly but not condescending prose for the puzzle book had given me new admiration for all the children's authors whose works I'd read aloud to my students without sufficient regard for their talent and skills. And left me despairing of ever finding my own narrative voice.

On Friday morning, a haggard-looking Patrick asked me at Bagel Haven if I could meet him that afternoon after he'd walked the dogs, to talk.

"Sure," I said. "If I'm not on the phone accepting congratulations from fans."

"What?"

"I'm kidding. The *Rose Park Monthly*'s coming out with my story in it today."

He made no reply, just stood there looking haunted.

I said, "Are you okay?"

"No."

"What's wrong?"

"That's what I want to talk to you about."

"This is starting to sound serious. Is it?"

"I'll meet you at Cawley Gardens at four."

"And then will this cryptic act of yours end?"

In answer, he put his arms around me and held on, in plain sight of Arthur and several customers.

"It's a bit early in the day for that sort of thing, don't you think?" Arthur said, in a not-really-joking voice.

~

As of one-thirty on publication day, no one had said a word to me about the article in the newspaper. No one talked to me about it at Bagel Haven, though there was a stack of papers in the rack by the shop door, though I'd shown the article to Arthur, and he'd acted interested, and promised to read it when he had a minute. No one called with praise and hosannas, though I'd alerted my parents that the issue with my article would land on their porch that day, though I'd run an extra copy over to Jane's house and slipped it in her mail slot, with a note attached directing her to page twenty-one.

I swallowed the disappointment, sent it down my gullet to join the unease growing in my gut over what exactly Patrick was going to tell me at four o'clock. I filled the time until then engaged in internet research — I visited websites about children's literature, read on-line reviews, and scoured interviews with children's lit authors for helpful hints, tried to absorb every tip and guideline available.

I raved on nervously to Patrick about the wealth of information I'd found when we met at Cawley Gardens. "You really should join the computer generation," I said. "Before you become the only person in the world who isn't online."

He said, "I have an email account."

"You do? Since when?"

"I've had it a long time. I access it through a domain website."

"Using what computer?"

"Whatever computer I want. A library computer sometimes."

"But I thought you told me — "

"I told you lots of things. Let's go. I'll tell you some more."

He slid off the bench and walked away fast, toward the street. I had to run to keep up, and dodge the trotting Buck while I did so. "Could you slow down a little? And explain what's going on?"

He kept walking, stared straight ahead. "I work for your brother."

"What?"

"Correction: I used to work for your brother. I did my last job a week ago."

"Worked for him how? You've joined the diplomatic corps?"

Daggers came at me from his eyes. "Not that kind of work. Noel runs a business on the side."

I pulled on Patrick's arm. "Stop walking so fast!"

He stopped and turned to face me.

I said, "What kind of business?"

"Artifact smuggling."

"Oh, come on."

"I'm not kidding."

I passed my hand over my face. "Can we please sit down and talk calmly about whatever it is you're trying to tell me?"

"My truck's around the corner. We can sit there. I'll drive somewhere."

"And start at the beginning."

~

About five years before, Patrick told me, Noel had shown up one day at the donut shop towards the end of Patrick's shift, struck up a conversation, and offered to drive him home. Noel inquired after Ryan (then in jail), expressed his condolences, asked Patrick how he was doing and what were his prospects. When Noel ascertained that Patrick wasn't on a high-income track, and that Mrs. Hennessy's health wasn't improving, he asked Patrick if he would be interested in earning some extra cash.

I interrupted. "Did he say doing what? Did he say, 'Do you want to help smuggle artifacts into the country?'"

"No, he didn't. He asked me if I could use some extra cash, and I said yes."

"Without knowing if the work would be illegal?"

"I figured as much, Blithe. People like Noel Morrison don't ask people like me to work for cash unless there's something shady going on."

Wealthy, privileged people, he meant, versus his more working-class, heroic type. I felt a chill that could not be warmed by the sight of the idyllic scene visible through the windshield. He'd pulled over on a side street. Nearby, a gardener cut a lawn, flowers bloomed, a teenage boy shot hoops in a driveway. "And you didn't care about the right and wrong of the situation?"

He hit the steering wheel with both hands. "I cared about my mother's arthritis, and three kids still at home, and no disability pension. Where's the right and wrong in that?"

I looked at his angry face and made my voice come out calm in the hope he'd copy me. "So what did you do for Noel, exactly?"

"I was his courier."

"Go on."

Noel had arranged to have small stolen artifacts smuggled into North America, hidden inside gift packages sent to my parents. When a delivery had cleared customs and made it to my parents' house, Patrick's job was to separate the smuggled item from the legitimate one and deliver it to an art dealer downtown.

"Why not ship the piece right to the dealer?"

"The dealer was jittery, Noel said. He didn't want to take the risk of receiving the shipment directly."

"And you did?"

"It didn't happen very often. Only nine times in five years. And I didn't have to break in. Your mother gave me a key because I walked Tup when she was out."

There's Tup now, waiting for Patrick by the front door of my parents' house. He sees Patrick, wags his tail, and pants a hello from behind the glass panel in the vestibule. Patrick lets himself in with the key, pats Tup on the head, goes inside, and finds the contraband. He clips Tup's lead to his collar, takes Tup out, and stows the object — sealed in a cardboard tube, say, or a large padded envelope — in the truck. Then he goes to collect the next dog in his troupe, Tup beside him.

Except Patrick didn't walk Tup anymore. Not since I'd moved home. And before the right side of my brain could work the problem through, the left side figured it out, made my head spin, strangled my voice. "But you said you just did your last job for Noel. How was that possible if you no longer had an excuse ..."

I didn't need to complete the question. There'd been something hidden behind the sun-kissed Mediterranean landscape my mother had given me, the item Noel had suggested should be my gift, the picture I had found in Patrick's hands when I came out of the bathroom. The picture Patrick could only have had access to if he were dating me.

My face flushed hot and an awful sobbing noise came out of my mouth. I fumbled with the door handle, tried to jump out of the truck, caught my foot on the seat belt, lost my balance, and fell hard onto the sidewalk, legs and arms akimbo, face down.

Patrick called my name in alarm, and I heard the truck door open and close, the sound of his rapid footsteps coming to my side. "Are you all right?" Was I? I lay still, sprawled on the warm concrete, my eyes closed, and listened to my various body parts shriek in pain. My left cheek hurt the loudest, but significant noise of the stinging and burning variety came from my right arm and right knee as well. Mixed in with the sounds of a crow cawing overhead, and a car driving by, and more footsteps.

I rolled onto my side, and saw Patrick's concerned face floating above me, the fluffy cloud sky as backdrop. Buck's head was there too, sniffing at my shoulder. And Molly Greer. Was I dreaming her? No, that was her cool hand on my forehead and her voice saying, "I was out walking and I saw you fall from down the street. Are you okay?"

I mumbled yes, but stayed put.

Molly said to Patrick, "Has she had anything to drink?"

"Alcohol?"

"I meant, could she be dehydrated?"

"I don't know. She just came from her apartment."

"And what were you two doing?"

"When?"

"When she fell."

Pause. "We were talking in my truck."

"With the windows open?"

"Yeah. It wasn't hot. The truck's in the shade."

"Were you fighting?"

Another pause. "Our conversation was a little tense. Blithe tripped on her way out of the truck."

I said, "My face hurts."

Molly said, "You've got a bad scrape on your cheek. How are you feeling otherwise? Any other pain? Anything feel broken?"

"No. A little bruised, maybe."

"Do you think you could sit up?"

I lifted my head an inch. The sky shifted sideways. I said no, not yet.

I heard a car drive up, stop and idle, and Molly said to someone I couldn't see, "Everything's fine here. Our friend just slipped and fell, but she's all right, thanks." Whoever it was drove away.

"I'll try to get up," I said, and Molly told me to take it slow.

"That scrape looks like it needs some disinfectant," she said. "Why don't you come to my house and I'll dress it for you?"

Patrick drove us the short distance to Molly's house, dropped us off, hesitated when Molly asked him if he wanted to come in, said no, he wouldn't, he'd call later.

"Do you want to talk about it?" Molly said, when I was installed on her couch with pillows behind my head, a glass of water, and a disinfected cheek.

"About why I fell, you mean? The seat belt was hanging down, it wasn't retracted. My foot got caught."

"About why you were fighting."

"No, I can't — no. I'd rather not talk about that. I'm sorry."

Molly said, "I want to make sure you're safe with Patrick."

"Safe? Of course I'm safe. You don't think he threw me out of the truck, do you? God, no. He just said something that upset me and I bolted." Something that had, in an instant, made all my old insecurities resurface, made me feel like I was reliving the breakup with Gerald. "Thank you for looking after me. I'll just sit another minute or two, if you don't mind, then go."

I took a sip of water. Molly plumped the cushions on an armchair. Then another. She sat down, crossed her legs, folded her hands in her lap, cleared her throat. Said, "Did you know that when we lived in Chicago, before we moved here, Hannah had a whole other secret life?"

I shook my head, felt a painful pull in the abraded skin of my cheek. I wasn't sure I wanted her to continue, didn't know how many more past secrets I could stand to hear.

"She had boyfriends," Molly said — tremulous intake of breath — "and lovers, I think, even at the age of fifteen or sixteen. She was never home in the evenings, and Larry and I didn't know where she went or what she did. She said she had a job working at a bar bussing tables for cash, she wouldn't tell us where. We thought she might be into drugs, or worse. But she always came home to sleep, and she passed her courses at school, showed real talent with her photography, and never got into serious trouble, either at school or with the police. She just went out a lot and didn't talk to us." She gripped the arms of the chair, then released them. "We moved here partly to remove her from whatever crowd she'd fallen in with, and I was so glad when she became friends with you, because you seemed so nice."

Everybody hates the teacher's pet except the teacher. "Nice?"

"You were such a good girl, I mean. So normal and pleasant and not brimming with attitude. When Hannah brought you home and you spoke to me as if I were a human being, I thought she might start talking to me again when you weren't here, when I was alone with her. But she didn't. That's why I never knew about her dating your brother until I saw them at the footbridge. Unless she was with you, I didn't know any more about what she was up to than I'd known in Chicago. And always, I wondered if one day there'd be a knock on the door, or a phone call to say she'd been caught doing something illegal. Even now I sometimes expect it."

And so she should, since Hannah must be part of the smuggling ring, too.

Molly said, "I should have told you this on the day you showed me the locker in the ravine, but I couldn't. So here goes." More vibrato breathing. "I think Hannah might have found the Glenwood treasure years ago. And never told anyone."

I said, "*I* think Noel found it. But Hannah is in on it too, somehow."

She made an uncomfortable sound, a half-laugh, half-cry. "You knew?"

"I only guessed on Sunday, here, in your basement, when I saw pictures of Noel in Hannah's binder." My backpack was on the floor beside the couch. I leaned over, unzipped the top pocket, reached inside, pulled out the contact sheet, passed it to her. "I didn't know how to tell you."

Molly picked up her reading glasses from the coffee table, put them on, examined the contact sheet for a long moment, said, "Him, too?" then, "I'll be right back," and went upstairs.

I sat up off the pillows, and was relieved to feel no woozi-ness in my head other than my confused feelings about Patrick. How angry did I have a right to be at him? How bad had he been? Compared to Hannah and Noel, say? Compared to Gerald? Compared to me?

Molly came back down and handed me a picture frame. "Hannah always liked this photograph," she said. It was a picture of the willow trees. No people in the frame. No big black X marking the spot, either. She said, "I thought of that picture as soon as you took me there."

There wasn't much more to say. We wondered what they'd done with the money. "Used it to live luxuriously, I guess," she said. "In Europe, where we can't know what they're up to." I asked if she thought we should mention the treasure to Hannah and Noel, ask them about it, and — cowards both, or maybe wise women both — we agreed there was no point.

"But Molly," I said, "if you thought Hannah had found the money, why did you encourage me to write the newspaper arti-cle about it, and bring the subject back into the light?"

"If Hannah had kept the discovery secret this long, I thought she could keep it secret forever. And how could I not encourage you, when you were the one who cracked the puz-zle, and uncovered the clues? When you deserved recognition for your achievement?" She'd wanted me to have my moment in the sun.

I said, "You're very kind."

"No, not very. But I try to be fair."

~

I accepted Molly's offer of a ride home, but I ignored her sug-gestion to let my parents know about my spill, to stop in and show them my wound. The wetness of the exposed subcuta-neous tissue lent my face a traumatized air that would invite too much fuss and bother. They weren't home when I arrived, anyway. And I wanted to call Patrick, hear the rest of his story.

He answered on the first ring. "Are you okay?"

"I'm temporarily disfigured but otherwise fine. What do you know about the treasure?"

"Huh?"

"And what about Hannah? What really happened the night you drove her home from the Ranch House? Is she involved in the smuggling business?"

"Hold on. I didn't know anything about the treasure until we dug up the locker. Noel must have found it before I started working for him."

"And Hannah?"

"Yes, she's part of the smuggling ring. She was a source of some of the objects. She travels a lot, doesn't she?"

Watch Hannah, in a flak vest over a tank top and adventure-gear shorts, and with two cameras around her neck, run across an under-siege Third World village square. Her arms are sinewy and tanned, her wristwatch war-resistant, her hiking boots worked-in. She dodges a sniper's bullet and dashes through a beaded curtain into a smoky café where Arab music plays and Sidney Greenstreet sits at a table in a white suit and a fez.

STOP.

"This story is so fantastic — do you actually expect me to buy it?"

"I don't know what to expect. But I swear — on my mother's arthritis — that I didn't know Noel and Hannah had anything to do with the treasure until I saw the note he left. I can only guess they must have used some of the treasure fund as seed money for the smuggling business and worried that if you knew who found the treasure, you'd find out about the smuggling."

"Because I'm such a master of deductive reasoning?"

"Because you're smart, yeah. That must be why Hannah came back to steer you wrong. Though she never told me that part of her plan."

He sounded so serious, and so relieved to be talking openly about the subject, and so perplexed — all at once — that I started to believe him. Until I remembered my pawn-like function in the scheme. "You haven't explained what went on with her at the Ranch House."

"Another reason she came here was to see me."

Noel had notified him, by coded e-mail — "He loved his decoder-ring when he was a kid," I said — of Hannah's visit, had set up the meeting at the Ranch House in advance.

"Why?"

"They were checking up on me, since Hannah was in town. And she wanted to tell me how to handle you, how I could get access to your parents' house with you home."

For a second, the anger in me shoved aside the blob of self-pity occupying centre stage. "How to handle me?"

"Let me finish. Don't hang up."

The idea of hanging up hadn't occurred to me. But maybe it should have, since tears had started to run down my face.

"The idea was not for me to seduce you," he said. "I was just supposed to become your friend."

The tears stung my oozing cheek on their way to my chin. "Why did you seduce me, then?" I said. "To see if you could?"

"No, that wasn't it at all." And did I hear a catch in his voice, too? "Haven't you been listening to what I've been saying the last few days?"

Had I? "I have to go," I said. "I need to think." I hung up the phone — no big, dramatic gesture — turned off the ringer, thought, jumped up and washed my face with cold water (which hurt, a lot), and thought some more. I ran a bath, lay in it until the hot water cooled, put on my pyjamas, curled up on the couch, stared out the window at the branches on the trees, and came to the shaky conclusion that Patrick deserved another chance, and so did I.

I stayed curled, imagined picking up the phone and dialling, couldn't think what to say, how to begin. I was startled out of my mind-fog by an aggressive knock on my door — a demanding, masculine knock that had to be Patrick, unable to stay away, come rushing over to beg my forgiveness, to make amends, to put everything right. I ran to the door, opened it, and almost choked at the sight of Noel, leaning in the doorframe, his head swathed in smoke from a French cigarette affixed to his louche lips.

He drawled, "Hello there, sis," strolled past me into the apartment, glanced at my face, and recoiled. "What the devil happened to you?"

~ Chapter 13 ~

Noel looked around the room, flopped down on the couch, put his feet up on the coffee table. "I see the old flat has retained its rustic charm. Be a good girl and get me an ashtray, would you?"

I've already mentioned that Noel was the tall, blond, blue-eyed, square-jawed type. Even I, who despised him, could not deny he possessed Adonis-like physical qualities. So I was shocked to see how his looks had faded since I'd seen him last.

He said, "Blithe, are you all here? I asked for an ashtray."

Before I could check myself, I did his bidding: ran for a cheap glass ashtray that was in one of my cupboards and handed it to him. There was a new looseness to his jaw, a perceptible sag around his middle. And the European style clothing he wore — an off-white linen shirt and trousers, and woven leather sandals — made him look more a roué than a leading man.

I said, "What are you doing here?"

There were the beginnings of jowls in his cheeks, and his skilful hair-combing couldn't hide the thinning. He pointed with a nicotine-stained finger. "Do you like the painting I had sent over? I knew it would suit that mantel."

"I asked what you're doing here."

"Saying hello to my only sister, what do you think? It's been a while." He stared at me. "But what is the explanation for that gaping wound on your face? Ought it to be looked at by a professional?"

"It's fine. I fell down."

"Isn't that what they all say?" He stubbed out his cigarette. "A shame about your divorce, by the way. Though I had Gerald pegged as a weak and unworthy bounder from the moment I met him."

His gall was breathtaking. "A bounder?"

"You know what bounder means, don't you? It rhymes with cad, and ne'er-do-well, and Patrick Hennessy."

I turned my back to hide the emotions that threatened to collapse my face, and cursed him for finding my Achilles heel so soon and so easily. With as much vocal aggression as I could muster (not near enough), I said, "You haven't answered my question: why are you in Rose Park?"

"You don't accept the notion that I'm here to offer you solace in your time of need? Can't say that I blame you. Let's see. Would you believe I crossed the ocean to bond with the parents? No? Then why am I here, I wonder?" He felt around in his pockets for his pack of cigarettes, pulled out another. "Oh yes. I remember now. To do business."

"Not with me."

"Yes, with you. I've decided the local operation could use your acumen."

"What are you talking about? What local operation?" But my voice betrayed me.

"Don't plead ignorance. I know Patrick told you about our working relationship. He warned me he would. Did you send him packing the moment you realized you were being used?"

How considerate of him to provide me, in his arrogance, with a new reason to be angry. "No, I didn't. Not that it's any of your business."

"It's completely my business. Now that I've seen what you're capable of, Patrick may be expendable. I'd much prefer a collaborator with brains to that tech school graduate."

Is this why he'd come? To jab at me and torment me? I said, "You're amazing."

"Yes I am, and so are you, to a lesser degree. Look how you found the site of the Glenwood Treasure when all others have failed. Except for the one other person, of course. Hard luck, that." His gaze was steady, his face unreadable. He either didn't know I knew about him and the treasure, or he didn't care.

"Yeah, I'm brilliant, all right."

He squinted at me through the unfiltered blue smoke. "Do you know what your IQ is, Blithe?"

"Do you?"

"Why, yes. Mother had us both tested as children, and I took it as my solemn duty to pilfer the file she kept on us and check our results."

I had no recollection of being tested, but I wanted to see where he'd go with this tactic. "And what were they?"

"I can't remember the exact number, but I confess to being appalled when I learned that your score was ten points higher than mine."

"Is that your idea of a joke?" I said.

"I tell the truth." He crossed his legs. "Scout's honour. I was a scout once, do you remember? When we were young and pure and life was a bowl of ripe fruit waiting to be gorged upon."

I sat down on the closest chair, covered my face with my hands, touched the sore spot by mistake, winced. "I need to lie down."

"Had a rough day, have you? I won't stay. I'll shoulder my filial burden and return to the drawing room for another bout of conversation with Dad. He bored me so over drinks that I was tempted to liven the atmosphere by telling him what the word 'tup' means in Scotland. Should I have, do you think?" He didn't wait for a reply. "I almost dozed off when he took the opportunity of your little article appearing in that two-bit newspaper to wax on about the legal issues surrounding buried treasure. And he seemed to have no recollection that I persuaded him to have his associates prepare a summary paper on those very issues years ago. Has he suffered many such memory lapses lately?"

I picked out the one sentence in this speech that mattered to me. "Why did you have him prepare a summary paper on the issues?"

A broad smile. "I was curious. And things were slow for him at work at the time — I gave him something to do." He stood up. "I gather you won't be joining us for dinner, in your scarred state. I'll make your apologies. And we'll talk tomorrow, shall we? About how best to integrate you into the family firm, and about how to dispose of Patrick?"

He headed for the door. I followed close behind, eager to throw the deadbolt, but he stopped at the kitchen table and picked up Trixie, whom Jane had dropped over a few days before.

"What the bloody hell?" He turned her over in his hand. "Is this my old Venus? I believe it is. I thought I'd thrown this away years ago. Where'd you find it?"

"Wedged into the back of a kitchen cupboard. Why?"

He tossed the figure in the air. "Now herein lies a cautionary tale. From my early days in the business. Would you care to hear it?"

I watched Trixie jump in his hand. "Could you put her down, please?"

"Don't worry. I won't let her drop. Even if she did almost cost me my reputation — the only thing that matters in the trade — when I was starting out."

I said nothing.

"Come on, Blithe. Play your part. Say: How did you get started in the business, Noel?"

Sulkily, I said, "How did you?"

"I met some people at college from abroad who had contacts, who knew where to acquire valuable objects of murky origin that private collectors would pay top dollar for, no questions asked. And this figure was one such object, for which I paid slightly less than top dollar, but a high enough price, under the impression, given by one of my sources, that it was the real thing, stolen from the Berlin museum."

He tossed Trixie up and down, in rhythm. I couldn't watch — the motion made me dizzy.

"I came very close to selling this figure to a semi-shady dealer. But he didn't know or trust me, and he wanted to double-check the authenticity of the piece. So I took it to an acquaintance at Harvard who was studying archeology, told him it was a family heirloom with a questionable provenance, asked if he could get it assessed for me, on the quiet, and found out it was plastic." He threw Trixie up high and caught her with two hands. "Poor me: I had to have one of my new friends beaten up before I could get my money back. The moral of this story being that one should only work with people who can be trusted, such as one's blood relatives. Have you become attached to this thing? Would you like to keep it?"

I thought of Alexandra and the pink sweater and said yes.

He set Trixie down on the table. "Please accept it as my gift to you, then. An incentive, as it were."

I said, "Whether or not the figure turned out to be fake, I don't understand where a college student could get enough money to buy something purported to be of such value."

He turned in the doorway, showed me the beginnings of a sneer. "You understand, all right."

I may have yawned at that point. Not from tiredness. But in order to replace some of the extra oxygen my brain had used to stay on top of the conversation. "So you did find the treasure."

"Of course I did. I'll tell you all about it tomorrow. Sweet dreams."

~

All I wanted to do after Noel left was go to bed, to oblivion, and submit to the exhaustion that had seeped into every part of me, heart and soul especially. I locked and double-locked, turned off lamps, ignored the flashing message light on my phone, went to the bathroom, brushed my teeth, and glanced in the mirror at my reflection. I spat, and swilled water around in my mouth — not vigorously, because to do so would hurt my cheek too much — and spat again, and made my mirror face, tried to see if my appearance spoke as clearly as Noel's had of damage done and glory lost.

I couldn't tell, couldn't see beyond the worried folds in my forehead, the red and swollen eyes, the hair matted with tears and sweat and some of Molly's disinfectant, the ugly, wet wound that had developed a pus-y shade of yellow around the edges, in artful contrast to its purple and red interior shades. Though, as I had never possessed head-turning, beauteous looks to begin with, maybe there was nothing to lose. Maybe I had an advantage over Noel at last.

I stumbled out of the bathroom, flopped onto the bed, and fell into the kind of deep, dreamless sleep the body requires in order to repair extremes of emotional and physical wear.

Anxiety woke me at 4:00 a.m. I lay in bed for an hour or so, thinking anxious, lovelorn thoughts about Patrick, and paranoid, apprehensive thoughts about Noel, until I couldn't stand to be alone in the dark with my mind anymore. I got up, turned on a light, made myself some peppermint tea, examined my face once more, saw that my cheek still oozed, though it also felt tight and itchy — an unpleasant mixture of sensations that matched my mood.

I listened to the five phone messages Patrick had left since I'd turned off the phone, which all implored me to call him back. I erased them, looked up the word "tup" in the dictionary, and found to my displeasure it was a slang word used to describe the sex act of sheep. I wrapped myself in a thin blanket, set my mug of tea on the kitchen table, pulled out a pad of paper, and wrote:

Why is Noel here?
  1. *Because he thinks I could contribute something valuable to his smuggling enterprise (hah!).*
  2. *To throw me down the slope into the ravine because I know too much.*
  3. *To shut me up by any means possible.*
  4. *All of the above.*

I tried to ignore the worried swilling of my gastric juices, and started a new page:

What to do about Noel:
  1. *Report him to the police. Watch Patrick, Hannah, and possibly Mom and Dad be immolated along with him. Make Molly's nightmare come true.*
  2. *Join his merry band of thieves.*
  3. *Refuse to join him and look the other way.*

I read the options over. Number one sounded far too confrontational, and too upsetting all around, besides. Option two was beyond my capabilities — moral or ethical qualms aside, I would become a tic-ridden shambling wreck within the first month of my life of crime. And number three? I had a feeling Noel would make number three more than difficult, would blackmail me into complicity if I didn't willingly agree.

I thought about everything that had happened that day, and added one more point to the list:

4. *Thwart him.*

I picked up Trixie and nestled her bulk in the palm of my hand. Number four was the best option, but how to achieve it? If only Noel's bald lie about my superior intelligence were true and I could devise a brilliant plan.

~

I called Patrick three hours later, at eight o'clock. "Can we meet?" I said.

"Yes. I love you."

"I'd like to believe you. I'd like to believe you didn't sleep with me just to gain access to my apartment to steal whatever was inside the picture frame."

"It was an Egyptian papyrus. And I slept with you because I wanted to. I could have been in and out of your apartment within five minutes and taken the papyrus anytime."

His words rang true, cheered me. But I said, "Never mind that. Can we meet or not? I need to ask you some questions."

"Where? When?"

"Now. In the parking lot behind Smithy's garage." A place where Noel should have no reason to tread.

"I can be there in fifteen minutes."

"Make it twenty."

I rode my bicycle to Smithy's. Patrick drove. I directed him to park his truck around behind the mechanic's bay, in a back part of the lot that was out of sight of the road. I leaned my bike on a wall, climbed into the truck cab with Patrick, and took out a notebook.

"Let's get started," I said.

"Okay, but you should know that I'm only going to tell you the truth from now on, no matter what you ask."

"Damn right you are. First question: how did the smuggling operation work?"

"Why?"

"Because I want to know. You said that Noel sent you coded email messages. What was his email name?"

"JeremiahB at ..." he supplied a common domain name.

"Are you serious?"

"Nothing but the truth, remember?"

"What a fool. And I bet I can guess his password. All right, next. How did the art dealer here know to expect a parcel from you when you were ready to deliver?"

"I sent him a coded message."

"What was your email name?"

"MarloweP."

"Marlowe, as in Philip Marlowe?"

"Yeah."

Were Noel and Patrick both fifteen years old? "Which is your password? Raymond? Chandler? or Samspade?"

He looked in awe of my clairvoyance. "Chandler."

"What was the dealer's email name? Peter Lorre?"

"Who's that?"

"Never mind. What was the dealer's email name?"

"JohnSmith497."

I wrote that down. "What would your message to the dealer say?"

"Tonight. The usual place. Seven."

"What was the usual place?"

"We met at Beachside Park."

"Would he reply to you?"

"He'd just send the word 'okay' as confirmation."

"And how would he know what to expect, what the object was?"

"Noel handled that end of it, gave him the specs in his own email."

"Did you ever see those messages?"

"He sent me blind copies. They were in code, though."

"Let me guess. A=1, B=2?"

"How do you know all this stuff?"

I tapped my head with my pencil. "I have a high IQ. Did you keep any of Noel's messages on your computer?"

"I don't have a computer, remember?"

"On whatever computer you used."

"No."

"Did you ever print them out?"

"No."

"Do your recall what they were like, what format, how much information he included?"

"Not much. Just identifying facts."

"No style to it? Good."

So Noel would send the item to Mom, advise the dealer what was coming, have Patrick make both pickup and drop, and put everyone but himself at risk.

"What about Hannah?" I said. "I thought you said she sourced some of the items. What'd she do — pass things on to Noel?"

"That's what she said that night at the Ranch House."

I kept my eyes on the pad. "And did you sleep with her?"

"No. I told you that before."

"How am I supposed to know which of the many things you told me were true?"

"I only lied or left out information about Noel and the smuggling. Everything else I've said or done was for real."

A few of the weights of sadness I'd worn on my shoulders for the last day and a half lifted off. "Okay. Just a few more questions. Why did you want to quit working for Noel?"

"So I could stop lying to you."

"What reason did you give him?"

"That reason."

"What was his reaction to that?"

"Don't ask. The prick."

"I did ask."

"He didn't like it. He said he'd have to come here and straighten us both out."

"Which would be why he invited me last night to join his gang."

"You?"

"Me. I could be the local brains of the outfit, seems to be the idea. Hannah having already signed up for the job of moll."

"Shit. He didn't say anything about recruiting you when he called me last night. He did ask how I thought my mother would feel to have another son up on charges, though."

"He did?" The prick, indeed. "But if he implicated you, couldn't you just turn around and finger him?"

"You think he couldn't find a way to get me into trouble and keep his own nose clean? People like Noel are protected."

"Last question: did the dealer ever see you?"

"Maybe from a distance, but not up close. Our arrangement was that I left the item for him in a bag under a picnic table where he took his dog for a walk every day. And I wore hats and kept my head down."

"I'd feel better if you hadn't been within view, but we'll have to live with it."

"What do you mean?"

"I'm not sure yet. I have to think about this. Decide what's best."

I let a silence develop, inhaled deeply, gave my next lines a better read than when I'd tried and failed to deceive Noel. "Maybe joining Noel's gang isn't such a bad idea. I could make some extra cash, we could work together. What do you think?"

His reaction was immediate, his sincerity obvious. "No! Don't do it."

I felt a fluttering inside my chest that was hope making a comeback, but all I said was, "I'll have to see."

~

Noel was waiting in the driveway with Tup — whose name I would always equate with tuppence, no matter what — when I returned from Smithy's. "You're out early," he said.

"I needed some air."

"Why don't you come to the park with Tup and me, then? Get some more."

In the sunny light of day, he looked less sinister — and more wasted — than he had the night before. And he had a good story to tell. About how he'd found the treasure on his own, and never figured out the man with a dog clue, or seen the map hidden inside the cornerstone.

I said, "Then how did you know where the treasure was hidden?" We were sitting in Cawley Gardens.

"I happened across the trove more than anything. I'd always been interested in the ravine lodge — I'd read about it and seen the photos. I even did a history project about it in middle school. That's when I found the map in the city archive and identified the site location. But I didn't come across the locker until one long weekend when I was home from my freshman year at Harvard."

"When Hannah and I were in our last year at Northside."

"What a hassle that was, incidentally, to sneak her in and out of the coach house flat without you knowing."

I risked a question irrelevant to my plan. "What did you care if I knew?"

"It was Hannah's idea to keep you in the dark." He pulled a deep drag on his cigarette. "She thought you'd drop her if you knew about our couplings — I can't think why. And she needed you. You were so buttoned-down that her mother gave her more freedom when she associated with you."

At last, a logical explanation for Hannah's friendship.

Noel said, "So I was down in the ravine alone day, cruising the lodge site — smoking a joint, I think — and I stumbled upon the locker, literally tripped over the ring in the trap door. Brown had stacked bundles of hundred dollar bills in a small wooden treasure chest inside, a tacky pirate-style thing. There it was, all that money, just waiting to be taken."

I stared off across the park. "As if it were meant for you."

"One of R.T.'s old diaries refers to Jeremiah wandering through the ravine during his later years. Now we know what he was up to."

"Why didn't you tell anyone? Take the glory, make news headlines — 'Local boy finds long-lost treasure.'"

"I was neither local nor a boy by then. I had big career plans, and I didn't want to be in the limelight for the wrong reasons." He stretched his arms out along the top of the bench. "I also didn't want the money to be tied up in court while my claim was contested."

"Contested by whom? The society for war widows and orphans? I can't imagine it would sue."

"Better safe than sorry." Which didn't strike me until later as being an odd position to take for someone who liked to live life on the edge. He said, "I covered my tracks fairly well — when I told Hannah about it, she had the bright idea to go down to the archives and alter the lodge location on the old town plan in case anyone ever started snooping around in the area, and she made sure her mother was given the doctored version for that lost-cause book she wanted to write. Plus she went the extra mile of taking you to the wrong place in the ravine, though in vain. It was clever of you to have penetrated our various ruses."

"Gee, thanks."

"Was the note I left in the locker still there? You made no mention of it in your article."

"It was still there."

"Good. I trust it inspired and entertained?"

"I should have recognized your kindly nature in its wording." Damn if I wasn't almost enjoying the parries and thrusts.

"Speaking of entertaining reading," he said, "do you have that diary of R.T.'s? I wanted to take another look at it for old times' sake, and Dad told me he'd given it to you as a birthday present. Your most appreciated gift, I'm sure. May I borrow it? Or did you throw it away?"

I could feel something hidden behind his words, feel it dull the sunshine. "I have it."

"Where? I looked through your bookshelves this morning and I didn't see it."

The sun was blotted out now. "You were in the flat?"

"When you weren't."

Let it go. Don't act suspicious. "I must have stashed the diary away somewhere. I'll look for it."

"I wish you would. I'd like to see it again."

And I'd have to find out why he wanted to get it away from me.

"So about your little smuggling ring," I said.

"My import-export business."

"That's a much better term. It sounds so much more criminal."

He eyed me through the haze of smoke that surrounded him. "Can that be disapproval I hear?"

"Tell me why do you do this."

He shrugged. "I needed a place to invest my windfall."

"Couldn't you open an offshore bank account like other possessors of ill-gotten gains?"

"I've spread the money around — some spending, some saving. But neither is as thrilling as engaging in illegal activity."

"I would have thought you'd use it to indulge in more commonplace vices, like sex, or drugs."

"I tried those. But their appeal palled, after a time." After a moment's silence, he said, with less of a drawl, "You don't know what my job's like, once the exotica of each new posting wears off. The boredom, the bullshit, the meetings and dinners and protocol, the fast fading of the blooms among the local flora." He peered up through the tree branches at the sky. "Not quite what I expected when I signed up for foreign affairs."

"So you became a criminal on the side?"

"It was that or indulge in a self-pitying bout of despair, and I didn't want to steal your act."

I said, "The smuggling is a lucrative enterprise, I hope?"

"It can be, when everything goes right. I wouldn't do it otherwise. But hold on a sec, are you actually considering throwing in with us?"

"I might."

"And Patrick?"

"You want me, you get Patrick, too."

"Splendid. Now I won't have to dismember you two and bury your remains in the game locker."

I must have blanched, because he reached out and touched me on the arm — a gesture meant to be reassuring. "I'm joking. Now. Let's discuss the details, starting with the next shipment."

"You've got one scheduled already?"

"For a week from now, when I'll be back in London. Hannah's making the arrangements. Her wager was that you would refuse to sign up, by the way. She said you were not a joiner, never had been. Wait till I tell her."

Be careful here. Sound convincing. "Tell her living on a teacher's income can change a person's ideas about the importance of lucre."

"Right, then. Listen up and I'll explain how the shipments work."

~

When Noel and I turned the corner onto our street, we came into view of Dad, seated at the wheel of his car in the driveway. Mom stood behind the open door on the passenger side, a hand to her forehead, the better to scan the horizon for a sign of the crown prince.

"Noel, darling," she called, "you didn't forget about our lunch with the Vaillancourts, did you?"

"How could I? I just need half a minute to freshen up." He trotted up to the house, turned back on the porch, said, "Don't forget to look out that diary for me, Blithe," and slipped inside.

Mom said, "My goodness, Blithe! What happened to your face?"

"I fell off my bike yesterday and scraped it on the road."

She examined the wound up close, carefully touched the skin around it. "You'll want to watch that, keep it moist. Terrible place to have a scar. I've got some vitamin E creme I'll lend you for it."

"Thanks."

"What's Noel doing? Toot your horn, Charles, and hurry him up."

"Say, Mom, did you ever have my IQ tested?"

"What are you talking about?"

"Think back. Do you remember having Noel and me test-ed for intelligence or not?"

From within the car, Dad said, "You were both tested as children. And achieved high scores, I recall."

"Noel, yes. But me, too?"

Mom touched her coif, tamed a stray hair I couldn't see. "Of course you, too."

"Wasn't Blithe's result higher than Noel's?" Dad said.

Mom dusted some invisible particles off her suit jacket. "I don't remember. Maybe by a few points. Those tests aren't a hundred percent accurate. Could you toot your horn again, Charles? Twice this time?"

Dad tooted, Noel emerged from the house with water-slicked hair and different clothes, and I bid them all goodbye, bounded up the coach house stairs to my porch, didn't unlock my door and go inside until Noel was safely in the car, till they'd driven away and around the corner.

Even so, I waited a minute before taking the diary from its accidental hiding place behind the top moulding of the book-case. Not until I was sure I was alone in the flat, sure they weren't coming back, did I pull the book out, sit down in my most com-fortable chair, and begin to read.

~ Chapter 14 ~

I had close to two hours of reading time before Noel would be back from lunch, and it took me almost that long to find what I was looking for in my grandfather's diary.

R.T.'s habit was to sit down after dinner and list, in the driest possible manner, the events of his day. I read about his golf games — "Played two under par today" — and his wife Frances's "fine cooking, as always." He also made discreet references to his legal work, with comments like, "Saw Fraser MacDonald about the sale of his house. He's moving to Boston," or, "Simon Rawlings called to consult about setting up a trust fund for his children."

Most entries were one or two plainly written short paragraphs, but the exceptional meal or spell of good weather moved R.T. to embellish his writing with a descriptive phrase, as in, "Frances outdid herself this evening with roast chicken in a toothsome gravy." Or, "Lovely day. My walk home from the office was invigorating."

I wanted to skip-read, but I had to pay closer attention. I'd skimmed and skipped through the Mary Elizabeth Bishop book, and had missed the key to the true treasure location. This time, I read every word, put the book down at one o'clock to make myself a toasted tomato sandwich, picked it up again to read while I ate.

After an hour or so, I struggled to stay awake. I moved to a hard wooden chair at the kitchen table instead of the sleep-inducing armchair, but the boring fare combined with my sleepless night made the work tedious.

At last, in July 1963, I came to an entry of interest: "Met with Jeremiah Brown today regarding his will." Careful reading led to a second short mention a few weeks later: "Discussed Brown's will with him at length. Unusual situation because he was an only child, was predeceased by his wife and children, and wishes to will the bulk of his estate to charity."

As the months wore on, Jeremiah Brown became a dominant theme of the diary, and R.T. began to lose some of his detachment. He wrote:

> *Brown's household staff informed me today that Brown has taken to wandering the far reaches of the property for hours at a time. Saw Brown, who appeared sane enough, but pressed upon me, for safe-keeping, a box of family artifacts — baby bracelets and locks of hair and christening gowns and such — that had belonged to his dead sons. Tonight at dinner (an excellent roast duck), I mentioned my concerns about Brown's state of mind, and Frances informed me Brown is referred to in the neighbourhood as the Bogey Man, someone to be avoided by fearful children when encountered on the street.*

Then, before Brown even died, before the treasure note came to light and all hell broke loose — R.T. in the thick of it, having to fend off reporters and fortune hunters and surveyors and god knows who else — came an entry that described another meeting between R.T. and Jeremiah. "During a visit to Glenwood today, I attempted to advise Brown on his handling of cash, after his bank manager had called me to advise of several large withdrawals. Brown glared at me with those unsettling white-veined blue eyes of his, and told me not to interfere in his personal affairs."

I stopped, said, "What?" and read the paragraph again. I pictured old Jeremiah staring R.T. down with eyes something like Patrick's. Or were they just like Patrick's? Could this be what Noel was trying to keep from me? That by some coincidence, Jeremiah Brown and Patrick had the same unusual blue and white pattern in their irises? Which would mean what, exactly? I closed my ordinary brown eyes and tried to think straight. Or rather, to think the way Noel would have done when he'd read the diary years before.

Could Jeremiah and Patrick possibly be related, their common eye type no coincidence, but a matter of inheritance? No, they couldn't be. Jeremiah Brown had died years before Patrick was born. And Jeremiah's sons had predeceased the old man — they couldn't have fathered Patrick either. Damn and hell. The answer to the puzzle was before me, I was sure, hidden in plain sight, if I could just find it.

Okay. What if one of Jeremiah's sons had, knowingly or not, fathered a child? Sometime between 1940, when the older boys went off to war, and 1950, when the youngest died in a car accident. And what if such a child, girl or boy, had grown up to become Patrick's mom or dad? No, wait, not his dad — Patrick had told me his late father's parents were Irish, from Ireland. His mother, then, who had grown up in Rose Park. If she were a Brown love child, Patrick and his siblings would be Jeremiah's great-grandchildren.

Was I crazy to even think of such a proposition? Probably. Was Noel crazy too? Most definitely. But the real question was whether I could come up with a single shred of corroborative evidence for the idea. I did a mental search through every little thing I knew about Jeremiah Brown, his sons, Patrick, and his parents — and came across a memory of Gillian Whitney's voice, on that rainy day at the Market, making what I'd thought was idle chatter. Eureka.

I checked the kitchen clock. Help, it was one-forty-five. Noel could return any minute. I jumped up, tossed the journal in my backpack, ran out to my bike, and rode the four blocks to Gillian Whitney's house on William Street.

Gillian was home, came to the door with an apron on. "Why hello there," she said. "How are you?"

"It's Blithe Morrison," I said. "Patrick's friend, Jane's neighbour, Alexandra's babysitter."

"Of course dear, I remember. Jane showed me your article in the *Rose Park Monthly* yesterday. I enjoyed it very much. And Alexandra was tickled to be written about. Won't you come in?"

"Actually, I wanted to ask you a question. A couple of questions. But if you don't mind, I will come in for a minute."

"Please." She led the way through the hall into her living room. "Have a seat. And please excuse my apron. I was about to start some baking."

I stopped halfway to sitting down on her couch. "I'm sorry — should we go into the kitchen? Does anything need tending?"

"No, no. I was just measuring. No chemical changes have occurred yet. I'm all yours."

"Good. Thank you. I'm doing some research for a book about Rose Park — a local history sort of book, and I thought maybe I could interview you for it, as a long-time resident." This cover story needed a prop to authenticate it. I reached inside my backpack, and pulled out a pen and a pad I had placed there a few days before, in case inspiration struck on the puzzle book text. "Okay. The first question is: how long have you lived in Rose Park?"

"Let's see, now — I was twenty on my wedding day, and we moved into this house right after, which would have been in 1948. So, I've lived here more than fifty years."

She'd moved to the neighbourhood in time to meet the youngest Brown son, but not the older two. I wrote down "1948" on the page. "Good. And what were your first impressions of Rose Park?"

She answered, I made notes and came up with a few more innocuous questions, and I wrapped up the fake part of the interview. "Thanks so much for your time. You've been a great help."

"You're very welcome. It's not every day someone your age takes an interest in my memories."

Not the perfect opening, but I ran with it. "It's funny you should mention memories, because I was thinking on my way over here about your comment the other day, the one about Patrick Hennessy's eyes?"

"He's a love, isn't he?" she said. "A nice, polite young man, and such a quick study."

"Yes, but what I found interesting was when you said you'd only seen his kind of variegated iris once or twice before." I strived to sound nonchalant. "On whom did you see it?"

"You know, I wondered the same thing myself after I started baking with Patrick, and I spent a few evenings pondering that very question."

I leaned forward. I might have begun to drool. "And?"

"I knew I'd seen eyes like Patrick's before, but for the life of me, I couldn't recall on whom. All I could remember was that the first time had also been in a young man's face." So much for my corroborating evidence.

"You couldn't remember which young man?"

"Well, eventually I did, after much pondering." She looked pleased with herself. "He was a boy named Tommy. Like Tommy Dorsey. Good-looking fellow, a ladies' man. Everyone loved Tommy. I was happily married at the time, of course, but all the girls were mad about him. He was so charming, and a great dancer."

"And he was the only man you knew who had the same eyes as Patrick?"

"I remember people said at the time his looks ran in the family, but I never met his relatives." She sighed. "It was a terrible tragedy when he died so young. In a car accident, you know."

"What a shame." We bowed our heads in a respectful memorial silence for a second, then I said, "What was the family name, do you recall?"

"Get to be my age, my dear, and you'll see what tricks your memory plays on you. I tried and tried to remember Tommy's surname. I could see his variegated eyes so clearly in my mind, but not his name. I finally went through my old photo albums and found a picture of him — would you like to see it?"

To put it mildly, "Love to."

She went over to a bookshelf, pulled out an old leather-bound photo album with black pages, sat down with it in her lap, raised to her face the reading glasses she wore on a chain around her neck, and began to turn the pages. "It's here somewhere — a picture at a golf club dinner. One of those table shots where they send a girl around with a flash camera. Where is it now? Maybe in the other book." She stood up again, pulled out another photo album, opened it. "You can't tell what his eyes are like from the picture, but you can see how handsome he was." She sat back down, and turned more pages, and I controlled an urge to snatch the book out of her hands.

She said, "I'm sure his last name was a common one, like White, or Smith, or Jones. I just wish I could remember it."

My entire future seemed to depend on not prompting her with the name. "I wonder what name could be like White."

"Black?" she said, and smiled. "But that wasn't it."
She turned the page. "Ah. Here's Tommy. He had a bit of the
look of a young Frank Sinatra, don't you think?" She passed
over the open album. A pretty young version of Gillian sat on
the left side of the picture, another woman in a fifties hairdo
was on the right, and in the middle was the man who had to
be Jeremiah Brown's youngest son — and Patrick's grandfather.
Gillian was right in saying the photograph didn't capture the
quality of his eyes, but I could see they were light in colour. I
could also see Patrick's mouth and chin on his face, recogniza-
ble despite Tommy's darker, straighter hair, and larger nose.

One last stimulus to jog Gillian's memory. "His hair looks
dark here," I said. "What colour was it?"

She took back the album, and looked at the picture. "The
photo doesn't do him justice. I remember his hair as brown —
a rich, chestnut brown."

The synapses fired soon enough, though when she spoke, it
was with the resigned aspect of someone who has given up on
her ability to reliably remember anything. "Oh dear. His surname
was Brown, Tommy Brown. How could I have forgotten that?"

~

I called my parents' number from a pay phone on the street near
the Market. My great luck — Dad answered.

"Hi, Dad, it's Blithe. But don't say my name out loud."

"Why not?"

"Never mind. Is Noel near you? A simple yes or no, please."

"No. He's in the flat with your mother. Where are you?"

"I'm out shopping. What are they doing over there?"

"Looking for my father's journal. Do you know where it is?"

"No. I seem to have misplaced it. But it'll turn up, I'm sure."

"Noel wanted to take a look at it before he goes to
the airport."

"When is he leaving?"

"He's ordered a car for three-thirty."

So I only had an hour to kill before I could go home. "Thank you. That's all I wanted to know. And do me a favour? Don't tell Noel about this conversation."

"Why not?"

"I can't explain right now. But please."

"All right, all right."

I said goodbye, hung up, and cycled off to the city reference library — a twenty-five-minute ride away — where I spent the time that remained before Noel's departure looking up various birth and death announcements in the newspaper files, examining all historic photos within the library's collection that might contain images of Rose Park Browns, and converting my hitherto non-profit, thwart-Noel plan into a more gainful venture. Now that I had a long-lost heir on my side of the bargaining table.

~

My parents were having drinks in the back garden when I got home. My mother called out when she heard me wheel up the bike. "Blithe, you missed saying goodbye to Noel!"

"Did I? I must have lost track of time."

"He so wanted to see you, too, about R.T.'s journal. I don't know what you can have done with it. We looked everywhere."

"It's probably under the couch."

"We looked under the couch."

I said, "Hey Dad, didn't you say you had a box of R.T.'s effects in the house?"

Mom frowned. "What would be the point of looking for the journal there?"

"I was more wondering if the box contained anything pertaining to Jeremiah Brown."

Dad swallowed some Scotch. "You've taken a keen interest in old Jeremiah, haven't you?"

"I'm just trying to be thorough in my research for Molly Greer's book." To my ear, I sounded about as convincing as one of my grade twos saying the punch he'd just thrown at another kid was accidental, but Dad said, "Would you like to see my father's files on Brown? I have them stored away in the spare room."

"I'd love to, thanks. Don't get up. I'll go find them."

Dad stood. "I'll come with you."

"What, now?" Mom said. "Really, Blithe, you've not had the greatest timing today."

Twenty minutes later, I walked into my flat and called Patrick. "I want to meet your mother."

"Why?"

"Because I've decided you're not a cad and a cur but a good guy who can be trusted."

"You still thinking about joining Noel's gang?"

"Maybe. Can I come over and explain everything?" Almost everything.

He was silent.

"Please?"

His voice broke. "You know I want you to come over."

"Then I will. I'll make you dinner. We'll talk. And Patrick, seriously — can you arrange for me to meet your mother? Tomorrow?"

~

Patrick hugged me with great ardour when he saw me. He raved about the spaghetti with anchovies, red peppers, arugula, and fresh breadcrumbs that I cooked on his stove. But he wasn't keen on my thwart-Noel plan. "It's too risky," he said. "And I don't think you should get involved with him."

"With my own brother?"

"How about we don't talk about this? Not tonight."

"Why not?"

"Because we have to make up."

~

Patrick's mother had his eyes, but was otherwise unlike him physically — she was petite and (dyed) blonde. And not as old as I'd thought she would be, with the talk of arthritis and multiple children. She was fifty-two, the right age to be Tommy Brown's illegitimate daughter, fathered a few months before he crashed his car on an icy road.

"So you're the Morrison girl," she said, when we'd settled into her small living room. It was furnished in the same modern style as Patrick's.

"Did you know my father Charles when you were growing up?" I doubted it. Dad was eight years her senior.

"No, I don't think so, though I've heard of the family. They're lawyers at one of the big downtown firms, aren't they?"

"Until my generation, yes. But you have the advantage of me. I don't know much about your family. Were you born and raised in Rose Park?"

"Yes, as was my mother before me." She smiled, with some mischief in her eyes. "I come from a long line of housekeepers."

"Mom," Patrick said.

"Patrick is embarrassed about my former profession, I don't know why. It served us well enough until my arthritis developed." She held up her hands, showed her misshapen fingers. "I work in a doctor's office now, as a receptionist, answering phones. But I think your parents may have dined at the last house I kept. That was for the Gordons, Deborah and Donald. Do you know them?"

A couple slightly older than my parents. "Yes, I do. Isn't Mr.

Gordon in the financial business?" The last I'd heard, he was CEO of a large investment bank.

"Yes, and doing well by it, too. I tried to convince Patrick to go into banking, but no, he wanted to make a living with his hands." The words weren't kind, but she looked at Patrick with great fondness when she said them.

"Patrick's a wonderful baker," I said. "And I'm told he has a good touch."

"If you're his girlfriend, I hope you'd know!" she said, and fell about laughing. Patrick rolled his eyes, said, "I'm going to get us something to drink," and left for the kitchen.

When Mrs. Hennessy had recovered from her joke, I said to her, "Did I understand you to say your mother was a house-keeper in Rose Park, too?"

"She was, and not just for anyone, either. Only the better families. Why, when she was young, she worked for the man you wrote that article about in the newspaper — Jeremiah Brown. Bet you didn't know that."

Bet I did. "How'd you like the article?"

"You had a good story there. I remember when the old man died, all everybody talked about was the treasure, but no one could find it. Guess someone did, though. I wish my mother was alive to have heard about that."

Patrick came back in and handed us each a glass of iced tea. I don't like iced tea, but I drank some to wet my throat. "What about your father?" I said. "Is he still living?"

"No. He died in 1995. Four years after my mother passed away." She showed no sign of hesitation when she spoke of her father, no sign of knowing of another.

I said, "How long were your parents married?"

"Forty-one years when my mother died. They married the year I was born." She winked at me. "I came a little ear-lier than expected."

I spat up some of my tea, they both asked if I was all right, and I assured them I was fine, wiped at the stains on my shirt with a napkin Patrick handed me.

Mrs. Hennessy said, "Of course, young people today don't worry about timing issues anymore, what with everyone practising safe sex. Isn't that right, Patrick?"

A comment that Patrick for some reason took as our cue to leave.

~

I had a date with Alexandra, so I didn't get a chance to tell Patrick my theory about his paternity — make that grandpaternity — until later, when we met at my place and played at being spies on a mission who can't speak freely for fear of the enemy eavesdroppers lurking outside in the surveillance truck.

I had loud music playing on the stereo when Patrick and Buck arrived. I shushed them at the door, took Patrick to my bedroom, gestured to him to lie down on the bed with me, put my arms around him as best as one can when lying face-to-face on one's side, and whispered in his ear, "Let's talk this way."

His hands found my waist and rested there. "Why?"

"Because it's more fun." Not because I believed Noel could have planted an electronic listening device in my apartment. He may have been a decoder-ring aficionado, but he was in no way mechanical. My security precautions aside, Patrick sat right up and yelled, "No!" when I whispered to him that he might be one of the missing heirs to the Brown estate.

He got up, turned off the music, and suggested we go for a walk outside where we could talk freely and I could explain the vast amount of circumstantial evidence I'd collected in support of his case. An hour of discussion passed before he would concede my theory might have some credence, and that was only after we'd concluded his grandmother must have kept her secret to the grave. Though why had she not said anything when the news of the treasure hunt came out? "Maybe she didn't realize your mother might have a legal claim," I said.

"Maybe she didn't want her husband to know."

We accepted both those explanations, and Patrick seconded my belief his mother knew nothing, said he was sure she would have told him if she did.

"But you realize who does know, don't you?" I said. We were walking back to the flat. The sun was low in the sky, the lawn sprinklers were running, the neighbourhood was wreathed in peace and quiet. "Noel. Noel knows. That's why he never told anyone he found the treasure. In case your family might take it away from him. And that's why he didn't want me to read my grandfather's journal. In case I figured out you were related."

Patrick scowled, gripped my hand tighter, flexed and reflexed his arm muscles. And I said, "Can we talk some more about how to thwart him now?"

~ Chapter 15 ~

We laid our plans and refined and finessed them, and I tried not to be too jumpy every day when checking email, tried not to combust with frustration when my internet connection went down for an evening, and took an hour and a half of help-line time to fix the next day — an hour and a half of a polite and patient technical person six hundred miles away telling me try this, try that, open this, close that, restart and see if it works now.

No emails had come from Noel in the interim, but two days after the system was restored, Noel did send a terse message in one of his infantile codes (A=Z, B=Y, etc) saying the expected shipment had been delayed by a few weeks, so to hold tight till we heard from him.

Had he cottoned onto us? Was this a triple-cross intended to defeat our double? Patrick and I debated the subtext of this development at length, and I tortured myself conjuring up ever more unlikely and implausible scenarios to explain the delay, scenarios based on the assumptions that Noel's plans were labyrinthine, his intentions malicious. What if Noel needed the extra time so he could arrange for Interpol agents — or whatever kind of agents had jurisdiction over missing art pieces — to be waiting in ambush to nab Patrick when he tried to hand over the goods to the dealer? What if the artifacts Patrick had been passing weren't artifacts at all, but were fakes like Trixie, implanted with state secrets inscribed on hidden microchips, or infused somehow with high-grade heroin?

After a few days of listening to me gabble on about ever more outlandish suspicions, Patrick demanded I stop all speculation, not traffic in paranoia. We could do nothing but sit and wait and drive ourselves insane, or we could carry on, behave normally, and pretend there wasn't a current of apprehension electrifying our daily routines.

I took his point. So while Patrick baked bagels and dog-walked and met with Gillian to continue his pastry chef apprenticeship, I wrested my imaginative energy away from the dark side, and applied it instead to the difficult task of drafting some puzzle book text.

I sat down with each of Molly's drawings in turn and spent hours coming up with an opening line, an opening approach. How to start with the footbridge, for instance? Should I mention its popularity as a kissing venue off the top? Should I be talking about kissing at all if the target audience were children? Could I do something clever with alliteration, using words starting with "A" to hint at the A's in the pattern of the bridgework? If I used a limerick to start off the Glenwood page — "There once was an old man named Brown" — I could hardly employ the same device (There once was an old man named Morrison?) for the picture of my parents' house. But which page would a limerick better suit?

The possibilities were endless, the decision-making process a jumble of either/or alternatives. I worked away, juggled words and phrases, dealt with the domino effect every time I changed a sentence or gambit, and finally finished a showable version. The effort had been powered by nervous energy accumulated in anticipation of our impending caper, but I'd passed the time and produced a tolerable first draft. My next step was to get feedback from a reader other than Molly, someone who knew a bit about children's books, and could be relied upon to be kind but honest, neither too partial nor too dismissive: Alexandra.

~

"I brought something for you to read today," I said, on the way to the park the next Sunday. "A new book I'd like your opinion on."

She held Tup's lead comfortably now, an old hand. "Another one about the twins?"

"It's more of a picture book than a chapter book. And it's not quite finished. The author wants some feedback on this draft."

"Is it the puzzle book about Rose Park you were doing the research for?"

"Yes, it is."

"Good," she said. "I wanted to see it."

At the playground, I tied Tup up to the fence, made him lie down, cleared off a picnic table of dirt and someone's crumbs, and spread out my mockup on the tabletop.

"You know who else could look at this, if you want?" Alexandra said. "My friend Margaret. She reads a lot. And she wants to meet you anyway, since I showed her your newspaper article about me and you and the treasure."

"I haven't heard you mention Margaret before. Is she a new friend?"

"I met her at Creative Writing camp last week."

"There is such a thing? How was it?"

"Margaret wrote the best story — about a girl who finds a secret door in a library that leads to the fantasy worlds in books."

Margaret, Schmargaret. "What did you write about?"

"My story was about a girl and a dog who save another girl's life when she almost drowns in a river."

"That sounds just as good to me. And exciting."

"It was okay. Is this page one?"

I read over her shoulder. By page three, I'd found a dozen things wrong. I gave up and waited for Alexandra to finish, looked over at Tup panting on the ground and a kid playing with the water fountain, and listened to the pongs of the tennis balls on the courts nearby.

After reading the page about Glenwood, Alexandra said, "Well, of course you had to do the cornerstone." About the footbridge, she said, "I get it! I see the A's! That's cool." At the Smithy's garage page, she said, "We had to memorize a poem about a blacksmith for school." And so on.

When she'd finished, and I'd made various notes about her reactions and mine, I said, "So, what's your overall rating? What would you give this book out of ten?"

She thought for a moment. "An eight."

"An eight's not bad. Thank you."

"Wait. Did you write it?"

"Oh, well, yes. I did."

"In that case, I'd give it a nine."

"Why?"

"Because teachers always give the students they like a better mark."

~

Jane's husband had taken Joshua out, and Jane had spent the babysitting time at her office. "How did your work go?" I said, when I brought Alexandra home.

"It went well. I get so much more done when I'm there alone."

"Was the museum busy?"

"Not very. The visitors outnumbered the security guards about three to one."

"The museum still has guards? I would have thought there'd be a sophisticated video surveillance system that watched every room in the place."

"There's that, as well, including a camera that runs in my office. I always forget it's there. I hope I haven't picked my nose recently."

"Mom!" Alexandra said. "That's gross!"

I said, "Do they have cameras in the washrooms, too?" Jane must have wondered why I cared, but I painted a sociable, conversational look on my face that would have made my mother proud.

"There are cameras in the washrooms, but not in the stalls, I don't think. I hope not, anyway."

"There are cameras in the washrooms?" Alexandra said. "Remind me never to go there again."

I said, "Next week, same time?" Jane said yes, please, and Alexandra asked if I could bring Trixie along. When I needed her to be under wraps, backstage, waiting to play a key role in the upcoming spectacle.

"Actually," I said, "I probably can't, because ..." They waited to hear the reason I hadn't come up with yet. "Because I've misplaced her. Maybe Tup hid her somewhere. I'll look again." I tried a smile. "Hey, Alexandra. It sounds like a case for Molly Greer's crime-solving twins, doesn't it? The Disappearance of Trixie?"

She wouldn't be cajoled. "Do you think she's lost? I wanted to show her to Margaret."

"I sure hope not." I had, I'm ashamed to say, become an expert liar.

~

I worked on the puzzle book text over the next few days, fixed the problems I'd noticed when I'd looked at it through Alexandra's eyes, and addressed her issues, too. That is, when I wasn't checking for email.

Noel had shown me how to set up a pseudo-anonymous email account, for which I used the name "Spirit," as in Blithe, in keeping with the alter egos of my partners-in-crime (Hannah's email account name, Noel had informed me, was MaggieBW, in honour of photojournalist Margaret Bourke-White — a fact I did not find in any way touching). And spirited I was: I turned on my computer every morning at seven, and checked it at far too frequent intervals throughout the day.

On a Tuesday morning, I gave the printed puzzle book material one last look-over while my modem connected with the server, and had just decided I was ready to turn it over to Molly for comments when I heard the incoming mail signal and saw two messages listed on my screen, both from JeremiahB.

The first, addressed to me, contained the date of the shipment — in three days time — and nothing more. The second was a blind copy of the message he'd sent the local dealer, JohnSmith497. Decoded, it read like this: *Page from medieval illuminated manuscript on its way.*

I clucked with annoyance about the obviousness of the message. How unimaginative could Noel be, if his idea of master criminal tactics was to use an email moniker like JeremiahB, a password I guessed in three tries (it was not Glenwood, nor my mother's maiden name, but Angus, the name of our childhood dog), and to make the content of his coded messages so direct? Though his simpleton approach made it easy for me to break into his email account and send this new coded message to JohnSmith497: *Change in plan. Paleolithic era goddess figurine coming instead.* It was also easy to temporarily forward Noel's mail to a third account I'd set up, named after a meaningless six-digit number that contained no significant birthdates or numbers. A smart precaution, it turned out, for that's where I received a request that afternoon for confirmation of the item details from JohnSmith497, who wanted to know the place of origin and dating of the figurine. I replied to that message, received back an acceptance, advised JohnSmith497 against any further contact for the week, removed the forward instruction from Noel's JeremiahB account, shut off my computer, and went out.

I found Patrick in the ravine with the dog pack. I ran over and clutched him by the arms. "I heard from Noel."

He frowned. "I have a bad feeling about this. How about we do the switch next time? Treat this shipment as a test run, see how it goes."

I let go of his arms, which I saw from the white marks left behind on his skin I might have gripped a little hard. "It's too late for that. I've already told JohnSmith497 about the change in object."

"Shit."

"What?"

"I wish I knew for sure your plan was going to work."

"How many times have we gone over it?"

"About twenty."

"Don't be so literal. We've gone over it a hundred times and it's foolproof." No wonder Noel engaged in the smuggling business, if it provided the drug-like high I was feeling. "There's no stopping us now," I said. "Operation Thwart is under way."

~

The shipment was scheduled for Friday, to be sent to me at my parents' address. On Thursday evening, I dropped in on Mom and Dad on the pretext of borrowing a cup of sugar, chatted with them awhile, mentioned I expected a package from Noel the next day. "He's sending me a box of some special English chocolate he told me about."

Mom said, "He's so thoughtful."

"But I'd like to open the package myself," I said, "when it arrives."

"Of course, dear. You don't think I'd open a package addressed to you, do you? Anyway, I won't be here tomorrow morning. I have a hair appointment."

The groundwork laid (and sugar obtained), I stood up to leave. Mom accompanied me to the door, said, "How's everything going with your young man?"

"Patrick? Fine. Why?"

She stood behind me and pulled my shoulders back. "Stand up straight. Dad suggested we have the two of you over for dinner sometime."

The thought of Patrick in his baseball cap, sitting at my mother's table — set for the occasion with a full complement of silver, china, and crystal, in order to send a not so subtle message about the socioeconomic differences between us — was too stressful to bear, under my current tense circumstances. "I think it's a bit early in the relationship for dinner with the parents."

"Have you met his mother?" she said.

Only because I wanted to check out her irises. "Once. And it's different with you and Dad — you knew Patrick before I did because of the dog-walking. You gave him a key to your house." Similar to the one I would use to retrieve my shipment the next day.

"We never saw him when he walked Tup. And Dad thinks it would be a good idea to get to know him better."

"What do you think?"

She waited a fraction too long before replying. "I think that if you're serious about him, we should become better acquainted."

Dad had twisted her arm, in other words. "Can I let you know when the timing feels more right?"

"Whenever."

"What time are you leaving for the hairdresser in the morning, did you say?"

"Nine o'clock. Why?"

"I'm just wondering when I should be here to look out for my package."

"What a fuss for some chocolate! I'll have to try a piece. Though I rarely touch it, and nor should you. A chocolate a day equals ten pounds in a year, you know."

Patrick and I had agreed that his talented hands should be the ones to separate the manuscript page from the lining of the box of chocolates, which meant that I wouldn't be able to open the package until he got off work at ten-thirty. No problem there — the package hadn't arrived by ten-thirty. Or eleven. Or eleven-thirty, when my mother came home with her hair coloured, cut, and blown dry.

"You don't need to wait around," she said, when she found me pacing in her front hall. "I'll call you when the package comes."

She'd call me and ask me to open the box, so she could view the chocolate in all its splendour. I said, "Are you going out again this afternoon?"

"At two. I have a late tee-off with Marge. Her son is dating someone, you'll be interested to hear — a lovely young woman of about twenty-five or so. Men like Phil get snapped up fast these days, divorced with children or not."

"I'm glad for him. But if you're going to be here to receive the package, I think I'll go out now, do a few errands."

"I'll leave it at your place if it comes while you're gone."

Precisely.

~

The courier came near three o'clock, when Patrick and I were both there, Mom was at her golf game, and Dad was safely ensconced at his office downtown. I signed the packing slip, and we ran a very large box of chocolate — Noel had spared no expense — over to my place. With the blinds drawn, the door double-locked, and my breath held, I watched Patrick, wearing latex gloves, slit open the lining of the box with a razor blade and carefully remove a thin envelope that had been inserted inside. The envelope, made of acid-free paper, was fitted so the paper within couldn't move, was sealed shut, and was stiffened with thin pieces of acid-free cardboard so it couldn't crease.

I said, "Can't we take a look at the illustration before we pass it on?"

"Our job is to deliver it, not appreciate it."

"But how do we know for certain what's inside the packaging?"

"What's inside is not our concern. The dealer would blame Noel if the shipment is faulty, not us, remember? The idea your whole plan is based on?"

When Patrick had placed the package inside the envelope we had readied for the purpose, and glued the box back together, we sat for a minute, and rested, and each tried a chocolate, found them to be bitter. We didn't need to discuss our next steps. Patrick went home to prepare for his Beachside Park rendezvous with JohnSmith497 to hand over Trixie — minus her pink sweater, swaddled instead in a protective cloth and packed in bubble wrap. And I, once I controlled the twitch in my left temple and calmed the muscle spasms in my right calf, was off to the museum.

~

There was no logical reason to leave a page from a medieval illuminated manuscript in the Classical Greek section of the museum, but I'd harboured great affection for the museum's Athenian gallery since childhood, specifically for a scale model of the Parthenon on display in a glass case. The model was constructed in such a way that you could bend down and look through the columned entranceway of the temple to the interior, to where the colossal statue of Athena — painted in a gaudy garb of white and gold and blue and red, and bearing a colossal shield and matching spear — towered over the inner chamber.

I'd taken a survey course on ancient art and architecture as an elective for my undergraduate degree, and learned about more obscure and better-preserved temples and theatres and stadiums in Greece. I'd visited the Elgin marbles in the British Museum, I'd gone to Athens and climbed the Acropolis and witnessed the elegance the Parthenon exudes in its present, crumbled, time-worn state. But that model in the museum — the fluting of every column detailed in plaster of Paris, the famous friezes on the pediments crudely recreated in primary colours — spoke to me still, reminded me of an innocent young girl who had stood entranced before an object that fired her imagination.

And the chest-high glass-topped surface of the display case, located in a back corner of the gallery, made the perfect place for a drop.

I'd considered all of a blonde wig, a pillow pregnancy, and the basic baseball cap and sunglasses rig as possible costumes for the videotaped portion of our caper, but decided to rely on some uncharacteristic wardrobe pieces as my best means of disguise. In my bag, a canvas carryall that could pass as a purse if the museum staff suggested that bags must be checked, I packed a long floral-print dress I'd bought for five dollars at a thrift shop, a straw hat with a large brim under which I could tuck all my hair and hide much of my face, and a disposable pair of white canvas sneakers.

Mindful of Jane's advice about the museum's washroom surveillance cameras, I changed outfits in a busy public washroom at a subway interchange, a place where I gambled that my pass-through would go unnoticed. Into the bag went my sandals. Over my own clothes — a white T-shirt and knee-length cotton skirt — went the girly dress. The sneakers were tied onto my feet, the hat firmly fixed on my head with a hatpin.

No one noticed me on the walk to the museum from the subway station. The pedestrians I walked through and past were more interested in the shop window displays and their own reflections than the sight of me in a flowered dress.

I entered the museum at four-fifteen and sussed out the activity at the membership desk. Using my own gloves, I had placed the manila envelope containing the acid-free envelope in my bag. I'd also cut from a museum brochure the conveniently printed museum director's name and address, and glued it on to the front of the envelope. My ultimate intent was to leave the drawing within the Greek gallery, but I had factored in the possibility that I might be able to drop it on a counter in the museum lobby instead, if the people working there were busy enough serving customers that they wouldn't notice the envelope until I had slipped away.

No go on that idea. There were two staff people at the membership desk, two at the general admission booth, and the only other customers in the lobby were a woman with a young boy who was clamouring to visit the bat cave.

I paid my admission with cash, made no memorable small talk, clipped the museum button to the neckline of the dress, and headed to the top floor, where I strolled into the temple gallery, past the guard stationed in the doorway between this room and the next, and made a slow turn around the room. I stopped to study every object on show, and waited for the guard to move on, to rotate to his next position, to decide I was no threat and could be left alone for a few minutes.

When he'd checked his watch and walked away at last, I reached inside the outer pocket of my bag, found my pair of latex gloves, pulled one onto my right hand, used the gloved hand to feel around in the inner pocket of the bag and take hold of the manila envelope, draw it out, carry it in front of me. I approached the case that contained the Parthenon model, rested my elbows on top, pretended to gaze within, and used my peripheral vision to check one last time that I was alone.

I was careful not to touch the envelope with my ungloved hand, not to make any sudden moves, to let the envelope slide slowly from my fingers and rest on top of the display case. The effort required not to run away at top speed was gargantuan, but I stood still while an interminable thirty seconds ticked by, and forced myself to proceed at a slow pace when I did move. I stopped at the next case and mimed an interest in the contents, and did the same for another before I cruised out of the room, through the galleries, towards the exit.

There are two concrete staircases in the middle of the museum, across a wide landing from each other, each one built around a pair of antique wooden totem poles imported from the west coast a century before. When I was young, the steps seemed to go up forever, around and around the fierce totem pole faces, faces that scared me if I looked at them too long up close.

I wasn't frightened by the totem pole faces anymore, but I had no desire to study them, to unlock the secret of their power. All I wanted was to leave the museum, and the illuminated manuscript page, behind, now, quickly. I walked down a flight, then a landing, another flight and another landing — how much farther to ground level? I measured my pace, didn't whip around the corners or to race the way I had with Noel, when we were kids. He would take one set of stairs, I the other, and down we'd go, feet flying, hands sliding down the curved metal handrail. What part of the museum would we have come from? Not the bat cave — it didn't exist then. Maybe we'd visited the dinosaurs, or the mummies, or the knights' armour, or Athena's temple. Who cared, as long as we could compete, going there and back? I'd been giddy with excitement on the stairs then, and I was close to giddy now. I heard footsteps coming down the stairs behind me and was positive they belonged to a guard who held my envelope in his hand, who was chasing me to ask if I'd left it behind. No. The owner of the footsteps left the stairwell at the second floor. I kept going, heard the sound of voices drift up from the bottom of the totem pole, voices that became louder as I descended, voices I was approaching. One of those voices must belong to an observant guard who monitored the video surveillance cameras, who had seen me leave the envelope and had emerged from security central to find me, to tap me on the shoulder, to ask me to please come along and explain where I had obtained an artifact known to all museum people around the world as stolen.

The conversation was close enough now that I could catch the occasional word. I heard something familiar in the voices that I couldn't place, but there was no urgency in the tones, no suggestion of pursuit. They weren't after me. Were they? Of course not. I needed to calm down, go slow, behave as if I were an innocent tourist in a straw hat and flowered dress who had spent a pleasant sojourn in the study of ancient objects. There — the final flight of stairs was ahead, the final hurdle. All I had to do was go down those stairs and into the lobby, through the doors and outside.

I rounded the last bit of totem pole and spotted a group of three people standing and talking in the main floor hallway at the foot of the stairs. One of the people was Jane, who should have been tucked away in her behind-the-scenes office, not loose in the public part of the museum. I floated by, head down and turned away from her, hat brim effect maximized on her side. She didn't notice me, I was sure — she was too involved with her conversation. I glided past, through the lobby and out the front doors to the street. I did not hear her stop and call my name, I was not apprehended by any guard or staff member or bystander. I was home-free. I had won the race.

~

I walked back to the subway, changed once more in the busy washroom, stuffed the dress, hat, and shoes into a plastic bag, disposed of the latex gloves in a garbage can on the street, walked home, deposited my costume in a Goodwill drop-off bin I passed on the way.

Two horribly slow hours later, when Patrick called, I snatched the phone off the cradle, said hello. "Hi," he said, "it's Patrick. How are you? Had a good day?" Following our script.

"Great. You?"

"Same. Buck and I will be over in fifteen."

I met them on the street and we walked around, and talked, and told each other how our respective outings had gone — hitchlessly. We came back home, and to keep my hands busy, I made grilled cheese and chutney sandwiches. We ate them, passed on any more of the chocolate for dessert, went to bed early, and lay there in spoon-position, not sleepy, unable to do much except wait for the fallout of our switcheroo.

~ Chapter 16 ~

We didn't have to wait long.

On Sunday, in her front hall, Jane said to me, "The strangest thing happened at work this week."

Alexandra said, "Someone left a piece of paper that had been stolen from another museum in Mommy's museum."

I worked hard to look perplexed. "A piece of paper?"

"A drawing of Adam and Eve and the serpent," Alexandra said. "A very old and valuable one."

I kept my brow knit. "How old?"

Jane explained that a sealed manila envelope addressed to the museum director had been left in the Athenian gallery, and found to contain a page from a medieval illuminated manuscript.

I bent down to tie Alexandra's shoes, ignored her surprise I was doing so. "So who left it, does anyone know? Did the security cameras catch anything?"

Jane said, "Only some images of a woman in a long dress and a large hat who dropped the envelope containing the work on a display case sometime Friday afternoon. A couple of staff people remember seeing her, but no one talked with her. And now the matter's been turned over to the police."

I stood up, partly to make sure I didn't fall down. "Why the police?"

"Because the illustration was stolen property."

"But it sounds like someone was trying to return it."

"It's an odd situation, all right."

I fumbled in my bag for my sunglasses. Play-acting would be easier if I could hide my eyes. "I didn't read about this in the newspaper. Is it supposed to be a secret?" I hoped not. The sooner Noel found out what we'd done, the better.

"I don't see how the news media could not get hold of it," Jane said. "The police were at the museum for hours on Friday questioning everyone from the desk clerks to the janitors. Someone's sure to tell a reporter. They even questioned me."

I found the sunglasses, put them on. "Oh, my." *Oh my?* "What was that like?"

"Interesting. They showed me a piece of videotape in which the suspect walked right by me."

I sorted out my respiratory system, said, "Really? And had you noticed the person at the time?"

"Not at all. I guess I'm not cut out for detective work. You two off to the park today?"

"Sure are," I said, and put up a hand up to rub the very tense muscles in the back of my neck.

~

That night in bed, I said to Patrick, "Leaving the illustration at the museum may not have been the best idea. I shouldn't have risked running into Jane."

"I thought she didn't see you."

"She didn't. But I can't take any more of this deception. I hate not being able to look my decent, truth-telling friends in the eye."

He smiled in the dark. "You're not finding the life of crime exciting anymore?"

"No. I prefer to sleep through the night."

Good man — he resisted the urge to say he'd told me so. "Me too, but we will, soon. After we deal with Noel."

I kicked off the bedclothes. "Alexandra asked me about Trixie again today. Do you think we can get her back when this is all over?"

"You know we can't."

I cursed Noel for throwing his cloak of bad deeds around me, for enveloping me in its folds, and I settled in for a restless night of troubled sleep.

~

Our guess was that the local dealer might have had his doubts about Trixie on the weekend, but couldn't do anything about them until Monday. Monday he could have her tested — he must know someone who could handle the job. That meant Tuesday would be the earliest he could contact Noel to unleash his wrath and pass on the news that the package he'd received did not contain the illustration. Therefore Tuesday was the earliest I expected Noel to call or email to unleash *his* wrath.

I did not hear from Noel on Tuesday. I did read a brief item in the newspaper that said an artwork stolen from an Italian museum a few months before had turned up under mysterious circumstances in our own museum. How long till a wire service picked up the story and sent it around the world? And what were the odds Noel would read it?

There was no word Wednesday. "Maybe the test is taking longer than we estimated," I said to Patrick, who made an annoying comment about the virtue of patience in reply.

Nothing Thursday or Friday, though I sent myself several emails to make sure the account was working. No new messages over the weekend. I was so desperate for information I was driven to mention to Jane on Sunday that I'd seen the news story in the paper and was anything happening with the case that she knew of?

"I think the trail's run cold. All anyone at work is talking about is how to get the work back to Rome securely."

By the weekend, I was certain my plan had backfired, that the unsuspecting dealer had taken Trixie as genuine and sold her to an equally unsuspecting collector, which meant I couldn't spring my closer on Noel, and what a muddle that was — now we'd have to live in the state of uncertainty until the next time he asked for help with a shipment. Such a dilemma being what happens when amateurs try to do the job of a professional, said a voice in my ear that sounded an awful lot like Patrick's.

I was preoccupied at Bagel Haven during my Monday morning visit, had no time for Arthur's opinions on current events, was not in the mood for Curly and Earring's noise, took my bagel to go so I could run home to my computer and sit by the screen. When I bumped into Molly on the way out, I had to make myself stop and speak to her cordially about the puzzle book. She had left a phone message the week before saying my words looked good at first glance, that she would go over them in detail and get back to me with ideas for revision. Those ideas seemed to be what she was handing me in an envelope now.

"Read my comments over, and let me know what you think," she said. "But what you've done is super."

"Thanks. I'll call you." I made to go.

"And guess what?" she said.

I may have failed to hide my disinterest. "What?"

"Hannah's in town!"

"What?"

Quickly and quietly, she said, "I haven't spoken to her about the treasure, as we agreed. Okay?"

In lieu of saying what for a third time, I stared at her with my mouth open.

Molly said, "Here she is!" and held the door for Hannah to walk in. "Look, Hannah. I told you we'd find Blithe here."

Hannah smiled with her big white teeth in that tanned face, did a good impression of someone pleased to see me. "Hi, Blithe. What's new?"

I looked at Molly. Her face showed nothing but maternal affection, seemingly aimed at both of us. I turned to see if Patrick was within view — he wasn't — so I could warn him and/or summon him over. All this looking around took only a second or two, and then the mother with the baby I saw every morning appeared next to Hannah and asked if we'd ordered yet, because she'd like to, and we three moved aside and I untied my tongue and tried to respond to the new question Hannah had posed, which was: "When can we get together today? I'd love to chat."

What could I say? Well, I wouldn't?

Molly said, "How about this afternoon? I have a tennis game at one."

"Sounds good to me," Hannah said.

I swallowed, produced a fake smile for Molly's benefit, and agreed to meet at one. Molly went off to see about her bagel, and in a low voice, Hannah said, "Oh, good. Here comes your little boyfriend. I need to talk to that fucker too."

Patrick was pushing the bagel trolley, didn't see Hannah until he'd come up beside us. He stopped the trolley, took in the sight of her with hooded eyes, and, unfazed, began to load bagels into the baskets.

"Patrick," I said, or rather, screeched, in a voice raw with nerves, "Hannah wants to meet with us this afternoon to talk."

Patrick said, "I have dogs to walk."

Hannah said, "You can't avoid me. I've come here for the sole purpose of setting you two straight."

Patrick made a derisive snorting sound I hadn't heard from him before. "Ooh," he said, "I'm scared."

Hannah said, "We'll meet at the sports park. One o'clock. You can bring your goddamned dogs along."

She left us to join Molly at the cash. I stood, rooted to the floor, my mouth again agape. Patrick said, "Why should we even show up?"

I kept my eye on Hannah, though she did not turn to check on us, made it obvious by the set of her shoulders that she didn't need to, that we posed no threat. "We have to show up, hear her out, see what she has to say. And then we can drop the bomb about your claim to the treasure."

Patrick's eyes glared defiance. "Maybe we should refuse to talk to her at all. Tell her we'll only talk to the big boss himself, not his lackey."

"No, let's resolve this, get it over with, today. Before I lose what little courage I have left."

~

The sun shone, a group of kids in white shorts and T-shirts hit flocks of tennis balls across the nets on the tennis courts, and Hannah, Patrick, and I, surrounded by dogs, sat on a long bench under a tree.

I asked Hannah what I'd asked Noel. "Why are you here?"

"You know why."

Patrick said, "Is there any way you could be a bit less melodramatic?"

She scowled. "Noel's angry about the switch you pulled. More than angry. He's livid."

Patrick again. "And where is he?"

"He sent me to speak for him. It wouldn't look right if he came back so soon."

I said, "But you were just here, too."

"I know. Keeping an eye on you guys has become a real pain in the ass."

I smiled. Ha ha on them. "That was the general idea."

"This isn't funny, Blithe. If you think Noel's going to sit by and let you idiots ruin his fun, you're mistaken."

"You're starting to sound melodramatic again," Patrick said.

Hannah pointed at him. "As for you, you shit — this whole situation is your fault. Why you had to go and get involved with Blithe, I'll never know."

I said, "Why did you have to go and get involved with Noel?"

She shrugged. "He knew how to have a good time better than anyone else around here."

"You mean he was the only person you could find who wanted to cheat and steal?"

Hannah sighed. "Talk about melodrama. Maybe if you two stopped thinking of yourselves as white knights battling dragons, you might realize all Noel and I are doing is supplementing our income by providing business services to well-paying clients. We don't steal anything."

I said, "What about the treasure?"

"What about it? Noel found it fair and square. So what that he didn't tell anyone? Why should he?"

I said, "You do know the real reason Noel couldn't boast to the world that he'd found the treasure, don't you?"

I felt Patrick's body tense on one side of me, and Hannah's tighten on the other. I said, "You know that Patrick is Jeremiah Brown's great-grandson, right?"

She hadn't known — I saw it on her face for the second before she drew a blind over what looked a mixture of shock and anger. Anger at Noel, I assumed. She couldn't help sneaking a peek at Patrick, either, before she said, "Bullshit, he is. Brown's sons died childless before Brown did."

"You don't have to believe me. But I'm sure a good lawyer could spin gold out of the matching thread of DNA we've found in a lock of hair that came from Brown's son." I was, of course, bluffing. I *had* found a lock of hair in R.T.'s file, but I hadn't yet dropped it off at the corner DNA lab for testing. "I'm sure we could make an interesting and drawn-out legal case out of Patrick's claim to the treasure."

"Yeah," Patrick said. "We could. And we will, if necessary."

Hannah swore, loud enough to attract a disapproving shake of the head from two women walking by. The women moved on, the dogs snuffled, and Hannah said, "I'll have to speak to Noel about this, and get back to you."

"Don't you want to know our terms?" I said.

She looked pained. "You *would* have terms."

It took less than a minute to explain what we wanted: a half share of the original treasure amount paid to an account in Patrick's name, and for both of us to be left out of their smuggling ring without fear of being blackmailed for our parts in it to date.

Hannah said, "Let me get this straight. You've virtually destroyed our business, you did away with a hefty chunk of profit when you donated the illustration to the museum, and now you expect to get money from Noel for this guy?"

I reached for Patrick's hand, but I couldn't hold it — he had it too tightly clenched in a fist. "It's a good deal," I said. "We're not charging a cent of interest. We'll never bother either of you about this again, we swear. And it's time you both found an alternate hobby. For the parents' sakes."

Patrick said to me, "Don't forget about the letter we've left in the safety deposit box, with instructions to be opened in the event of our deaths."

Patrick and I had never discussed any such letter, but from the wild cast to his eye, I deduced he was travelling on a my-style fantastic voyage to what-if land. "Right," I said. And to Hannah, "In case you or Noel are considering arranging some kind of retaliatory accident for us, an untimely death, say — we've hidden away a letter that explains all, and incriminates you both."

"For Christ's sake," Hannah said. "An accident? An untimely death? Your imagination has gotten the better of you, Blithe, as usual. Noel and I are not psychopaths." She stood up, brushed the specks of lint that were us off of her shorts, and turned her back on the green field, the children, the bird-twitterings in the air. "You'll be hearing from me," she said, and stalked away.

When she was safely across the street, I turned to Patrick. "A letter in a safety deposit box to be opened in the event of our deaths?"

"I know," Patrick said. "It was a lame idea. But better safe than sorry." Us and Noel both.

~

I gnawed on the inside of my mouth — ate it instead of dinner — for the five hours until Hannah dropped by my place to tell us Noel had caved when he found out we knew from whom Patrick had inherited his cracked blue eyes. He dickered with the price a bit, lowered the cost of our silence to two hundred thousand dollars, based on a deduction he felt was justified by our "theft" of the medieval picture. We accepted his offer, or, I should say, Patrick accepted, on behalf of his family. Two hundred thousand could provide some supplemental interest income to his mother's salary, help support the kids she still had living at home. And giving up a portion of that financial responsibility would allow Patrick to rent some baking time and space from Arthur in the early evenings, so he could produce the fancy baked goods that he would soon begin to sell to upscale grocery stores and restaurants around town.

Patrick and I performed a victory dance around the apartment after Hannah, in a cloud of profanity, left us, but later, in bed, I couldn't sleep. Again and still.

"What now?" Patrick said, but gently.

I tucked my knees up to my chest. "If only we hadn't had to weave such a web of lies."

"What the mothers don't know won't hurt them."

"There are so many mothers involved, though — yours, mine, Molly, Jane, Gillian."

I heard nothing in the room but the sound of Buck's breathing for a moment, then Patrick said, "Do you know when I first started to like you?"

"Are you trying to change the subject?"

"No."

"Was it when I used too many big words?"

"It was when you were talking about Brat Farrar and you said you liked him because though he had done bad things, he was basically a good person."

"And you think we're basically good people, too?"

"I know we are."

~

Alexandra stopped asking me about Trixie, partly because I saw her less. She went with her family on vacation for a few weeks in August, and she was invited to the cottage of her new friend Margaret a couple of weekends, then September came, and Jane thanked me for my summer babysitting, wished me luck in the upcoming school year, in effect said au revoir.

I faltered a few moments with the fear of discovery in the face of Jane's graceful goodbye, wondered if she could have reviewed the museum security videotapes and guessed the true identity of the woman in the flowered dress. Maybe, I said to Patrick, she had decided not to report me to the authorities, but not to associate with me any longer either, was echoing my approach to Noel.

Patrick disagreed. "Most people don't think about things as much as you, don't let their minds go so wild."

He must have been right. Because when I saw Jane on the street one evening in mid-September, she was warm and friend-ly — we spoke for a good fifteen minutes, and she showed no sign of discomfort, didn't try to edge away. I told her Patrick and I were planning to move in together, were looking for a new apartment we could make our own, and she said she and Alexandra missed us, would love to have us over for dinner. On a specific date.

That left only Molly to feel guilty about. Did I owe it to her to reveal the final resolution of the quest she had assigned to me all those years ago at Glenwood? Or to stay quiet? I couldn't decide.

The first time I saw her after Hannah left, Molly said, "Hannah's stay was so short. Did you two have a nice visit together, at least?"

"It was a little awkward. We don't have much in common anymore. You know how that can happen."

She wouldn't meet my eye. "I'm afraid Hannah said more or less the same about you."

The pit of nervousness I would be jumping into at the slightest provocation for months to come opened up before my feet. "What else did she say?"

Molly breathed out a sigh. "Hannah thinks anyone who doesn't live life the way she does — dangerously — isn't really living. But she doesn't see what you have that she doesn't."

Good old Molly — champion of my cause, my own non-magical, irreligious fairy godmother. I said, "What is it that I have, according to you?"

"Just everything that matters more than excitement. Corny, boring things like love, friends, family, a place you belong." She patted my arm twice, and steered the conversation over to the puzzle book. The mushy part of our talk — and any further discussion between us about the treasure — was over.

~

In early October, Patrick and his mother went to Niagara Falls on a weekend trip to visit Ryan, a pilgrimage they made once a year in the interest of maintaining family ties. That same weekend, my parents were in San Francisco, on another of my father's law conferences, which left me dog-sitting both Buck and Tup. I was still living in the coach house — Patrick and I would move into a west-end duplex on October 15 — so it was from my parents' street that I set off, on a cloudy Saturday morning, with the two dogs, for a ramble in the ravine.

There was an autumnal chill in the air, and the sky was grey and ominous-looking, but the leaves were still green, the trees still full with foliage. The path through Cawley Gardens down into the ravine was lush with summerweight plant life, the sightlines down the slope and across the creek obscured by thick bushes. I ploughed through, made my way to the footpath on the ravine floor. It was muddy in patches, but navigable, so I turned north, to take my customary route, up to the old lodge site and back, fearless ravine walker that I had become.

I saw no one on my way, none of the usual denizens. The cool temperature must have kept them home, and the mud, and the early hour. Ravine habitué or not, the lack of adult company in the woods might have unsettled me more if the dogs hadn't charged along, noisy and unafraid, at my side. But when I came into view of the lodge site, and spotted a lone adult-sized figure, standing and leaning against one of the willow trees, I didn't know whether to feel relief or alarm. I squinted at the person from afar — could it be a runner, resting between laps? or a mugger, resting between mugs? — but all I could make out was that his or her clothes appeared to be black. Including a hat, unless he or she had black hair.

I came nearer, the person disengaged himself from the tree, his maleness and identity became plain, and he spoke. Noel called out, "Ahoy there, Blithe."

Tup performed his recognition trick and greeted him with enthusiasm, Buck ran over for a friendly sniff, my body went on alert, and my mind leapt into overdrive. A part of me — the imagination gone amok part — had expected Noel to appear in search of retribution sooner or later, and that same part triggered my defence mechanisms. What did he want? What would he do? How close was the nearest path out of the ravine? Why hadn't I brought a cell phone? If I yelled or screamed, would anyone come?

I wracked the brain for something safe to say. Better not to mention any of our treasure deal, Patrick, Hannah, or that Mom and Dad were out of town. Though I had a hunch he knew the parents' whereabouts. Maybe he knew Patrick was away too, and had chosen this moment so he could confront me alone and exact his revenge.

I said hello throatily, kept on walking, fast. There was more chance of meeting someone else that way. And of getting out of the ravine. He fell into step, a tall, black bulk towering over me. What would I say if I weren't afraid of him? "This is a surprise. Where have you come from?"

"I watched you leave the house. I was sitting in a rental car on the street, waiting. You walked right by without noticing. And here I thought you were so quick and observant."

There was a touch of the old tease in his voice, but not much.

"If you were sitting in a car when I walked by, how did you beat me here?" I charged ahead while I talked, scanned the path ahead for any sign of walkers, joggers, cyclists. Where was everyone?

He said, "I made sure you were headed into the ravine, then I drove up to the King's Bridge and came down the path there. I knew you'd make for the treasure site. Its siren call is strong, isn't it? Hard to resist." He didn't look himself, in black pants, a black cotton windbreaker over a black T-shirt, black loafers. The cheap wool cap he wore covered his hair and forehead, came down to just above his pale eyebrows and his watery eyes. Watery, bloodshot, protruding eyes that showed more signs of wreckage than they had two months before.

Pretend all this is normal. Pretend he's normal. "Why didn't you just come to the door when you arrived? When did you arrive?"

"Last night."

"Last night? Where did you sleep?"

"In the car." While I'd slept in the coach house with the two dogs, cozy and unworried, he'd waited for me outside, in the car, like some crazed stalker.

"Why would you do that?" Said as if I didn't think he'd come home to harm me, as if there were a shred of a normal fraternal relationship between us.

He said, "So I'd be sure not to miss you when you came out."

The path ahead was still deserted, also the path behind. But coming up was the side-path that led across the creek to the old quarry site — the reclaimed meadow — a space more likely to be populated with walkers. I called Buck and Tup back from where they roamed ahead, took the fork, Noel still dogging me.

He said, "Aren't you wondering what brings me here?"

I nodded, too scared of the answer to speak.

"I came to tell you," he said, "that I was sacked from my job. I wanted you to know."

He wanted me to know because he thought it was my fault. And he *had* come to harm me. I hurried down the path, anxious to get out into the open, out from under the shadow of the trees, away from the thickets. He kept up. "Why were you fired?" I said. "What happened?"

"My dismissal letter cited non-performance of job duties, submission of fraudulent expense reports, and conduct unbecoming to a consular officer. Which last was a quaint way of describing what happened when the consul's wife found me *in flagrante delicto* with her fifteen-year-old daughter."

We had emerged onto the quarry site, and though there were no people visible, the unobstructed view of sky was calming, made me relax my guard a second, allowed space for the fleeting and unexpected thought that anything good about Noel was gone forever to me. When we might have been clever, bantering, Noel Coward–style siblings under different circumstances.

I said, "Is there any point in asking whether you committed the crimes you were accused of?"

"I'm guilty of all those and more. For years now. But the business with the nubile daughter was what lifted my superiors' asses off their chairs."

The dogs sniffed the tall grass in search of rodents to chase, or sitting birds to rout. We walked by a pond. I said, "Why, Noel?"

"Why what?"

"Why did you do those things?"

"Because there was nothing else to do since you sabotaged the smuggling business and Hannah has taken up with a French playboy she met in Cap d'Antibes or somewhere. Can we sit down? I'm exhausted." He sat on a bench overlooking another pond and pulled out a rumpled pack of cigarettes, lit up. A stiff breeze made the match flame falter, and blew in my direction the taste of tobacco smoke and the scent of his unwashed body.

I said, "So now what?"

He leaned back on the bench. The hits of tobacco seemed to have strengthened him a little, slowed his tremors. "What do you live for, Blithe?"

"What do I live for?" The wind gusted, and I shivered. A heron flew out of a stand of bulrushes, with a great flap of wings, but there was still no one in sight who might save me from the red-eyed, unshaven, dissolute, runny-nosed creature sitting before me. I offered it a tissue from my pocket.

He took the tissue and blew his nose. He said, "I've been making inquiries lately, asking everyone I meet the same question. And I've been stunned by the mundane, the artless, the woefully commonplace reasons that people give for enduring large daily doses of mind-numbing monotony."

When was the last time anyone had uttered such a pleasingly extravagant sentence in my presence? And when would be the next?

"Like what?" I said.

He pulled his jacket closer to him. "Bloody cold out. We'd better keep walking. Shall we climb that ridge?" He pointed to a gently sloped, flat-topped hill that lined the quarry on the east side — a path up led to the top, to a view of another valley beyond, and the busy arterial road that cut through it. A road on which cars would be passing.

"Yes, let's," I said, and led the way.

"For instance," he said, "the last time I spoke to Hannah, she said that her raison d'être was to mix danger with the good life. Two things I've tired of."

He sucked hungrily on his cigarette, and I saw that his nails were bitten, the cuticles ragged.

"When did this firing of yours take place?" I said.

"Three weeks ago."

"Do the parents know?"

He shook his head.

"And what have you been doing since then?"

"Sorting things out, asking around. Would you believe I met a fellow in a pub who told me he lived for his pint of bitter after work?" A sneer of contempt transformed his face into that of the Noel I knew and loathed. "Some other moron said all he needed to get through his day was the thought of the smile on his missus's face when he came in the door. He actually referred to her as his 'missus.'"

Where he was going with this? And what could I say to pacify him, to keep him from turning on me? Another minute and we would be on the ridge, in view of the cars on the road. I said, "What do you live for, Noel?"

"There's the rub, isn't it? What *do* I live for? I'm certainly not waiting for my unborn children to undergo prosaic and meaningless rituals like those poor sods with terminal cancer who keep themselves alive until their son's high school graduation ceremony or daughter's wedding day. I'm not labouring under the pathetic illusion that any of that nonsense matters."

The mention of wedding days — the reminder of the effect he'd had on mine — caused a chemical reaction in the fear heating up my system, converted it to anger, made me erupt. "You've got some nerve, you know, you really do, acting all anguished and existential, after the privileged life you've lived — going to Harvard *and* Oxford, for pity's sake, and the treasure, and Mom's blind devotion, and otherwise intelligent people falling for that cheap act of yours —" The sentence had gotten away from me, but I didn't care, started another. "How dare you complain about anything when you've been dishonest and mean-spirited and selfish your whole life? And when we all know you'll bounce back from this setback the way bastards like you always do, while better, nobler people suffer."

"My god, Blithe — 'better, nobler people'? — how sanctimonious have you become?" His words dripped with some of the old irony. "And was that noise I just heard the sound of an axe grinding? It's not my fault I was born the better-looking, more charismatic sibling, you know."

We were at the top of the hill now, walking along its broad, flat surface, making for the north end of the quarry. The cars I'd expected — the drivers my witnesses, if need be — were moving along on the road at the base of the hill on my right, and to our left, down below, entering the park, I saw, at last, not only a person, but someone I recognized, a woman dog walker of Patrick's acquaintance, accompanied by four dogs. I wasn't alone anymore. Or afraid.

I stopped, said, "I'm going back," and turned, but Noel reached out and grabbed my arm. "Don't go yet," he said. "Come a bit farther. Look, the dogs have gone up the path already. We'll fetch them."

I looked down at where he held my wrist. His grip was not strong. I said, all icy calm, "Let go of me."

He did, right away, put his hands up in the air in a gesture of mock surrender. "Just up to the top and back. Please?"

I looked down into the quarry. The dog walker was seated on a bench smoking her own cigarette — we were fully within her view. And a dogless middle-aged couple had appeared, were strolling along the path. I stepped aside. "You first."

The path narrowed up ahead, and turned, moved off the flat hilltop to encircle the north end of the quarry, which stretched out some eighty feet below. The path meandered up and across a bit of woods, was stymied by a wire fence and doubled back, gave walkers no choice but to return the way they had come. The dogs, ahead, figured that out, stopped to consider descending the steep slope — with its broken-off bits of turf and exposed layers of shale and clay — and trotted over to Noel and me, ready to retreat. But Noel said, "We'll just go as far as the crest there, that green bit that juts out, do you see?"

The bit he indicated was on the very edge of the precipice, not ten feet away. I pictured him luring me nearer, telling me that another few inches meant all the difference to an appreciation of the landscape, urging me to feel the invigorating breeze — and pushing me over. I put my right hand in my pocket, grasped my keys, pushed them through my fingers to make my fist a spiked weapon, anchored myself between a bush and a small tree, held on to the tree with my left hand. "You go ahead. I'll wait here."

He made no effort to coax me away from the tree, but went on alone, stumbled on the rocky path, recovered, kicked off his loafers, gained the crest, and stood there in his stocking feet, arms spread wide, embracing the view. His nearness to the edge, the strong gusts of wind, the glowering sky, all made me more uneasy than I already felt, but I didn't move. I hung onto the tree and to my keys and called out, "Come on, Noel. That's enough. Let's go."

He turned around, carefully, so that his feet still touched only the mound. What was he up to? He said, "You didn't tell me what you live for."

Unbidden, a montage unreeled in my mind of making cookies with Alexandra, of Molly telling me in her upbeat, coach-like way that I'd done a wonderful job with the puzzle book text, of Patrick — who had taken a bite from Noel's apple and resisted corruption — presenting me with a slice of cake. I said, "What I live for is not anything you'd understand, or relate to, or want."

"More nonsense along the lines of a pint of bitter and the smile of your mister, I suppose?" His expression was rueful, and for a strange second, I liked him a little.

He turned back around to face the quarry, and curled his toes underneath the edge of the mound, and shouted, "Did you know that I was once asked to join the diving team at Harvard?"

Then, before I realized what was happening, before I could get past fear for my own safety and decipher his last, throwaway clue — before I could stop him — he dove, headfirst, arms outspread, to his death on the quarry floor.

~ Chapter 17 ~

Noel had left a short note, handwritten, addressed to my parents, sealed in an envelope, pushed inside their mail slot. It explained he'd been fired with just cause from his job, through no one's fault but his own. It said, "I can't think of a reason to live." And, "I apologize for any burden that my passing will place on you." That was all.

No one cried more at Noel's funeral than I did. I cried so much people looked at me strangely, or would have if they weren't following funeral protocol and permitting the family to grieve in any manner it so chose, even a theatrical, sobbing, tears-streaming-down-the-face-for-the-entire-service manner.

My extreme display of emotion excused me from having to speak to most of the three hundred or so people who attended the church service and the reception at the house afterwards. An exception was Molly, who sought me out, hugged me — made me cry some more — and said, deep sympathy in her voice, her touch, her eyes, "I'm so sorry, Blithe. I didn't know how much he meant to you."

Hannah came to the funeral, too. For the third time in five months, she flew home. Dressed in an ill-fitting black suit she must have borrowed from Molly, she attended the service next to her parents, came to the reception, and found me, alone, in the library. She pushed open the door, walked in, sat down in one of the shabby old leather chairs, and said, "Got a minute? I need to talk to you before I go."

I was lying in a chair with my head back, listening to my crying-caused congested breathing, trying not to think about Noel not breathing, about what his body had looked like, crumpled on the quarry floor, when the dog walker and the middle-aged couple and I had all run down, and I'd had to put my fingers to his throat and search for a pulse that wasn't there.

I said, "Leaving so soon?"

She said, "Look. All that shit we went through a few months ago — forget all that. I have one thing to say to you, and this is it: Don't feel guilty."

I raised my heavy head a few inches. The message conveyed by the grief counsellor my parents had brought in had been the same — that we, the survivors, should not take any responsibility for Noel's suicide. We must accept that Noel had chosen his own fate, the motherly psychologist had explained, we must understand that we had been powerless to stop him. Easy for her to say — she didn't know what good reasons I had to suffer from guilt. But Hannah did.

"Why shouldn't I feel guilty?" I said to Hannah. Whispered.

"I knew you would." She didn't sound as pissed-off as I might have expected, as she'd sounded an eon ago in the park, when I'd wanted to recite to her the terms of the thwart plan I'd thought was so clever, so harmless to all concerned.

"You shouldn't feel guilty," she said, "because Noel's been depressive ever since I've known him, always on uppers and downers, drinking too much, doing whatever wild thing he could think of to escape the blues. He was always chasing after something he couldn't find."

What she said made perfect sense, though before that moment, I had never interpreted Noel's behaviour the way she did, had never seen beyond the successful face — the arrogant face — he'd presented to the world.

She said, "It wasn't you putting a stop to the smuggling or finding out about the treasure that sent him over the edge. He'd been perched there so long it was just a matter of time until he fell." She stood up and faced the window where Noel had stood, wearing his devilish grin and beckoning her to him, all those years before. There were no signs of recent crying on her face — no sign she'd cried in her life — but she looked tired, like she'd taken a few too many transatlantic flights.

I said, "If I'd only turned a blind eye, if I hadn't tried to beat him at his own stupid game —"

"No!" She shook her head, and became again the impatient, hard-hearted Hannah I thought I knew. "I came all the way here, for what I hope is the last time this decade, to tell you to get over him, and move on, and control your own destiny. You want to live a parochial, conventional life with a husband, a house, and babies? Go ahead. Noel did what he wanted to do, from start to finish, and you should do the same. We all should." She stared at me for an intense second, then looked away. "That's it, I'm done. Goodbye." She turned on her heel, any guilt *she* might have felt apparently discharged.

I stopped her before she reached the door. "Wait, Hannah. What about you? How much are you like Noel? How close to the edge are you?" How long till Molly got the phone call she'd been dreading, the one my mother hadn't known to expect?

She laughed a brittle laugh. "Me? I'm nowhere near the edge. I know what I want and it's not to self-destruct. Don't worry."

Was the French playboy what she wanted? Was there a French playboy? Regardless, there was little I could do to affect her outcome, less than the nothing I was being told I could have done to save Noel. "All right, then," I said. And lamely, "Good luck."

"You too," she said. Almost as if she meant it.

That evening, alone with Patrick, I said, "I made such a spectacle of myself today."

He handed me a cold, wet facecloth. "You're allowed."

My eyes were dry, but red and swollen. I laid the cloth over my lids. "But everyone thinks I carried on like that because I loved Noel so much and will miss him and was so destroyed by the loss."

He sat down beside me and held my hand. "When the real reason was?"

The tears pricked at my painful eyes once more. "I don't know," I said, but I did. I didn't need to sign up for years of therapy to understand that I'd cried for what could have been, for the closeness we'd never had, for the person Noel never was.

~

It's spring now. When I come home after school and stand outside on the tiny third-floor deck of our new apartment, in my winter coat, and try to soak up some of the weak sunlight, and look out over our cheek-by-jowl, multi-ethnic, mixed-use neighbourhood, I see signs of budding on the old oak tree close to the street, and on the young Chinese elm growing wild in our own house's backyard.

The fall and a long winter have passed, time enough that my mother no longer cries over Noel every day (only every other), and my father has stopped stupefying himself quite so much with liquor, has reduced his evening consumption of drinks from five or six to his traditional two or three. Enough time has passed that my emotional upset over Noel's death has become a small intermittent ache that only flares when I exercise specific, infrequently used muscles — when I hear someone use an Anglicism in conversation, say, or when I glimpse, on the street, a tall man with yellow hair.

I've tried to take Hannah's advice — the last token of whatever friendship we once had — and I've begun to look forward more, instead of back. To the puzzle book coming out in May, for example. I don't expect it to be a best-seller or to attract much notice outside Rose Park, but I'm proud of my work on it, happy I've done it.

I've also begun to allow myself, in small, rationed spurts, to imagine a real, long-term future with Patrick. I can see us fixing up a small, rundown Gothic Revival house together, something like the model Patrick gave me, but located in a neighbourhood anywhere but Rose Park. I see the house bright and suffused with light, filled with new furniture and rugs and window dressings — nothing antique. With sturdy new plates and glasses and silverware, no heirloom anything.

If I narrow my mind's eye and look farther ahead, I can almost see two children living in that house with us. Whether they're boys or girls or one of each I can't tell, but they don't wear precious English or European clothes, and they're not so gracious in their manners that dissembling comes naturally, that lying masquerades as politeness.

I try to imagine those children sitting by the fireplace, listening in fascination while I tell them the story of the Glenwood treasure, about Jeremiah Brown and the man with the dog who sees a light in the valley, but I can't, quite. If those kids ever come into being, they'll probably run off in search of their own obsessions, their own adventures. They'll probably leave my past — mine and Noel's — far behind. And just as well.

~ Author's Note ~

The neighbourhood of Rose Park featured in *The Glenwood Treasure* is a fictional amalgam of the Toronto neighbourhoods of Rosedale (North and South) and Moore Park. Some of the landmarks visited by Blithe for inclusion in the puzzle book are real, some modified, some invented.

Cawley Gardens is an exact duplicate of the real Chorley Park, where I was pleased to find one stone column from the original estate still standing by the Roxborough Drive entrance. The Field Street footbridge is the Heath Street footbridge that bridges Moore Park and Bennington Heights; the steel framework does indeed look like a row of printing exercise book A's when viewed from the ravine below. The former clubhouse of the Rosedale Golf Club still stands on Glen Road at Beaumont, but alas, does not sport golf balls in its gingerbread trim. The white stone in the wall at the made-up Adams house is a reference to a distinctive white stone in the wall at Toronto's Casa Loma, which I learned about from Sheldon Oberman's children's book, *The White Stone in the Castle Wall*.

The exterior of Glenwood is modelled after the John Thom House, at 54 South Drive in South Rosedale, built in 1880, not the 1854 I needed to make the mnemonic work. I numbered Glenwood #51 in honour of 51 Glen Road, the South Rosedale house lived in by the infamous Ambrose Small, a theatre owner who mysteriously disappeared in 1909. The old quarry site can be easily identified as the reclaimed Don Valley Brickworks, and habitués of the Rosedale ravine will recognize its byways and thickets. The lodge was inspired by a haunting photograph, from William Dendy's book *Lost Toronto*, of the deserted Moore Park Belt Line train station that once stood in the ravine near the Heath Street footbridge. Of the station, I have not been able to find any physical remainder.

The last time I checked, the Royal Ontario Museum in Toronto (soon to undergo extensive renovations) still contained two pairs of antique totem poles in its stairwells and a model of the Parthenon in its Greek gallery. The model differs in its details from the one I created from my childhood memories.

Patricia McHugh's book, *Toronto Architecture, A City Guide* was a valuable information resource on Rosedale architecture. Also helpful was Bess Hillery Crawford's *Rosedale*. And like Blithe, I highly recommend Josephine Tey's 1949 novel *Brat Farrar* and Mary Stewart's 1961 variation on a theme, *The Ivy Tree*.

~

Thanks to Ehoud Farine, Joe Kertes, Helen McLean, Louise Moritsugu, and Antanas Sileika for reading early drafts of the novel. Thanks also to Margaret Hart of the Humber Literary Agency for her dedicated work on my behalf, to Barry Jowett for his thoughtful editing, and to all the staff at Dundurn for their support of the book.

Photo by Ken Mulveney

Kim Moritsugu was born in Toronto, where she now lives with her husband and children. She holds B.A. and M.B.A. degrees from the University of Toronto, and worked several years in a corporate setting before turning to the writing of fiction. She is the author of the novels *Looks Perfect* (shortlisted for the City of Toronto Book Award) and *Old Flames,* and teaches creative writing at The Humber School for Writers.